D0837755

"So, what's got you all atwitter?" I asked as Karla Faye joined the Velcro tabs of the cape around my neck. The rest of the stylists were still whispering by the shampoo sink, and I caught several of them casting sideways glances in our direction.

JUL 2 9 2011

"Are you ready for this?" She rested her hands on my shoulders, as though she was steadying me for a blow. "That little hussy who's been playing house with your Wayne?"

I didn't bother to point out that he definitely wasn't my Wayne anymore. "Britannie? What about her?"

Karla Faye leaned in so close that her breath, sharp with the scent of menthol cigarettes, stirred the delicate hairs at my temple when she whispered, "She's dead."

"What?"

"Dead. As in doornail. Vonda Hudson, who works in the 911 call center, came in for a manicure over her lunch break. All that typing is hell on her nails. Well, anyway, Vonda said a 911 call came in from Wayne himself at around ten thirty."

"But I just saw her last night," I whispered.

1st book in a series

I Scream,
You Scream

A Mystery à la Mode

Wendy Lyn Watson

PEARL RIVER PUBLIC LIBRARY
80 FRANKLIN AVENUE
PEARL RIVER, NEW YORK 10965

AN OBSIDIAN MYSTERY

OBSIDIAN
Published by New American Library, a division of
Penguin Group (USA) Inc., 375 Hudson Street,
New York, New York 10014, USA
Penguin Group (Canada), 90 Eglinton Avenue East, Suite 700, Toronto,
Ontario M4P 2Y3, Canada (a division of Pearson Penguin Canada Inc.)
Penguin Books Ltd., 80 Strand, London WC2R 0RL, England
Penguin Ireland, 25 St. Stephen's Green, Dublin 2,
Ireland (a division of Penguin Books Ltd.)
Penguin Group (Australia), 250 Camberwell Road, Camberwell, Victoria 3124,
Australia (a division of Pearson Australia Group Pty. Ltd.)
Penguin Books India Pvt. Ltd., 11 Community Centre, Panchsheel Park,
New Delhi - 110 017, India
Penguin Group (NZ), 67 Apollo Drive, Rosedale, North Shore 0632,
New Zealand (a division of Pearson New Zealand Ltd.)
Penguin Books (South Africa) (Pty.) Ltd., 24 Sturdee Avenue,
Rosebank, Johannesburg 2196, South Africa

Penguin Books Ltd., Registered Offices:
80 Strand, London WC2R 0RL, England

First published by Obsidian, an imprint of New American Library,
a division of Penguin Group (USA) Inc.

First Printing, October 2009
10 9 8 7 6 5 4 3 2 1

Copyright © Wendy Lyn Watson, 2009
All rights reserved

OBSIDIAN and logo are trademarks of Penguin Group (USA) Inc.

Printed in the United States of America

Without limiting the rights under copyright reserved above, no part of this publica-
tion may be reproduced, stored in or introduced into a retrieval system, or transmit-
ted, in any form, or by any means (electronic, mechanical, photocopying, recording,
or otherwise), without the prior written permission of both the copyright owner and
the above publisher of this book.

PUBLISHER'S NOTE
This is a work of fiction. Names, characters, places, and incidents either are the
product of the author's imagination or are used fictitiously, and any resemblance to
actual persons, living or dead, business establishments, events, or locales is entirely
coincidental.

    The publisher does not have any control over and does not assume any respon-
sibility for author or third-party Web sites or their content.

The recipe contained in this book is to be followed exactly as written. The publisher
is not responsible for your specific health or allergy needs that may require medical
supervision. The publisher is not responsible for any adverse reactions to the recipe
contained in this book.

If you purchased this book without a cover you should be aware that this book is stolen
property. It was reported as "unsold and destroyed" to the publisher and neither the
author nor the publisher has received any payment for this "stripped book."

The scanning, uploading, and distribution of this book via the Internet or via any
other means without the permission of the publisher is illegal and punishable by
law. Please purchase only authorized electronic editions, and do not participate in or
encourage electronic piracy of copyrighted materials. Your support of the author's
rights is appreciated.

To Peter, always

Acknowledgments

So many people to thank, so little time . . .

First, I owe an immeasurable debt to the teachers who gave me a love of language and a passion for books: Shari Graham, Ann Mitchell, Ned Creeth (who would hate this), Bert Froysland, and, of course, my mom.

Many thanks to my cheerleaders, including my sister, Karen, Marty, Chris, Emily, Liz, and Cleone. Without you all, I would have given up long ago. A very special thanks to Judge Donovan Frank, both for supporting my dream of writing and for nurturing my obsession with ice cream.

Kim Lionetti has been the best agent I could have hoped for. Her patience with me and enthusiasm for my work have made all the difference. And she brought me to Kristen Weber, who has been a dream to work with. You both made the book infinitely better. Thank you.

Last but not least, my thanks to my dearest husband, who understands the need to create and has given me the space to do it. Love you, darlin'.

chapter 1

From the day I could hold a crayon in my chubby little hands, I have colored inside the lines.

I *yes*, *ma'am*ed and *no*, *sir*red and *pardon me*'ed. I smiled the right smile at all the right people. I dated the right boys and never let any of them get past second base until the day I married the right man. I shoved every last mean or petty impulse down deep into the darkest recesses of my soul, until I was as perfectly perfect as I could possibly be.

Yet still somehow I found myself up to my armpits in a vat of toasted praline pecan, scooping sundaes for my perfectly smug ex-husband and his perfectly bodacious girlfriend.

Proving beyond a shadow of a doubt that life just ain't fair.

"What kind of topping you want on that, Wayne?

We got salted caramel, brown sugar pineapple, bitter-sweet fudge, and brandied cherries, all homemade."

Wayne Jones, my two-timing rat-bastard of an ex, hooked his left thumb through a belt loop on his Dockers and draped his right arm over the shoulder of the living Barbie doll at his side.

"What do you think, Brittanie?"

Because of course the little love muffin was a Brittanie. What else could she possibly be?

Brittanie heaved a sigh that sent her gazongas bouncing. "I don't know." She skimmed her coral-tipped fingers over her nonexistent hips. "I hardly ever eat sweets."

Wayne's lips curled. "Well, Tally is an expert on sweets. Why, I bet she's tried every possible combination. So why don't we let her decide?" He patted Brittanie's perky little butt. "What do you recommend, Tally?"

I recommend you kiss my ample be-hind.

Honestly, if the entire staff of Remember the A-la-mode hadn't been watching the exchange with eyes as big as low-hanging moons, if my biggest display freezer didn't need a new motor, if we'd had more than two paying customers that Saturday afternoon, and if Wayne wasn't thinking about hiring me to provide dessert for the annual employee picnic at Wayne's Weed and Seed . . . well, if it hadn't been for all that, I would have told Wayne and Little Miss Fancy Britches exactly what I recommended.

As it was, I bit the inside of my lip and counted to eleven in my head—counting to ten was never quite enough with Wayne—before plastering a bland smile on my face.

"With the praline pecan, I would go with the bittersweet fudge. The caramel would be redundant, you're allergic to the pineapple, and the cherry would just be gross."

"All righty, then. Let's give that a go."

I dragged my scoop through the luscious French pot ice cream that would put Remember the A-la-mode on the map, filled the pressed-glass sundae dish with two perfect globes of praline pecan, then ladled warm fudge sauce from the dipping well. With a slow, sensuous slide, the chocolate oozed down the sides of the scoops, forming a puddle of melted ice cream and fudge in the base of the glass dish.

Hand to God, there's something downright sexual about ice-cream sundaes, about the creamy, melty decadence of them. I felt like a pervert handing that sundae across the counter to my ex and his new girlfriend. Like I was handing them a sex toy or something.

I kept reminding myself how much money—and publicity—I could finagle out of the Weed and Seed employee picnic.

Outside of Texas, folks may not think of lawn care as a big deal, or a company picnic as a society affair. But the residents of Dalliance, Texas, take their grass seriously, and they're fighting a never-ending battle with nature to keep it green and free of nut grass and fire ants.

And while Wayne may have been a crap husband, he was a savvy businessman. He'd turned Wayne's Weed and Seed into the CNN of Dalliance; the distinctive lime green trucks were always plastered with birthday and anniversary wishes, announcements about the latest Rotary event, and admonishments to support the troops and get right with Jesus. In just under two decades, Wayne had parlayed a couple of riding mowers and a Leaf Hog into a Dalliance institution.

When Wayne's employees and his best customers got together to celebrate victory over another scorching Texas summer, the *Dalliance News-Letter* would be there to record the event. Having my ice cream dished up to all those people would mark an important step in my transformation from Tallulah Jones, Woman Scorned, to Tallulah Jones, Successful Entrepreneur.

Fingers crossed.

Wayne spooned up a big glob of ice cream and sucked it in. Wayne's sweet tooth rivaled my own, so I was eager to know what he thought. "Damn, Tally. That's some fine ice cream. What do you think, sugar?"

I almost responded. After all, I'd been Wayne's "sugar" for most of my adult life. But I caught myself just in time as Wayne handed the spoon to Brittanie.

She dipped the tip of the spoon into the ice cream and held it to her lips. She shuddered. "Ooh, it's way too rich for me."

Wayne rolled his eyes. "Ah, geez, Brit. Lighten up and have just a bite."

Brittanie thinned her glossy lips and narrowed her deep blue eyes. In a heartbeat, the curvy coed went from looking like butter wouldn't melt in her mouth to looking meaner than a skillet full of rattlesnakes. I dang near got whiplash watching the transformation.

"I would think you'd be happy if I didn't pig out on ice cream, Wayne. I mean, you don't want *me* to get fat, do you?"

Whoa. Low blow. Behind me, I heard the synchronized gasps of Alice, Kyle, and Bree.

Apparently I was going to have to learn to count to twelve with Miss Fancy Britches Brittanie.

Wayne had the good grace to look abashed. He clicked his tongue against his teeth. "Dang it, Brit. Don't be a sore winner."

Winner? *Winner?* I couldn't count high enough to let that one slide.

"Lord a-mighty, Wayne, do you really think you're some kinda prize? I hate to bust your bubble, but I washed your BVDs for over fifteen years, and you ain't a prize."

That drew muffled snorts of laughter from the peanut gallery.

Needless to say, Wayne was not amused.

He flushed a shade of red I've only ever seen on baboon butts and the faces of self-important middle-aged men. A sort of precoronary crimson.

"Now, dammit, Tally—"

"Oh, hush, Wayne," Brittanie snapped. "You had that coming."

Wayne's lips thinned and a vein in his temple popped out. His eyes slid back and forth between me and Brittanie, and I could see the tiny wheels turning as he tried to decide who had pissed him off more, me or the twinkie.

I wanted to kick myself. With every pulse of that vein in Wayne's forehead, I saw my chances of catering the Weed and Seed picnic growing smaller.

Thankfully, Wayne decided the twinkie was the larger thorn in his side.

"Jesus, Brit," he growled. "You forget who butters your bread, little girl?"

Brittanie stroked the pendant at her throat—a delicate gold trio of Greek letters stacked one atop another—before tucking her arm through his and leaning toward him. She tipped her head down and looked up through mile-long lashes.

I'd seen this dance a hundred times. *Done* this dance a hundred times: the Ego-Strokin' Two-Step.

"Don't be angry, baby," she cooed. "Let's just sign that ol' contract with Tally and get ourselves home."

Wayne grunted assent. A wave of conflicting emotions overwhelmed me, leaving me light-headed and a little queasy. Gratitude and relief that, with Brittanie's help, I would get my contract. Shame that I had to sign the dang thing after Wayne and Brittanie walked all over my dignity. Revulsion at the thought of Wayne and Brittanie having make-up sex within the next thirty minutes or so.

Some images, a woman shouldn't have to endure.

Bree, Alice, and Kyle were still lurking behind me. I shot them a dirty look, and my niece, Alice—chronologically the youngest, but the most mature by a mile—herded her nemesis-slash–major crush, Kyle, and her mom, Bree, into the back room. I ushered Wayne and Brittanie to a wrought-iron café table and spread out my preprinted contracts.

"I've already filled in most of the details," I said, trying to sound efficient instead of desperate. "You tell me what you want and for how many people, and I can give you a quote."

Wayne made a big production of shuffling through the papers, drawing a pair of dime-store reading glasses out of his shirt's breast pocket so he could read through the fine print on the contract.

I sat quietly until he slipped the glasses back in his pocket and pushed the stack of documents toward me. He folded his arms across his chest, the big man back in charge.

"Looks fine, Tally. Are you sure you can pull this off on such short notice? We usually have a couple hundred people." He coughed. "But I guess you know that."

Awkward.

"So what would you like to serve?" I asked.

Wayne rolled his eyes. "Brittanie decided we should do a—a whatcha call it?"

"A luau," Brittanie supplied.

"Right, a luau. Pig roast and flower necklaces and stuff."

While I shuddered to think what kind of poi you could get in North Texas, and I'm not usually a fan of theme parties, a luau at least had the potential to be classy.

"All right; then maybe something tropical? Everyone loves Tahitian vanilla ice cream, and we could top it with fresh pineapple, mango, and a gingered caramel sauce. How does that sound?" Wayne frowned, but before he could open his mouth, I added, "I'll do some without pineapple for you, Wayne."

Wayne shot a glance at Brittanie. Out of the corner of my eye, I saw her give a tiny nod.

"That sounds fine, Tally. But here's the thing. I want to put the Weed and Seed stamp on this hoedown. So I'd like the ice cream to be green."

"Green?"

"Yep. Wayne's Weed and Seed green."

Wayne's Weed and Seed green wasn't just green, but an intense chartreuse.

So much for classy.

"Wayne, I don't know. I'm not sure how to get all that ice cream a real bright green without it tasting funny." I held my breath, praying he would just let it go.

"Well, how about that sauce stuff? Could you make that green?"

"I don't know. That's a pretty tall order."

Brittanie leaned forward in her seat and drummed a manicured index finger on the top of the contract. "I hear what you're saying, Tally. I really do."

Oh, lordy. It was one thing if she wanted to manage Wayne, but I wasn't too pleased at Little Miss Fancy Britches managing *me*.

"But branding is really important for a growing business," she continued.

I turned to Wayne. He shrugged. "Brittanie just got her degree in marketing from Dickerson."

"Branding," Brittanie said, giving the word as much weight as a bottle blonde with big ta-tas could. "We need the green."

She rested her hand on Wayne's forearm. "Baby, I know you wanted to help Tally out, but I think we should go with the original plan and have bright green fondant-covered cupcakes. I was so disappointed when Petite Gateau canceled on us, but I bet Deena Silver could help us find someone else. Lord knows we're paying her enough to cater the meal; she ought to throw in the dessert for free."

I bristled at the notion of Wayne throwing me a bone, giving me the job out of pity. But the ominously erratic hum of the display freezer was a constant reminder that I was in debt up to my eyeballs. I needed this job badly, even if it meant working with Wayne and Brittanie. Even if it meant making Day-Glo green sundaes.

"I can do it," I blurted.

Brittanie sighed and shook her head. "Really, I don't think—"

"No, I'm serious. I can do it. I can use a coconut sauce instead of caramel. I'll tint the coconut sauce green, and with the fresh pineapple mixed in, the effect will be Wayne's Weed and Seed green."

Brittanie pouted, but Wayne reached for the contract. "Get me a pen so we can sign this thing."

I looked over at my display freezer, filled with tubs of ice cream—rosewater pistachio, raspberry mascarpone, peanut butter fudge. My own recipes, mixed by my own hands, in custom-made vertical batch freezers I'd designed myself. If I couldn't pay the bills and those freezers went kaput, my heart would melt right along with the banana caramel chip.

They say if you lie down with dogs, you'll get up with fleas. As I clicked my ballpoint and reached for the sheaf of contracts, I tried to pretend I didn't feel an itch coming on.

chapter 2

"I can't decide if you're a saint or just the ordinary type of martyr." Bree clicked her tongue against her teeth as she slipped the scrunchy from her hair and tried to finger fluff some life back into her flaming red mane.

I locked the service door and rattled it a few times just to be sure it was solid. I wasn't worried about burglars—I didn't have any cash in the store, the equipment wasn't worth much to anyone but me, and the ice cream was tough to steal—but I didn't have enough to cover my deductible if high school kids decided to break in and trash the place.

"How about 'none of the above'?" I grumbled. "Cash is cash, Bree. So unless you have a little nest egg tucked away somewhere that you want to pony up for the greater good, you can just put a sock in it."

Bree grasped the neck of her T-shirt and fanned herself with the damp material. The calendar said it was October, but the Texas summer was having one last ninety-degree hoorah. Still, I couldn't seem to lure people in to buy my ice cream.

"Sorry, darlin'," Bree said. "I'm broke."

No surprise there.

Technically, Bree Michaels was my cousin, but since we were close in age, we were both only children, and we'd spent every childhood summer together, we ended up more like sisters. I stood up for Bree in four of her five weddings (number three was a spur-of-the-moment Vegas thing that didn't last as long as Bree's hangover), and I sorted through the rubble after each one ended.

As a result, I was intimately familiar with the state of Bree's finances. They were worse than mine. And while I managed to scrape together minimum wage for Alice and Kyle, Bree was basically working for free: theoretically, she was in for a portion of profits, but thirty percent of nothing was still nothing.

Bree stuck her thumb and middle finger in her mouth and let loose a screeching whistle. "Yo, Alice. Let's hustle."

Alice Anders and Kyle Mason were deep in conversation at the end of the alley. Kyle straddled his bike, ready to fly north up Lantana to Ravenswood and his parents' Brady-era split-level ranch. Alice, Bree's daughter by husband number two, leaned against the back wall of Erma's Fry by Night Diner, her body canted awkwardly, as though she could just as easily bolt down the alley as throw herself into Kyle's gangly adolescent arms.

Kyle and Alice's relationship was every bit as awkward as my precocious niece's stance. Alice took after me more than she did Bree, a goody-goody from tip to tail, but spooky smart. At sixteen, she had a full-ride scholarship at Dickerson College. I just knew she'd get out of Dalliance and set the world on fire.

God willing, Kyle hoped to graduate from Dalliance High at the end of the school year, but a lot depended on the goodwill of his history teacher and his ability to pay restitution for a summer mailbox demolition spree. I was the only sucker in town willing to hire him, sullen attitude and all, but at the pitiful wage I could afford to give him, he'd still be making payments for those mailboxes with his Social Security checks.

Kyle and Alice had nothing in common but a powerful fascination. They alternated between making cow eyes at each other and vicious sniping.

Alice's head turned in our direction. "Fine," she snapped, contempt dripping from the single syllable. Genius or not, the child was a teenager, after all.

Beside me, Bree sighed. "That's trouble, right there," she said, nodding her head at the youngsters. Alice took a few hesitant steps away from Kyle, but you could tell she found it difficult to break free of his hormonal gravity.

I sighed. "Why should Alice be immune from the family curse?"

Bree snorted. "Amen."

We joked about the curse a lot, usually over margaritas or hot fudge sundaes. It wasn't anything tragic, like lunacy or crib death. Just a penchant for picking bad men.

Grandma Peachy had two daughters by Grandpa Clem before he got sent to the federal pen for selling phony war bonds. I was eight when Mama learned about Daddy's other family up in Tulsa. Bree didn't know exactly who her daddy was, but none of the options was particularly appealing.

Everyone thought I had broken the curse when I broke away from my hell-raising high school boyfriend, Finn Harper, and married the staid, upstanding Wayne Jones. But then Wayne came home with the clap and a line of bull a mile long, and it was clear the curse had caught me, after all.

When Alice finally schlumped up, we turned down the alley and headed to Jessamine Street, which would carry us south toward our home. Alice and Bree took the lead, Bree slinging her arm over her daughter's skinny shoulders. Alice shuffled along, hands thrust deep in her pockets, hunched over as though her mother's arm were a yoke over her neck. I followed, marveling at the complexity of mother-daughter relationships as we made our weary way home.

"Home" was the house I'd bought after Wayne and I separated. Tired of developer-designed McMansions, with their steep, hip roofs and bland neutral palettes, I strong-armed Wayne into buying me a cute little arts-and-crafts bungalow in the historic district near downtown Dalliance. Wayne paid cash for the house in lieu of alimony. It seemed like a great idea at the time. Bree was recently divorced, and she and Alice were crashing in a friend's spare bedroom. The historic district was within walking distance of Dickerson College, where Alice had just been admitted, and so it seemed like fate that we should all move into the old house together. But then the main sewer line collapsed, squirrels infested our attic, and the subflooring in the bathroom rotted clean through. After a few months, a McMansion and an alimony check started looking pretty good.

Our little procession made its way down Jessamine, away from the courthouse square, past a few silent storefronts. As the commercial hub of Dalliance gave way to the early-twentieth-century homes of the historic district, I felt the tension in my shoulders unwind. The post oaks cast gnarled shadows in the moonlight, and the bitter scent of charcoal grills and citronella candles lay heavy in the air. From somewhere a few blocks away, in the general direction of Dickerson College, I could hear the deep, throbbing bass of dance music. At half-past nine, the nightlife was changing shifts, with family barbecues giving way to fraternity parties.

As we rounded the corner onto Waxahachie, Bree and Alice came up so short, I nearly tripped over them.

"Speaking of the curse . . . ," Bree muttered.

There on my own front steps, just inside the circle of dim light cast by the porch fixture, sat my very own bad-boy heartthrob, Finn Harper. In the bright light of day, I'm sure I would have noticed threads of silver at his temples, a softening along his jawline, a net of fine lines around his eyes. But in the mellow glow of the porch light, he looked like the Finn of my adolescent dreams: a loose-limbed, lanky boy with a swoop of dark hair falling in his eyes.

He stood when he saw us, dusting off his khakis. That was new. My Finn wore only ratty jeans and T-shirts, not khakis and collared shirts.

He nodded a greeting. "Tally. Bree. Good to see you." His gaze settled on Alice, squinting at her as though she were one of those optical illusion pictures that look like a bunch of random dots until your eyes suddenly get the trick and you see the giraffe or whatever.

Bree rested her hands on Alice's shoulders. "Hey, Finn. This is my daughter, Alice." She ruffled Alice's strawberry bob. "Alice, honey, this is Fi—this is Mr. Harper, an old friend of your aunt Tally's."

Alice sized up the stranger with all the warmth of late-December creek water.

"Nice to meet you, Alice."

She dug one sneakered toe into the sidewalk. Finn's wide mouth kicked up in a tiny smile.

"Alice Marie Anders." Bree barely whispered her daughter's name, but the warning in her tone sounded as loud as a whip crack.

Alice heaved a mighty sigh. "Nice to meet you, too, Mr. Harper."

Finn's smile widened to a full-on grin. Then he

turned that devilish grin on me. "How ya been, Tally?"

"Fine."

What else could I say? That I was flat broke? That my husband had dumped me for a luscious piece of arm candy? That I was sweaty and sticky from mucking around in vats of ice cream, feeling like a total frump? I met the daring gaze of the one man who had ever made feel just a little bit dangerous, a little bit beautiful, feeling about as far from beautiful as a girl could get.

Finn's grin faded, and his straight, heavy eyebrows lowered. "Well. That's good." He glanced at Bree and Alice.

"Right," Bree said. "Come on, kiddo, let's get inside and get cleaned up. I think I might have a brandied cherry in my brassiere."

"Mom," Alice gasped, looking utterly mortified.

"Lighten up, Saint Alice. Finn's heard worse. From me, even." Bree cocked her head and pouted her lips, her inner Southern siren coming to the fore. "Ain't that right, sugar?"

Honest, I couldn't tell whose jaw fell farther, Finn's or poor, prissy Alice's.

Bree laughed, a rich, throaty chuckle. "Nice to see you, Finn," she said as she ushered her daughter up the steps. "You two behave."

I felt my face burning. If I'd been armed, Bree would have been in serious trouble right then.

"So." Finn bent to brush the dust from the second porch step, then held out a hand for me to sit. As I settled gingerly onto the step, Finn rested a hip on the concrete stoop.

After an awkward minute or two of silence, Finn cleared his throat. "Sorry to drop by unannounced. I got your address from my mom's Christmas card list. I, uh . . ." His voice trailed off, and he cleared his throat again. "I'm moving back to Dalliance."

A numbing warmth seeped through my veins until it felt as if my body had disappeared entirely.

"Actually, I've already moved back. You know, my mom had a stroke last month."

"Yeah," I said, though I couldn't feel my lips move. "I heard. I'm sorry."

"Thanks. It's her second. She needs help. So I'm back."

"Mmm."

"I got a job with the *News-Letter*."

"Mmm-hmm." Last I had seen Finn Harper, he was as pissed as hell and peeling out of the parking lot of the Tasty-Swirl. That was about two weeks before graduation. I'd heard, though, that he'd somehow made it to college; that he was working as a reporter someplace up north.

"Tally, listen. I wanted to see you because . . ." He trailed off again. "Look, we can't avoid each other in a town this small. I just didn't want to bump into you out there"—he waved his hand vaguely— "without first stopping by to say 'hey.'"

I met his gaze, hoping he couldn't see the utter desolation in my heart. "Hey," I whispered.

His mouth softened. "Hey."

We sat for another moment, the silence not quite so painful this time.

"I wanted to let you know I was back," Finn said, "because I'm supposed to cover the big to-do at Wayne's Weed and Seed next weekend. I don't know what you've said to Wayne about me, and it just seemed like a good idea to give you some warning." He smiled. "I probably should have called. I don't imagine Wayne will be too pleased to find his wife's ex hanging out on his front porch."

The sense of unreality returned in a dizzying wave.

"Wayne and I got divorced." The words came from far away. It didn't even sound like my voice.

"When?" There was a note of challenge in Finn's voice, as if he didn't believe me.

"Not quite a year ago. January eighteenth."

"Your birthday?"

"Yep. Happy birthday to me."

"That was just after my mom's first stroke. I guess she didn't think to tell me."

I shrugged.

"So you won't even be at the Weed and Seed thing." Finn sounded relieved, and I tried not to let that bother me.

"Actually, I will. I'm catering dessert. I bought the ice-cream place on the square."

"Dave's Dippery?"

"Yeah. Dave moved to San Antonio to be near his grandkids. It's mine now. Remember the A-la-mode."

"Cute."

I wanted to shrivel up and die. It *was* cute. Cute like gingham curtains and kitten posters. To a hard-nosed reporter from the big city, I must have sounded like a total bumpkin.

"So I guess I'll see you there after all," he said. He straightened and shoved his hands in his pockets. "I should get going. Mom goes to bed pretty early. But it was good seeing you, Tally."

Good seeing you too, Finn. That's what goody-goody Tally would say. But it would be a lie. It was excruciating seeing Finn again, knowing that the girl he loved was gone forever, all her promise and possibility reduced to the dull certainty of my life. I just couldn't force the words through my lips.

"Give your mom my best."

"Will do. G'night." With a hitch of his shoulders, he ambled down the walkway and climbed into a white Jeep.

As he pulled away from the curb, I rested my face in my hands.

Dear God. Finn Harper was back in Dalliance. Worse, he'd be there next weekend to see me standing beside Miss Fancy Britches Brittanie, who'd probably be wearing a grass skirt and a coconut bra, while I wore a stupid Remember the A-la-mode T-shirt and pineapple sauce in my hair.

If I got through that dang picnic without taking a life—or losing my own—it would be a blessed miracle.

chapter 3

In a fit of desperation, I let Bree give me highlights the day before the Weed and Seed luau. Here's a rule to live by: never let a woman who calls her own breasts "the twins" come near your head with a bottle of peroxide, especially when she's been knocking back margaritas. By the time she was done, my chestnut hair looked like the hide of an electrocuted zebra.

"Damn, Tally. You look like you been rode hard and put up wet."

I straightened from the folding table I was setting up, my hand still wrapped around the steel tube support brace, and squinted hard at Wayne. A snappish quip tickled my tongue, but I wasn't sure who I was talking to that day—the man whose toothbrush leaned against mine for seventeen years, the man who shamed me before every soul I knew, or the man who was signing my paycheck—so I swallowed it down and kept quiet.

"Brittanie got these shirts, and she wants you all to wear 'em." Wayne extended an arm, lime and fuchsia Hawaiian shirts hanging from each finger. "More branding," he added.

I sighed. "Sure, Wayne. Why not?" I couldn't look much more ridiculous, and maybe people would think my hairdo was intentional, part of some theme-party getup.

"How's this work?" Wayne asked. "It's still hotter than *h-e*-double-toothpicks, so how are you going to serve all that ice cream without it melting?"

I perked up a bit. I was pretty proud of my plan, formulated after a consultation with Deena Silver, owner of the Silver Spoon, Dalliance's most sought-after catering company, and the person responsible for the rest of the luau food.

"I actually scooped and packed all the ice cream last night. I got these disposable plastic plates shaped like seashells, and I put three perfect pearls of ice cream on each one. They have lids, so I could seal them up and stack them in the freezer. Then, I used little six-ounce to-go cups for the topping. So everything is already portioned and packaged."

I pulled one of the plastic ramekins filled with tidbits of fresh pineapple and neon green coconut cream out of the cooler at my feet. "I even have a half dozen with no pineapple, just for you. See, they have the red lids, so the servers don't get them mixed up. It's not the most elegant way to serve, but it's not bad. And this way the ice cream stays frozen, and the fruit and coconut cream stay neat, clean, and bug free. We'll be setting out bowls of toasted coconut and macadamia nuts on the tables, so folks can help themselves."

Wayne nodded along with my presentation, his lips pressed in a thin line of concentration. "Tally, to tell you the truth, I didn't want to hire you for the picnic." He held up a placating hand. "No hard feelings; I was just worried that you would get in over your head. I mean, you really dove into this business without a net."

I smiled a bit at Wayne's mixed metaphor. Big-city folks might mistake his bumbling good-ol'-boy persona for stupidity, but in Dalliance, Texas— "Little D" to the "Big D" of Dallas—it served him well. It fostered an immediate sense of trust in his clients. Early in our marriage, Wayne worked hard to nurture that down-home charm, but now it came as naturally as breathing. In fact, sometimes I forgot he hadn't always been an extra from *The Andy Griffith Show*, that he'd once been clever and sweetly sensitive and almost urbane.

"But I gotta say, I'm real impressed with what you've done. I wasn't blowin' smoke the other day. That was some damn fine ice cream. And it looks like you've got a handle on the more practical end of things, too. I just didn't know you had it in you."

I didn't bother reminding Wayne that I had helped him run a wildly successful lawn-care business for years. Granted, I never drew a salary, but I helped juggle shift requests and changes for two dozen workers, drafted employee manuals, and waded through all the tax schedules and work-sheets small businesses have to deal with. Back in the day, he even trusted me to fill out and file the incorporation papers for Wayne's Weed and Seed.

"Thanks, Wayne," I said. "That means a lot."

He nodded once, as though something important had been settled. That nod felt like the punctuation to a chapter in our life.

"Well, now, you and Alice and the boy oughta put on these shirts, before Brittanie sees you out of uniform and takes a strip out of my hide."

I chuckled as I took the shirts from him. "She's got you on a short leash, huh?"

The instant the words left my mouth, I regretted them. I shouldn't poke around in Wayne and Brit-tanie's relationship. Made me look like a scorned woman trying desperately to keep my claws in my ex-husband.

Which, I assure you, I was not.

I didn't expect Wayne to answer. And I guess he didn't, really. At least not directly.

He looked at the ground, and a faint flush stained his throat. "She's a good kid. Real ambitious. Real smart. A little set in her ways, but I guess I don't mind." He cleared his throat, shuffled his feet, and glanced at his watch. "Folks'll be showing up soon. I better scoot."

I watched Wayne walk away, marveling that my

two-timing rat-bastard of an ex-husband appeared to be at least a little bit in love with Miss Fancy Britches Brittanie.

I never liked parties much. Making chitchat with people you don't know, staying alert for candid photos, and eating standing up . . . None of that really appeals.

Turns out, working a party is even worse than being a guest. No one expected me to make small talk at the luau, and I got to sit down to eat—on a camp chair behind my van, with only Alice and Kyle to keep me company, but I did get to sit. Still, the awkward looks I got from all my former friends and neighbors—overly bright smiles beneath panic-stricken gazes—killed my appetite.

"Tally! Good heavens, I almost didn't recognize you!"

"I've been meaning to come by your little store, but you know how it is. Busy, busy, busy."

"I was going to call you last weekend, but the barbecue turned into such a couples thing."

I was grateful when dinner service rolled around and all the ladies in their linen shift dresses and the men in their golf shirts settled at their tables, while grass-skirt-clad coeds circulated with the food.

When the hula servers started clearing away the plates of roasted pork and bowls of suspiciously Middle-American potato salad, I dragged Kyle and Alice bodily from their whispering tête-à-tête in the shade of my old GMC van and stationed them by the portable freezer to hand out the shallow dishes of ice cream, while I took up a position behind the table, stacking cups of sundae topping on round trays. Dessert service was more chaotic than dinner, with guests milling about between the tables and the waitresses dodging Junior Leaguers as they wended their way through the hubbub. Still, I soon fell into a rhythm that synched with my breathing, pushing nearly every other thought from my mind.

The only thing that got through, like a crack of lightning in a peaceful night sky, was Finn Harper. He sidled up to the table, a spark of mischief in his heavy-lidded green eyes, a half smile on his face, and a dish of ice cream in his left hand. I froze, a container of pineapple topping in each hand. He brushed my fingers lightly as he took one of them from me.

"Thanks, Tally."

That whole night, he was the only person who thought to say "thank you" to me, the hired help.

When the rush died down, I reached up to brush a sweaty strand of hair back from my brow and almost jumped out of my skin when I found Finn standing not two feet away, smiling that same lazy smile.

"Hey, Tally," he drawled.

"Oh. Hi." I wiped my fingers on my jeans, then smoothed my hair behind my ears again. "What's up?"

He jerked his head at the mingling partygoers behind him. "Hard-nosed journalism at its finest."

"Ah, yes. Must be a real drag to go from—" I paused because I wasn't sure what exactly Finn had been doing for the last eighteen years. I had shut that door in my life and didn't feel like peeking behind it, so I worked hard to avoid the inevitable small-town gossip. "Well, you know what I mean."

His smile widened. "Minneapolis. Crime and local politics." He shrugged. "This is a little tame, I suppose, but it has its advantages."

"Really?"

"Like the ice cream. Nothing that good in the Twin Cities." His voice dropped to an intimate rumble. "Decadent." Wrapped in the mellow twilight, his words made me feel things I had no business feeling.

I felt a blush burn my face, and I rushed to change the subject.

"So, uh, you get any juicy tidbits while you were circulating?"

"Hmm. Define *juicy*." He held up a hand and began ticking off items on his fingers. "Honey Jillson apparently wore an above-the-knee skirt to the Zeta Eta Chi pledge tea."

"Really?" I was genuinely shocked.

Finn shrugged. "She's got the legs to carry it off."

I shoved his shoulder. "Finn Harper! The mayor's wife is seventy if she's a day."

He laughed. "All the more reason for her to flaunt what God gave her."

"You're incorrigible. What else?"

He leaned in close, dropping his voice to a husky

whisper. "Folks seem real surprised Eddie Collins showed up."

Getting into the spirit of dishing dirt, I tipped my head close to his. "That *is* a surprise. Eddie Collins is one of Wayne's competitors now. He jumped on the whole 'live green' bandwagon and provides organic lawn care and pest removal. Charges a small fortune, from what I hear. I can't believe Wayne invited him."

Finn bobbled his eyebrows. "The buzz is that he didn't. Either Wayne's girlfriend—" He stopped short, looking at me in abject horror.

I couldn't hold back a wry chuckle. "It's okay. Her name's Brittanie."

He nodded slowly, all the while studying me as if he were looking for signs of hairline fractures, any underlying structural weakness that might lead me to shatter at the mention of the other woman. "So, either Brittanie invited good ol' Eddie, or he invited himself."

"Fascinating."

Finn continued to watch me closely until the silence between us grew uncomfortable. When he finally spoke, the words tumbled over one another in a rush. "Tally, are you okay?"

I put a hand to my cheek. "I'm fine. Why? Do I look sick?" My hand drifted up to my hair, and I silently cursed Bree's do-it-yourself highlights. I probably looked like I had jaundice.

Finn exhaled sharply, a sound I couldn't interpret. It might have been a laugh or a sigh of impatience. "You look fine." He shoved his hands deep in his pockets and hunched his shoulders. In that instant, I could see through the veil of years to the brooding teenager I had loved with a passion beyond reason. I had to look away.

"I just picked up bits and pieces about what happened between you and Wayne," he continued. "It must be hard to be here, watching him with Brittanie."

I kept my eyes fixed on a group of children swirling sparklers over the head of a frenzied Australian shepherd, writing their names in big looping letters of ephemeral light. "Brittanie didn't kill my marriage." I allowed myself a thin-lipped smile. "She swooped in while the body was still warm, but Wayne was tomcatting around long before that little girl showed up."

"I'm sorry, Tally."

I waved away his apology.

"For what it's worth," he said, "I heard JoAnne Simms call Brittanie a little whore."

That surprised a laugh out of me, and I clapped both my hands over my mouth. "Oh, I'm going to hell for making fun."

I glanced at Finn and found his smoky green eyes smoldering like a peat fire. Something dark and delicious stirred in their depths, and as he leaned forward, I caught a hint of his scent, brisk notes of juniper and mint and laundry soap.

I stood mesmerized as his lips parted, but I never learned what he planned to say, because Wayne picked that moment to strut up, chest puffed out like he was a bantam rooster, the thumb of one hand hooked in the waist of his chinos, the other hand grasping a sweating plastic cup of margarita slushy—tinted Wayne's Weed and Seed green.

He looped his free arm over Finn's shoulders as if they were old drinking buddies. "Hey, Scoop!" Wayne laughed loudly at his own joke. I recognized the way his lids drooped over fever-bright eyes. Wayne was drunk.

He took a swallow of margarita. "This little lady giving you an earful? Because you gotta take what she says with a grain of salt. She's still got her dander up pretty good."

Finn stiffened visibly. "Actually, Wayne, I was doing the talking. Tally was just being polite, listening to me ramble."

Wayne laughed again. "I guess that's a reporter's job, gossiping and such."

I braced myself, waiting for Finn to haul off and sock Wayne in the face. The teenage Finn would have swung first and thought second, but the years had apparently smoothed his rough edges. The muscle on one side of his jaw bunched up, as did his fists, but he didn't take a punch. He did, however, step out from under Wayne's arm and move away a few paces.

Some habits die hard. I moved around the table and took the glass out of Wayne's hand before I remembered it wasn't my job anymore to corral the man when he was drunk.

In for a penny, in for a pound, I thought.

Raising the glass to my own lips, I smiled and said, "Thanks for bringing me a drink, Wayne."

A bemused look on his face, Wayne simply nodded.

Out of the corner of my eye, I could see Finn's eyes narrow and his mouth flatten. Well, better he be peeved with me than fightin' mad at Wayne.

I had the cup raised to take another sip when Brittanie crashed our awkward little party.

"What's going on here?" she demanded, her words running together in a gentle slur. Her striking eyes, just a shade lighter than Liz Taylor violet, looked slightly unfocused.

Apparently Wayne wasn't the only one hitting the margarita machine pretty hard that night.

Her gaze slid from Wayne's scarlet face to my hand resting on his forearm. "Dammit, Wayne," she snapped, "I turn my back on you for five minutes and you're sniffing around her skirt like a stray dog."

Wayne raised his hand in a placating gesture. "Now, Brit, don't get your panties in a bunch. I was just making conversation."

Brittanie snorted. "Right. Tally may have bought your bull crap, but I'm wise to you. I know you can't keep your fly fastened, and I know that look on your face. You're flirting, and you're busted."

Wayne glanced nervously over his shoulder. Around us, party chatter died and guests turned our way.

"Brit, keep your voice down," he hissed.

"Oh, get over yourself, Wayne. Everyone here knows you ran around on Tally for years. But I'll be damned if I let you humiliate me the way you did her."

My eyes met Finn's for an instant, but I couldn't bear to hold his gaze.

"Please, Brit, you're jumping to conclusions."

"'Please, Brit,'" she mocked. For a second, she teetered in her strappy high-heel sandals, and she grabbed Wayne's arm to steady herself. "I saw your Visa statement, Wayne. A couple of hinky charges on there, you know? Including a big ol' bill from Sinclair's, but you haven't given me any jewelry since my birthday in July."

Wow. Miss Fancy Britches Brittanie was playing hardball, snooping through Wayne's mail. I suppose I should have been appalled, but if I'd taken that sort of initiative, I might have discovered Wayne's extracurricular activities a little sooner.

The color drained from Wayne's face. "Brittanie, this isn't the time or place to discuss that."

She snorted but turned her attention from Wayne to me.

"And you," she spat. "You just couldn't wait to crawl back into his bed, could you?"

Finn took a step in my direction, but I held up a hand to ward him off. I could handle one little girl, no matter how big her hair or her boobs were.

"Why don't you give it up? I mean, look at us." Brittanie waved a hand down the length of her body. She wore a formfitting dress—in Wayne's Weed and Seed green, of course—the delicate spaghetti straps just barely holding the bodice over her ginormous breasts. Her belly was as flat as the West Texas plains, her legs as long as the Rio Grande.

I didn't have to look at my own dumpy khaki shorts and wilted Hawaiian shirt to realize what a stark contrast they presented. But I couldn't let her attack slide. With half of Dalliance looking on—not to mention Finn Harper—I had to put Miss Fancy Britches in her place.

"Listen, honey, not every man will be blinded by your bodacious ta-tas. There's a little thing called character, and you can't get it from a personal trainer. Eventually, gravity will take its toll, and if you want to be able to face yourself in the mirror after that happens, you might want to focus a bit more energy on being less of a bitch."

I paused for breath, a little stunned at myself. I glanced to my side and found Finn looking at me as if I were a new species. Behind him, Kyle and Alice stood with their mouths hanging open.

But it was Wayne who spoke. "Brittanie is not a bitch. She's just not feeling herself tonight. Come on, baby, let's go." He gently grasped her elbow and started to steer her away.

For an instant, I thought Brittanie was going to protest. But then she swayed again, and suddenly she looked very sleepy. She leaned against Wayne, sheltered beneath his arm, and together they headed toward the parking lot.

I watched them go for a moment, then turned and clapped my hands in Kyle and Alice's direction. "Come on, troops. Let's get this mess cleaned up so we can hit the road."

As they scurried to work with uncharacteristic enthusiasm, I threw Finn a sheepish look.

"Still think your new beat is a little tame?" I asked.

He laughed. "Never underestimate small-town drama. I've got enough material to write a story that will have tongues wagging for weeks."

Sure enough, the next morning all the old-timers at the Fry by Night were jawin' over Denver omelets and Finn's story. But the buzz didn't even last through the day. By noon, a much bigger story had stolen all Finn's thunder.

chapter 4

Word spread faster than an Oklahoma twister.

I got the news from Karla Faye Hoffstead, who had done my hair since I got my first perm in the ninth grade. Karla Faye owned the Hair Apparent Salon, a no-frills beauty shop that always smelled of permanent wave solution and the overheated elements of the bubble-domed chair dryers. For years Wayne had pushed me to go to Artemis, an upscale spa complete with aromatherapy facials and hot-rock massages, but I didn't want to have to dress up to get my hair cut. I stayed loyal to Karla Faye, and eventually Wayne stopped complaining.

In the wee hours after the Weed and Seed luau, I had tried to fix Bree's highlighting job with a box of caramel-colored discount dye from the all-night drugstore. My efforts had backfired, and now my stripes were a sort of salmon pink. I called Karla Faye first thing Saturday morning in hysterics, and she agreed to stay after her regular shift to help me out.

At a little after three o'clock that afternoon, I slipped in the front door of the Hair Apparent wearing my floppy gardening hat and a pair of Jackie O sunglasses. The shop was quiet save for the rhythmic *whuffing* of a load of towels in the dryer and the low murmur of voices coming from a handful of women gathered by the shampoo sink. My sneaker squeaked on the linoleum floor, and every gaze snapped to me.

Karla Faye broke from the huddle and tottered across the salon on her three-inch spike heels to greet me. She wore skintight black jeans, an orange jersey tunic that hung off one bony shoulder, and a wide black leather belt slung low on her skinny hips. She might have been wearing the very same outfit when she gave me that perm in the ninth grade.

"Lord a-mercy, Tally. Have you heard the news?"

"What news?" I asked as I pulled off my hat.

"About that little—" Karla Faye gasped. "Bless your heart, what happened to your head?"

"Bree happened to my head," I moaned.

Karla Faye clucked softly. "How many times have I told you? Surgery, dentistry, and permanent hair color . . . the three things in this life you need a professional for."

"I know. And I'm sorry. But I was in a bad place

emotionally, and it seemed like a good idea at the time. Can you fix it?"

"Baby girl, I can fix anything."

She led me to her station and shook out a leopard-print cape while I settled in the chair.

"So, what's got you all atwitter?" I asked as Karla Faye joined the Velcro tabs of the cape around my neck. The rest of the stylists were still whispering by the shampoo sink, and I caught several of them casting sideways glances in our direction.

"Oh!" Karla Faye threw up her hands in alarm. "I can't believe I got sidetracked. But, honestly, pink stripes?"

"Karla Faye."

"Right. Are you ready for this?" She rested her hands on my shoulders, as though she was steadying me for a blow. "That little hussy who's been playing house with your Wayne?"

I didn't bother to point out that he definitely wasn't my Wayne anymore. "Brittanie? What about her?"

Karla Faye leaned in so close that her breath, sharp with the scent of menthol cigarettes, stirred the delicate hairs at my temple when she whispered.

"She's dead."

She may as well have been speaking Swahili. The words just didn't make any sense.

"What?"

"Dead. As in doornail."

"You're kidding."

"Nope. Vonda Hudson, who works in the 911 call

center, came in for a manicure over her lunch break. All that typing is hell on her nails. Well, anyway, Vonda said a 911 call came in from Wayne himself at around ten thirty. He said Brittanie had been feeling poorly when she went to bed last night so he let her sleep in this morning, but when he went in to check on her, she wouldn't wake up. He thought she wasn't breathing. Ambulance radioed back that she was DOA."

"But I just saw her last night," I whispered.

I don't know why people say that. *I just saw her* . . . As though people die only when you aren't looking.

"You and half of Dalliance." Karla Faye ran her fingers through my hair, studying the strands with a critical eye. "We're always busy on a Saturday, what with ladies getting ready for date night or wanting to get their hair done for church, but this place has been mobbed today. Ladies who didn't even have appointments just popped by to chew the fat."

She walked over to a recessed Formica counter and started shuffling through plastic bottles of colorant.

"Everyone says Brittanie was sauced at that picnic last night, but she was otherwise fit as a fiddle," Karla Faye threw over her shoulder. "Heck, Luanne Peters said the girl did two hours of cardio at the Lady Shapers yesterday."

"Two hours?" No wonder you could bounce a quarter off her behind.

"Oh, yeah. Luanne said she was in there every

day, working her little patoot off." Karla Faye
snorted as she started pouring glops of purple goo
into a glass dish. "I think that Lady Shapers thing is
a cult or something."

Karla Faye ruled over an all-female domain, but
she was deeply suspicious of any other organiza-
tion that excluded men. I'd heard her rant about
Lady Shapers, the women-only gym, before, along
with similar screeds about Mary Kay, Avon, and our
local quilters' guild, the Dalliance Fat Quarters.

I tried to keep the conversation on track. "Did
she have a stroke or something?"

Karla Faye shrugged. "No one knows. Did she
seem sick last night?"

"I don't think so. Drunk and cranky, but not
really sick."

She fixed me with a squint-eyed stare as she sashayed back to my chair, a stack of foil squares in
one hand and a paintbrush balanced on a dish of
dye in the other. "The scuttlebutt is, you two got
into a catfight over Wayne."

It was my turn to snort. "I wouldn't call it a catfight. Just a misunderstanding. Brittanie seemed to
think Wayne and I were flirting."

Karla Faye didn't say a word, but one eyebrow
shot up.

"We were *not* flirting. I wouldn't take Wayne
back if he begged me to, and I don't expect him to
come knocking anytime soon."

"Mmm-hmm," she hummed as she snapped on a
pair of gloves.

"Really, Karla Faye."

She didn't say a word, but she didn't look convinced.

Though my pride demanded I argue the point, I hushed up to let Karla Faye work. Color correction's a tricky business. Using a rattail comb to tease out sections of pinkish hair, she painted them with the colorant, then whacked a square of foil with the rattail to get a good crease before folding it around the treated hair. I ignored the purple goo and the halo of aluminum foil, because I knew the drill: hair had to get ugly before it got pretty.

When it looked as though Karla Faye had found her groove, I brought the conversation back to the big story. "So, what are people saying about Brittanie's death?"

Karla Faye paused to brush a strand of platinum hair from her eyes with the back of her wrist. "Oh, I don't know," she hedged.

"Bull pucky. You said yourself the shop's been buzzing all day."

She pulled a face. "Yeah, with a bunch of silly twits who don't know 'come here' from 'sic 'em.'"

I felt a niggling of unease fluttering in my gut. "I know it won't be gospel, but I'm still curious. You know I like to dish as well as the next girl."

Karla Faye sighed. "Just about everyone thinks Brittanie finally paid the piper for her many and varied bad deeds. But there's some disagreement over how, exactly, fate decided to collect on the debt."

"What do you mean?"

A grim smile spread across her face. "Well, there's a small but vocal minority who think God struck Brittanie down for adultery."

"How very Old Testament of them."

Karla Faye laughed.

"Besides," I continued, "Wayne and I were still technically married when he started dating Brittanie, but we weren't sharing a bed and I'd already seen my lawyer."

She grunted noncommittally.

"What about the others?" I prodded.

For a minute, I didn't think Karla Faye would answer. She seemed completely absorbed in making a perfect foil packet around a lock of my hair. Finally, she cleared her throat. "Well, twenty-three-year-old sorority girls don't usually just drop dead, not without a little help. Some folks think Brittanie crossed the wrong person."

"You mean . . . ?"

"Maybe someone murdered her," Karla Faye confirmed with a nod.

That fluttering in my gut came to a full boil. "That's ridiculous," I croaked. "Who would murder that little girl?"

Karla Faye rested her hands on my shoulders and met my gaze in the mirror. "Some say Wayne. Some say you."

chapter 5

To the best of my knowledge, Emily Post never addressed the tricky question of whether a woman should attend the funeral of her ex-husband's mistress. Proper protocol might depend on whether the mistress in question had been murdered and whether the woman was a suspect, but on the day of the funeral—two weeks to the day after Brittanie's death—the tricounty medical examiner's office continued to list the cause of death as "undetermined."

In the absence of a formal rule of etiquette, I fell back on one of my Grandma Peachy's maxims: you can't go wrong if you show up with a casserole.

Thus, I found myself knocking on what had once been my own front door, with a King Ranch casserole balanced on one hand, ready to make my contribution to the postburial dinner. As I waited for someone to open the door, I shifted my weight from foot to foot.

"Relax," Bree hissed from behind me.

"I can't relax," I whispered back. "Folks have been looking at me cockeyed all week."

"All the hubbub's been good for business."

"Bree, that's terrible!"

"Terrible but true," Bree protested, giving an indignant tug on the hem of her little peplum jacket.

I couldn't deny it. With the ME mum about the cause of death, outlandish rumors continued to swirl around town about the bad blood between me and Brittanie, and everyone wanted a peek at the woman who might be the subject of an upcoming Lifetime television movie. Popping by Remember the A-la-mode for a waffle cone gave the looky-loos license to gawk to their hearts' content.

Still, it seemed gauche to comment on our uptick in sales when we were waiting to pay our respects to Wayne.

I rang the doorbell for good measure. "My point is, it's bound to be a hundred times more uncomfortable in there"—I jerked my head at the frosted-and beveled-glass inset of my old front door—"than it was at the Sack 'n Save or the credit union."

"So we'll only stay a minute, give Wayne our regards, then dash back to the store. Besides, that's why we brought the casserole. To smooth things over."

"My King Ranch casserole is good, but it can't work miracles."

Bree frowned. "I told you we should have brought the cheesy funeral potatoes instead of the King Ranch."

Before I could snipe back at her, the front door swung open to reveal a little dollop of a woman, just a whisker over five feet tall. The unrelieved black of her ankle-length broomstick skirt and shiny knitted tunic matched the plaits wound around her head. The severe color and style of her hair seemed out of place atop a face as pale and undefined as a scoop of melting French vanilla.

"Good afternoon," I said gently. "I'm Tally and this is Bree. We came to pay our respects."

For a split second, a spark of something—recognition, surprise, guilt, anger—flashed in the woman's mahogany eyes before the watery veil of grief shifted back into place.

"Who is it, Linda?" Wayne stepped up behind the woman and cupped a hand gently around her shoulder. He wore an austere black suit that strained over his midsection enough to make the button-holes gape. Even to my untrained eye, his deep lavender tie looked expensive. I recognized the suit as the one I helped Wayne buy for his grandfather's funeral five years earlier. The tie, though, was new, and given the color and the quality, I suspected it had been a gift from Brittanie.

"Hi, Wayne," I said. "I am so sorry for your loss."

"Tally. Thank God." Wayne reached for me like a quarterback diving across a pileup for the touchdown. I don't know quite how I expected Wayne to greet me, but I never anticipated such naked relief.

As Wayne dragged me by my un-casserole-laden arm into the foyer of the mid-eighties colonial house we'd once shared, he introduced Linda. "Tally, this is Linda Brinkman, Brittanie's mother. And this," he continued, indicating a gray dumpling of a man in a navy sport coat and charcoal slacks, "this is Brittanie's father, Fred."

Fred Brinkman was as colorless as his wife, a soft man of indeterminate age. He kept his hands shoved deep in his pockets and his shoulders hunched, as though he were prepared to ward off a blow.

"Bree, meet the Brinkmans," Wayne muttered as he drew me farther into the house. He steered me into the formal dining room, where my mission oak table had been replaced by a heavy Spanish colonial monstrosity decorated with inlaid turquoise and now groaning beneath the weight of dozens of potluck dishes. I managed to nudge aside a glass-covered dish of broccoli rice casserole and slide my King Ranch onto a corner of a trivet before Wayne pulled me into the kitchen.

He skidded to a halt, turned to face me, and leaned in urgently.

"Tah—," he breathed, stopping short as his gaze swept our surroundings.

In the mid-nineties, Wayne and I had knocked down some walls to create a great room spanning the width of the house. From the kitchen, you could see all the way to the fieldstone fireplace on the far side of the family room. A bank of French doors opened onto the awning-covered patio, with views of the terraced yard and blue-tiled pool beyond.

That afternoon, clusters of somber mourners dotted the dining area and family room. I saw a few familiar faces from the Dalliance Chamber of Commerce crowd with whom Wayne socialized, including Mayor and Mrs. Jillson. But most of them were strangers, matronly women with helmets of tight gray pin curls and avuncular men wearing drab but tidy suits with the quiet pride of country folk. Probably friends of the family and members of Brittanie's church.

Outside on the patio, a few dozen of Brittanie's twentysomething peers huddled together, sharing cigarettes and bright red plastic cups, looking as though they'd rather be anywhere else in the world. The girls all wore black, but with glimpses of cleavage and sequins, as though they were too young to distinguish between church dressy and club dressy.

Funny how when we die, all the disparate elements of our lives—public and private, business and pleasure, old and new—coalesce, the fragments of our being pulled together into a rough collage that finally shows a true picture of who we were.

In Brittanie's case, the pieces of her life didn't seem to want to mingle. Yet, despite the stark differences between the inside and outside guests, at that moment they were united in their unabashed interest in me and Wayne.

Flummoxed, Wayne heaved a giant sigh and pulled me into the breezeway to the garage. He flopped down on the upholstered boot box and cradled his head in his hands.

"Tally, you have to help me."

"Oh, Wayne. I don't think it would look right for me to play hostess today. Besides, we left Kyle and Alice in charge of the store, so we have to hustle back before they eat all our profits."

He looked up at me with the most pitiful hang-dog expression I've ever seen. Heck, he didn't look half as guilty when I caught him dictating a memo to his secretary with his pants around his ankles.

"No, Tally. I did something stupid, and I need your help. If anybody asks, I need you to say I came to your house after the luau. I need you to say we were together the night Brittanie died."

chapter 6

"Lord a-mighty, Wayne, what have you done?" I had very few illusions left about my ex, but never in all my born years would I have imagined him needing an alibi.

Wayne groaned and dropped his head back into his hands. "It's complicated. See—"

The thunderous sound of someone pounding on the front door cut short his explanation. Wayne and I exchanged a glance. His eyes were rounded in alarm and his mouth hung open just a fraction. He looked like a scared kid, and some ingrained maternal instinct made me want to shield him from the monster at the door.

I took the lead, marching back past the Greek chorus of mourners in the great room, past the untouched smorgasbord of casseroles in the dining room, past Bree and the Brinkmans, still awkwardly sizing one another up in the foyer. As I reached for the brass handle, another volley of violent blows landed on the door, startling a yelp out of me.

"Oh, for the love of . . . What?" I barked as I jerked open the door.

A half dozen men crowded my front steps—or, rather, Wayne's front steps. In the lead, with his hand poised to knock again, stood another blast from my past, Cal McCormack.

Cal had always been Mr. Macho: junior rodeo calf-roping champ, star running back for the Dalliance Wildcatters, undefeated Texas 4-H small-bore rifle marksman. It hadn't surprised anyone when Cal finished up a stint in the army and became a cop or when he made detective in record time.

"Well, hey there, Tally," Cal drawled. The desultory breeze ruffled his short salt-and-pepper hair. "Didn't expect to see you here."

"Hey, Cal. Just paying my respects."

He nodded, then jerked his chin over his shoulder to indicate the uniformed officers behind him. "We're here on official business. Got a search warrant."

Oh, dear.

I turned around to look for Wayne just in time to watch Linda Brinkman collapse to the floor in a dead faint.

"Do you live here, ma'am?" The officer standing between me and Wayne tipped his head back so he could stare down his nose at me.

"Of course—" Bree elbowed me, hard, in the ribs. "What?" I snapped. I met her exasperated gaze. "Oh. No. I don't live here."

"In that case, I'm going to have to ask you to wait in the living room, there, with the rest of the folks, until we can figure out how to proceed." He leaned forward and lowered his voice, a note of childlike excitement creeping in. "I don't think we've ever served a search warrant during a party before."

"It's not a party. It's a funeral. Barging in here like this, it's disrespectful. That woman"—I jerked my head toward Linda Brinkman, almost lost in the cushions of an overstuffed leather sofa, her husband gently patting her hand— "she just buried her daughter, and you're detaining her like a common criminal. Didn't your mama teach you better?"

The poor kid flushed brick red, but he didn't back down. Instead, he squared his shoulders and got all formal on me again.

"Ma'am, I'm just doing my job. Detective Mc-Cormack told us to keep everyone together, and that's what I aim to do."

On the far side of the kitchen, Cal was speaking earnestly into his cell phone. With every fiber of my being, I wanted to march over there and give Cal a piece of my mind. The good boy I grew up with would never treat a grieving mother like that.

To Cal's left, Wayne stood flanked by two uniformed officers. He looked madder than a wet rabbit. When our eyes met, he squinted hard, then raised his eyebrows and jerked his head in Cal's direction. After all those years together, I knew how to interpret Wayne's charades: he was reminding me to lie for him to Cal.

I wanted to march over and give Wayne a piece of my mind, too. Lying to the police. What a damn-fool idea. How could Wayne even ask me to do such a thing?

But the young man with the gun on his hip wasn't going to let me anywhere near Cal or Wayne.

Bree tugged me away by the sleeve of my linen jacket. She snagged a plate piled high with pigs in blankets and a couple of diet sodas off the breakfast bar and led me into the midst of the crowd in the living room.

I caught Fred Brinkman's gaze, but he waved me away with a faint smile. Bree and I made our way through the milling guests to an empty ottoman. As we plumped ourselves down, she offered to share her bounty, but I wasn't in the mood.

"Suit yourself," she mumbled around a mouthful of Vienna sausage and crescent roll.

A few minutes later, Cal swaggered into the room.

"Listen up, folks," he announced, his brow wrinkled beneath the weight of his authority. "We are not going to detain you much longer, but we are going to need to get everyone's vitals before they leave. Name, address, phone number, and the like. I will have Officers McClusky and Tibert gathering that information." He indicated my friend from the kitchen and another boy so scrubbed and scrawny that he looked as though he were playing dress-up. "Y'all need to be patient, and speak with the officers one at a time. After you have been processed, you may leave."

"Processed," Bree snorted. "Sounds like we're meat." She set aside the plate of snacks and stood up. "I've gotta hit the ladies'."

She sashayed toward the powder room, pausing to flirt her way past a blushing lawman. I watched Cal McCormack pull Fred Brinkman away from his wife for some sort of tête-à-tête. Poor Fred hunched up so much his shoulders nearly brushed his earlobes. Cal managed to keep up his end of the conversation, alternating between speaking softly and nodding, while following the sway of Bree's hips with his eyes.

I was sighing to myself when Honey Jillson appeared at my side.

"Would you mind if I shared your seat?" she asked. "I think this is going to take a while."

"Oh, but . . . sure . . . of course," I stammered.

Hand to God, Honey Jillson scared the piddle out of me. She personified Southern aristocracy, both her wit and her backbone crafted of honey-dipped steel. I had never heard her raise her voice or say an unkind word about anyone. She didn't need to. With just the slightest tightening of her facial muscles, she could convey the sort of absolute, withering contempt that could reduce a Ladies Auxiliary president to tears (an event I had personally witnessed).

She sank to the ottoman with an ease that belied her age, her bony knees never breaking contact with each other, the skirt of her simple black sheath unmarred by a single wrinkle. She rested her pocketbook on her lap, opened the metal clasp with slightly palsied fingers, and began rooting around for something inside.

I took the opportunity to study her face. Honey wore her thinning hair, the color of pale apricots, teased high at the crown and layered tight at the sides. The cut emphasized her prominent cheekbones. Age had honed and hardened Honey rather than softening her. Deep wrinkles lined her skin, yet it wasn't loose but stretched taut on her skull, as though the blazing Texas sun were slowly mummifying her.

The only signs of human frailty were the faint tremor in her hands and the red-rimmed puffiness of her eyes.

She pulled a cellophane-wrapped piece of hard candy from her purse and extended it toward me.

"At the risk of sounding like a little old lady, would you care for a butterscotch?"

I took the offering with a mumbled thanks but didn't bother to unwrap it.

"How have you been, Tallulah Jones?"

"Fine, thank you, Miz Jillson. And you?"

She laughed, the sound of wind in autumn leaves. "My heavens, aren't we a couple of prim Southern belles. Here we are at a funeral, which the police have raided, about to be tagged and released like undersized bass, and we're making polite chit-chat."

I returned her smile. "My Grandma Peachy said you should always ignore unpleasantness in the hopes it will go away."

Her smile tightened a fraction. "I don't imagine this trouble is going to go anywhere for quite some time," she whispered.

"No, probably not." I sat for a moment, watching Dub Jillson, the mayor, bending solicitously over Linda Brinkman. His face wore an expression of bland, official concern, but Linda looked as though she was about to bolt. I felt bad for her. Grieving parents shouldn't have to make small talk with officious strangers.

When I glanced back at Honey, she, too, was watching her husband chat up Linda Brinkman. Her smile disappeared. I wondered briefly whether Dub had a wandering eye. Linda Brinkman wasn't man candy like her daughter, but as I knew only too well, cheaters weren't always particularly discriminating.

I felt a pang of sympathy for Honey Jillson.

"Did you know Brittanie well?" I asked her, hoping to distract her from watching her husband with another woman.

She startled momentarily at the sound of my voice.

"What? Oh, no." She paused to unwrap a second piece of butterscotch. "She was a Zeta, of course. And she spent a summer as an intern in Dub's office. Came to the house for dinner once." Her voice faltered. "I guess I won't ever get the chance to know her better."

We sat in silence a moment, while Honey stared into the middle distance and her butterscotch clicked softly against her teeth. Eventually, she brought her attention back to me. "Why do you ask?"

I shrugged. "More of that polite chitchat."

The wry smile lightened her face, but it didn't touch her eyes. "Of course."

For a full minute, she studied me with unnerving intensity. "Tallulah Jones, why have we never lunched together?"

Because I'm about a dozen rungs down from you on the social ladder, I thought.

"I don't know," I said.

"Let's remedy that," Honey replied. "Next week. I know it is short notice, but are you free on Monday?" I nodded. "Wonderful. Let's say noon at the Prickly Pear."

I nodded again, just as Bree sauntered up. "Hey, Tally. Miz Jillson. I explained to that officer over there"—she jerked her head in the direction of the blushing sentry at the powder-room door—"about how we have children to tend, and he's agreed to take down our particulars so we can skedaddle."

"I don't know if Alice and Kyle really count as 'children,'" I said, even as I stood up. "But I'll take what I can get. Miz Jillson?"

She made a shooing motion with her hand. "Call me Honey, and I'll see you on Monday. Now, scoot."

In two shakes, Bree and I were hustling down the sidewalk toward Bree's beat-up VW Rabbit.

"Tallulah Jones, did you just make a play date with the mayor's wife?" Bree asked.

"Apparently so," I answered as I slid into the passenger seat, resting my feet gingerly on a drift of empty soda bottles. "What do you think the cops were looking for?"

Bree craned her body up so she could see her face in the rearview mirror. She opened her mouth and dabbed at the corners with her fingertip. "I asked that sweet boy in there," she said as she settled back in her seat. "But either my feminine wiles are fading or he was just muscle, because he said he had no idea what they were looking for."

"Hmm."

She cast a sideways glance in my direction as she fired up the Rabbit. "I know who might be able to tell us." She plucked her phone from the cup holder, unhooked it from the charger dangling from the cigarette lighter, and thrust it toward me. "Finn Harper."

chapter 7

The Saturday afternoon crowd at the Bar None cackled and hollered, caught up in the throes of a mating ritual fueled by pitchers of beer, hip-shaking country music, and a bank of big-screen televisions broadcasting college football. I found a corner table, away from the throng watching Southern Methodist trounce UTEP up and down the football field and plastered my "I'm not interested" expression on my face to dissuade any beer-goggling cowboys from moseying my way.

A sly-eyed waitress in tight jeans and a tighter T-shirt slapped a laminated menu on my table, then cocked a hip and waited for my drink order.

I handed the menu back without even glancing at it. The Bar None serves the best fried pickles in Lantana County. I ordered a basket, with ranch dressing, and a longneck. Not exactly classy, but I didn't see much point in pretending around Finn. Between the ignominy of my luau performance, the bitterness of our high school breakup, and my general all-round middle-aged frumpiness, I couldn't imagine him making a pass.

I'd just taken my first pull from my beer and popped a fried pickle chip in my mouth when Finn slouched in. Even in a crisp white oxford shirt, he looked as though he'd just rolled out of bed, all rumpled hair and sleepy eyes. I nearly choked on my pickle.

Without a word, he slid into the chair opposite mine, plucked a pickle from my basket, and waggled my beer at the waitress to let her know he wanted one of his own.

"So," he said, turning his attention to me, "you were there when the shit hit the fan."

"You could say that." I grimaced. "I thought Wayne was going to stroke out when Cal handed him that warrant in front of God and everyone."

Finn studied me through narrowed eyes. "A bit of rough justice?"

"What do you mean?"

"Aw, come on, Tally. It must have felt just a little good to see Wayne brought down a peg."

That took me aback. I thought it over as the waitress returned with another beer for Finn. She set the bottle on a paper coaster, ran her finger up the glass in a teasing caress, then, with a slow wink, licked the condensation from her fingertip.

I watched her sashay away, dumbfounded.

"What was that?" I asked.

"Would you believe 'Southern hospitality'?"

"No."

He laughed. "Lighten up, Tally." Immediately, I felt like his prissy maiden aunt, and I forced a smile.

"So watching Wayne brought low didn't give you a tiny thrill?"

"Actually, no," I said. "I was so busy being ticked off at him for—" I stopped, suddenly remembering that I was talking to a reporter and that Wayne's request for an alibi for the night Brittanie died might end up a front-page headline. "Well, no. I don't take any pleasure in Wayne's public humiliation."

He didn't respond, but his lips twisted in amusement.

"So do you know what they were looking for?" I asked.

His expression sobered. He crooked his finger around the neck of his beer and shrugged. "I'm not exactly in the loop, but I made some calls." He tipped the beer back, and I watched the supple movement of his throat as he swallowed.

"The medical examiner's office finished the toxicology and microscopic tissue analyses yesterday. They determined that she died of acute ethylene glycol poisoning."

"Acute what?"

"Ethylene glycol poisoning. Antifreeze."

I don't know why, but ever since Karla Faye told me about Brittanie huffing and puffing at the Lady

Shapers, I had convinced myself that she exercised herself to death. Maybe I resented the fact that she spent so much time at the gym while I spent so much time sampling my own ice cream. Or maybe I just glommed on to the one thing I knew about her so I could quiet the troubling uncertainty of her death. Whatever the reason, that explanation had taken root, and I had trouble believing anything else.

Finn raised a hand, showing four fingers. "With a kid or a dog, antifreeze poisoning might be accidental— apparently it tastes sweet, so children and animals will get into it without realizing it's dangerous. But with an adult, an accident is unlikely." He folded one finger down. "And it's sure not natural." Another finger down.

He waggled the two remaining fingers. "That leaves suicide or murder."

"Murder?" I should have been prepared for that. After all, whispers of murder had rustled through Dalliance from the day Brittanie died, but I had attributed them to the overactive imaginations of gossips and busybodies. In my heart of hearts, I never thought it might be true. First the cops at the funeral, now an actual name to put to the poison . . . and suddenly those rumors seemed all too plausible.

I felt a little light-headed as Karla Faye's words echoed in my mind: *Some say Wayne. Some say you.*

"Tally, are you okay?" Finn leaned across the table and picked up my hand in his own. He gently chafed my wrist with his thumb. "You look like you saw a ghost."

I rustled up a smile and pulled my hand from his grasp. "I'm fine. It's just shocking."

I paused to eat another pickle chip, chewing contemplatively.

"Murder," I said, dropping my voice to the same superstitious whisper folks use to talk about cancer and teen pregnancy. "I just can't believe that. Stuff like that doesn't happen in little towns like Dalliance."

He tilted his head, unconvinced. "From what I've seen of the world, 'stuff like that' "—he sketched quotes in the air with his fingers—"happens just as much in little towns as it does in big cities."

I snorted. "How many years did you live in Minneapolis? You can't tell me y'all had less crime than we have in Dalliance."

He nodded, conceding the point. "There may be more crime in big cities, but most of it is impersonal. Some guy steals your stereo or your wallet. Maybe someone gets caught in the cross fire of a gang shooting. Ugly, but oddly businesslike. The sort of smoldering anger or greed or lust that leads a person to slip another person some poison? That's just as likely to happen in the crucible of a small town. Maybe even more likely."

"Still, you said it might have been suicide, right?"

Just then, SMU scored another touchdown and the Bar None erupted in cheers. A couple of red-and-blue-clad fans teetered to their feet and raised their arms above their heads, setting off a spontaneous wave that swept from one end of the bar to the other and back again.

Finn slugged back the last of his beer and fished his wallet out of his pocket. "Come on," he said as he tossed a few bills on the table, "let's get out of here."

He took my hand and helped me stand on un-steady legs. This time, I needed the warm pressure of his grip to anchor me, so I didn't pull away. In-stead, I let him lead me from the smoky dusk of the bar into the golden dappled light of the afternoon sun filtered through a canopy of pecan trees.

As we strolled along the sidewalk, he picked up the thread of our conversation.

"Mike Carberry has way more seniority at the *News-Letter* than I do—not to mention better connec-tions in the police department—so my editor as-signed the story to him. I'm getting my information secondhand, from Mike. But from what he said, it sounds like suicide is still technically on the table."

"Technically?"

"Meaning the ME didn't officially rule it out, but the cops don't think it's likely. They're treating her death as a homicide, and they have a pretty neat theory of how it happened."

"They think Wayne did it?"

Finn shook his head, then shrugged.

"But they searched his house," I insisted. "They had a warrant. That means they had reason to think they'd find something incriminating, right?"

I watched some internal struggle play out on Finn's expressive features. I suspected he knew something and he just couldn't decide whether to tell me.

We had crossed the street and were standing in front of the courthouse, kitty-corner across the square from Remember the A-la-mode. I watched as a couple paused outside my shop, studied the menu posted on the window, then kept on walking.

Finn pulled me to a park bench set on the grassy lawn surrounding the courthouse, a private spot nestled between two mature crepe myrtles. He sat down, but he didn't relax, his long body folded into uncomfortable angles on the hard iron bench.

I sat next to him, holding my breath and willing him to spill the beans.

Finally, he sighed. "Tally, this has to be between us, okay?" I nodded. "You can't even tell Bree." I shook my head. "Promise?" I nodded again.

Still, he hesitated. I struggled to keep my expression impassive, when I wanted to take him by the throat and shake it out of him.

"Like I said, Mike has carefully cultivated sources inside the Dalliance PD. They trust him not to disseminate information that might jeopardize an ongoing investigation, and I can't afford to tick off my colleagues by talking out of school. And," he added with a hard smile, "I don't want to be accused of tampering with a witness in a murder investigation my very first month back in town."

"Tampering with a witness? What are you talking about? I didn't witness anything!"

"I would like to believe you."

What he didn't say, but what I heard loud and clear, was that he had a tough time believing me. It had been more than eighteen years since I had broken Finn Harper's heart, but I had broken it bad. Maybe he could hold my hand or tuck my hair behind my ears, the casual gestures echoing the intimacy we once shared. But the foundation of trust between us had crumbled to dust eighteen years earlier in the Tasty-Swirl parking lot.

"Here's what I know," he said. And I accepted those words like the peace offering they were.

"Apparently, after Brittanie died, Wayne made a statement to the police. At that point, it was just a formality. There was no reason to suspect foul play.

"Wayne said that after the Weed and Seed luau, he took Brittanie home. She didn't feel well, and she threw up. He got her a bottle of this sports drink she liked, something called Vigor. He put the bottle in a can koozie, set it on the night table, tucked Brittanie in bed, and then crashed in the guest room next door. Slept like a baby all night long."

He stopped talking and stared at me hard, as if he expected some sort of reaction from me. I didn't get it.

"So?"

He nodded once, and a little of the tension drained from his posture.

"So there's a big hole in Wayne's story. See, the morning Brittanie died, the cops on the scene noted an empty bottle of Mountain Mist–flavored Vigor on the floor and dents in the drywall behind the bed that corresponded to the knobs on the headboard. One of the officers apparently made an off-color comment about Wayne needing to stay hydrated after bed-shaking sex."

Revulsion rippled through me, and I sucked in a hissing breath between my teeth.

Finn nodded. "Classy, huh? Anyway, they also noted that both bedside lamps were on the floor, their glass bases shattered. At the time, they chalked up the broken lamps to the paramedics' efforts to revive Brittanie, because the paramedics had arrived on the scene first. But the ME's report noted incipient bruising on Brittanie's arms and legs and lacerations to her tongue and the insides of her cheeks. Given the development of the bruises, the ME suspects she had at least one massive seizure six to eight hours before she actually died."

I shook my head in frustration. I didn't want to hear about Brittanie's suffering in the hours before she died, and I didn't understand why Finn felt compelled to tell me all that. "How does that contradict Wayne's story?"

"When the ME determined Brittanie had seized, Cal asked the paramedics about the lamps. They said the lamps were already broken when they got to the bedroom. That suggests that Brittanie seized so hard she knocked the lamps over. She probably shook the bed hard enough to put the dents in the drywall, too. But Wayne had told the police he slept the night away just on the other side of that wall."

Now the picture was becoming horribly clear.

"This morning, before the funeral," Finn continued, "Cal talked to Wayne again. He laid out the facts from the perspective of the cops. According to Wayne's own story, he gave Brittanie a bottle of antifreeze green sports drink, which she polished off. Then, apparently, Wayne ignored the sound of Brittanie's violent seizures. He said he looked in on her early Saturday morning, but again, he apparently ignored the broken lamps and left her for a few more hours, only calling the paramedics after it was too late to revive her."

I started shaking, my hands and arms vibrating unsteadily and my breath coming in irregular hitches. The picture Finn painted with his words was almost impossible to process.

Finn wrapped an arm around my shoulders and tucked me close to his heat. He pressed his lips to my hair and murmured softly. "Sounds bad, huh?"

I managed a nod.

"Yeah. Sounded bad to Wayne, too. So he changed his story. Now he says he put Brittanie to bed, and then he left the house. Didn't get back until midmorning on Saturday. That's when he found Brittanie and called 911." A beat of silence passed before Finn lowered the boom. "Wayne says he was with you all night."

That was why Wayne begged me to tell the cops we'd been together. He needed me to corroborate the story he'd already told. The story that made him look just a little bit less like a cold-blooded murderer.

"Cal's going to question you, Tally. He's going to want to know what happened that night."

And if I told the truth, I'd expose Wayne as a liar. He'd look guiltier than sin.

"I know Wayne lied," Finn said. "You didn't even flinch when I told you Wayne's original story, that he slept in the guest room. He wasn't with you that night."

So if I lied for Wayne, Finn would know.

"What are you going to tell the cops?" Finn asked, his voice barely more than a sigh.

As the silence stretched between us, I felt Finn pulling away, and I was bereft.

I pushed back, putting distance between us. A woman walking a pug was staring at us, her lips pressed tight in disapproval. I scooted away from Finn and tugged my jacket closed.

Before I could formulate an answer, my cell phone chirped. With an apologetic glance at Finn, I dug it out of my purse and flipped it open.

"Hello?"

"Hello, Tally? Tally Jones?"

"Yes."

"This is Cal McCormack. I need you to answer a few questions. I know tomorrow is Sunday and all, but are you free tomorrow morning?"

I met Finn's gaze. "Sure, Cal. You want to stop by the house or the store?" Finn gave me an "I told you so" look.

Cal kept his tone polite but formal. "I'd prefer you come in to the station so we can get this on the record."

chapter 8

The fresh interest in Remember the A-la-mode generated by Brittanie's death proved a mixed blessing. The clicking and chiming of the cash register eased my fear of losing my business, but the sly glances and furtive whispers of the customers frayed my last nerve.

In the evenings, though, when I locked the door of Remember the A-la-mode and pulled the roller blinds down over the storefront windows, I could lose myself in refilling the empty display freezers with fresh tubs of peach melba and coconut chip. Cooking the dense custard base, creating silky purees by pressing fruit through a delicate mesh chinoise, tempering dark chocolate—the mindful attention to a thousand careful details calmed my nerves better than yoga could.

The night after the funeral and my conversation with Finn, I needed something to center me, and making ice cream did the trick. By the time I began pouring the custard into the vertical batch freezers, I had achieved some measure of peace. The hypnotic rotation of the blades and the billowing swirls of soft color in the freezing custard restored my balance.

Alas, my delicious meditation competed with the usual end-of-day commotion. Bree teasing Kyle. Alice teasing Kyle. Kyle enduring it all with stoic, adolescent dignity. And, of course, Bree and Alice waging an epic mother-daughter power struggle.

"Yo, Alice." Bree paused in the act of wiping down the burner grates on the industrial stove to lob the opening salvo of that night's confrontation. "Don't forget to throw a load of unmentionables in the wash when you get home. Your mama doesn't want to have to wear ratty ol' granny panties tomorrow."

Alice cast a sideways glance at Kyle, who ducked his head over his mopping in mortification, before she heaved a dramatic sigh. "Geez, Mom. I'm not your slave."

Bree chuckled darkly. "Au contraire, *ma chère*. You are the fruit of my loins, and that means I own your skinny butt until you're eighteen. That's why they call it 'emancipation.' As in the freeing of slaves."

Alice disappeared into the walk-in cooler, putting away the leftover cream and eggs, then slammed her way back into the room. "I could divorce you. Kids can do that, you know."

"Whoo-ee, Tally, listen to that one," Bree said, jerking her thumb in Alice's direction. "She thinks she's all grown. Gonna live on her own."

"I could live on my own just fine," Alice snapped, dumping a dishpan full of spoons into the dishwasher with a mighty clatter. "I'm more responsible than you are. Isn't that right, Aunt Tally?"

Bree snorted, and they both looked at me expectantly.

"Whoa. Leave me out of this," I said, throwing up my hands in mock surrender.

Out of the corner of my eye, I caught Kyle slinking out the back door. Smart kid. If I hadn't had ice cream to make, I would have retreated, too.

Bree slapped a wet rag onto the counter by the stove and began mopping up the spatters of egg custard. "Miss Responsible Alice should remember that just last week she borrowed her aunt Tally's car to go to the movies and brought it back with an empty gas tank. Remember that, Saint Alice?"

Alice gave up the pretense of working, planting her feet in a fighting stance and bracing her fists on her hips. "Yeah, Mom, I remember that. And I apologized to Aunt Tally the next morning. Did you apologize to Aunt Tally for losing the notices from the code-enforcement people?"

Bree froze.

Alice's mouth turned up in a tiny smirk. "I'll take that as a no," she muttered.

"What code-enforcement notices?" I asked.

Bree sighed and tossed her rag in the sink. "Scram, Alice. And don't forget the laundry."

Alice drew her work apron over her head and hung it on the rack by the cooler. "My work here is done," she said, and threw us a little salute before she slipped her arms through the straps of her backpack and ducked out the back.

The heavy door shut with a resounding thud, leaving only the ambient hum of the freezers to fill the silence.

"What code-enforcement notices?" I asked again.

"I'm sorry, Tally. I screwed up."

"What code-enforcement notices?"

Bree sighed. "A few weeks ago, the historic district commission left a notice on the front door. Apparently, the color we painted the house last summer isn't historically accurate."

"The house is gray. What's wrong with gray?"

She looked at me as though I were an idiot. "Tally, you're the only person in the world who thinks that paint is gray. It's purple."

"It's gray."

"Tallulah Jones. The paint color is called lilac lullaby. It's purple." She waved her hand to dismiss the issue. "Whatever, the historic commission doesn't like it. The notice said we had two weeks to repaint the house or appeal the ruling."

I felt a wave of relief. I could hammer out some sort of appeal before bed, buy a little time to figure out my options.

"When is the appeal deadline?" I asked.

Bree winced. "A week ago." She cautiously opened one eye to gauge my reaction.

"Okay."

"I'm really sorry, Tally. I wanted to help, so I took the notice up to my room. I spent some time poking around on the Internet, looking for ideas of how to argue their ruling. And then I forgot."

"Okay."

Words tumbled from Bree's mouth in a cathartic rush. "Alice found another notice on the door after her morning classes today. It said we are now delinquent and will be fined twenty-five dollars every day until we get the house repainted."

"Okay."

Bree rolled her eyes. "Is that all you're going to say?"

I shook myself and turned back to the batch freezer churning away on the peach melba. The peach ice cream had frozen to the consistency of cake frosting, so I took the measuring cup filled with raspberry coulis and began pouring a slow, steady stream into the spinning canister. A fuchsia ribbon bloomed across the undulating mounds of pale blush ice cream.

I allowed the canister to make a half dozen more rotations, so the raspberry swirl would run through the entire batch, then pulled the lever to raise the blade from the freezer and powered it down. While the rotation of the canister slowed, I turned back to Bree.

"What do you want me to say? 'Thanks'?" I laughed sharply. "Tell you what. This time, you get to pick the paint color."

"Wow." Bree huffed in disbelief, then stalked over to the industrial sink. She cranked on the tap and began scouring the stainless steel for all she was worth. Like mother, like daughter: both Bree and Alice turned into cleaning machines when they were irked. "You are a piece of work," she muttered.

"Me? What did I do? Other than accrue interest on a fine I knew nothing about."

She threw down her sponge and turned to face me, striking the very same pose Alice had adopted earlier.

"That's exactly what I'm talking about."

All of my ice-cream Zen had dissipated in the wake of this new crisis, and I wanted nothing more than to go home to my purple house, crawl into a little nest of blankets on my sofa, and fall asleep to the soothing sounds of a home-shopping channel. So I turned my back on Bree, lifted the canister of peach melba ice cream off the freezer unit, and lugged it to the huge worktable we used for hand packing the pint and two-gallon containers we stored the ice cream in.

Bree followed me, taking up a position right by my elbow.

"You know what you are?" she asked.

I pulled a clean two-gallon tub and an ice-cream spade from the shelf below the table. "Oh, I can't wait to hear this."

"You're emotionally constipated."

"Bull pucky," I said, whamming the spade deep into the peach melba. "What does that even mean?"

"It means you don't experience authentic emotions."

I laughed as I threw my weight behind the task of transferring the ice cream from one container to another. "I'm experiencing a pretty authentic emotion right now."

"No, you're not. You should be angry."

"Uh-huh."

"But you're not angry. You're ticked, you're annoyed, but you're not experiencing authentic anger. So you're cracking wise instead of yelling at me."

I shoved a hank of hair out of my eyes and looked at Bree in disbelief. "You want me to yell at you?"

A grin wobbled slowly across her face. "No, not really. But I worry about you, Tally. It's not healthy to bury your emotions down so deep. You've got a lot on your plate, what with the business and the house and this whole thing with Wayne and Brittanie."

I wasn't sure how this recitation of my woes was supposed to improve my mental health.

"You've got to learn to let it out," she continued, "so you don't just explode."

I thumped the tub of ice cream against the work-table to eliminate any air bubbles and began scraping the freezer canister with a rubber spatula to get every last drop. "Tell you what, Bree. I'll let you emote for the both of us."

She pulled a face and opened her mouth to argue, but a knock on the back door stopped her short.

We exchanged puzzled glances. Alice and Kyle had keys, and no one else would stop by so late. Bree took a step toward the door, but I laid a cautioning hand on her arm.

A muffled voice called from the alley. "Tally?" Wayne. "Tally, you in there?"

"What the . . . ?" I opened the door. Wayne stood with one hand braced against the doorjamb, looking like death warmed over. Jeans and a Dallas Cowboys sweatshirt had replaced his funeral finery, and a ball cap advertising a fire-ant poison rested low over his eyes. "Wayne, what are you doing here?"

He all but fell on me, wrapping his arms around me in a smothering embrace.

"Tally, sugar, I'm in an awful mess."

I struggled to untangle myself and stepped out of range. "Don't you 'sugar' me, Wayne Jones. I know you're in a mess, and you've dragged me in right along with you."

"You gotta help me, Tally. Cal McCormack is gonna ask you about the night Brittanie died."

"Uh-huh. I have to go down to the station tomorrow morning." The color drained from Wayne's face, and he stumbled back a step. I admit, I didn't feel much sympathy for him at that moment. "The *police* station, Wayne. I'm not very happy about that."

"I'm real sorry, Tally. Cal wanted to know where I was that night, and I . . . I just couldn't tell him. I didn't know what to say. I panicked."

Out of the corner of my eye I could see Bree watching our exchange with lurid curiosity. Despite her pestering all evening, I'd been true to my word to Finn and had kept my mouth shut. This was all news to Bree.

"Tally, they think I killed Brittanie."

Bree gasped. I caught her attention and jerked my head to indicate she should give us some privacy. A mutinous look flashed across her features, but then she sighed and headed out to the dining area.

I waited a second, until I was sure she was out of earshot, before I spoke again. "Did you, Wayne? Did you kill her?"

"Shit, no! Of course I didn't kill her. That's why I need you to back me up, Tally. You have to tell Cal that I was with you that night."

"Why, Wayne?" I snapped.

He sagged back against the wall, his shoulders slumped and his hands dangling loose at his sides. Wayne was nearly ten years my senior, but I'd always thought of us as being roughly the same age. Now, though, he looked old. All the heat went out of my retort. "Why should I lie for you?"

I meant the question to be rhetorical, so his answer surprised me.

"Money," he said. "I'll pay you. Whatever you want."

Apparently Wayne didn't share Finn's concern for witness tampering.

To be brutally honest, I considered his offer and, for the space of a heartbeat, a *yes* tickled my tongue. The revenue from the luau and the recent increase in sales had helped, but I still had a mountain of bills, a display freezer in need of repair, house painters to hire, and fines to pay. Money was finally coming in, but it was going out faster.

But there were limits on what I would do to get money. I wouldn't sell my body, and I wouldn't sell my honor. "Sorry, Wayne. I'm not about to perjure myself for you or anyone else."

He closed his eyes and moaned.

"Why don't you tell Cal the truth? Were you home that night?"

He shook his head miserably.

"Where were you?"

"I can't tell you. I just can't."

What on earth could Wayne have been doing that night that he was willing to guard the secret so closely? I couldn't even imagine. But he wasn't my husband anymore, which meant it wasn't really my business.

"Wayne, you don't have to tell me, but you have to come clean with Cal."

"I can't." He moaned again and slid farther down the wall.

I went out to the front of the store and, ignoring Bree's questioning look, dragged back a couple of the wrought-iron café chairs.

I slid a chair next to Wayne and sat down in the other one.

"Wayne, if you stonewall Cal, he's going to assume you've got something to hide. He's not going to bother considering the possibility of suicide or looking for another suspect in Brittanie's murder. You don't have many options here."

Wayne sank into his seat and leaned forward to rest his head in his hands. "You think I don't know that? But I can't tell anyone where I was."

"And I can't lie."

Silence stretched between us, punctuating the end of our marriage more clearly than any legal decree. For months, we'd been building our separate lives, but the possibility of their converging again had remained. Now here was Wayne, reaching out a hand to pull us together, and if I didn't take it, that tenuous connection would be severed forever.

I stared at Wayne, seeing him for what he was: a middle-aged man who had spun an illusion of power out of nothing more than forced charm and his own sense of entitlement, and who was now faced with the reality of his own insignificance. A man who had cheated and lied and put his own needs above mine for years. A man I didn't want in my life anymore.

Still, I couldn't quite bear to turn my back on him. And so I made a foolish promise.

"Tell you what, Wayne."

He raised his head and the flash of triumph in his eyes almost made me change my mind.

"Don't get your hopes up, Wayne Jones. I said I wouldn't lie for you, and I meant it. But I'll poke around a bit and see what I can learn about Brittanie. Under the circumstances, folks might be more willing to talk to me than to you. And maybe I'll be able to find a little something to throw Cal off your scent for a while."

I narrowed my eyes and looked at him hard. I needed him to understand I was as serious as a heart attack.

"Wayne, you gotta think long and hard about keeping secrets from the police. It's the most harebrained, cockamamie notion I've ever heard, and I want absolutely no part of it. But, short of lying, I'll help you however I can."

32830003204874

chapter 9

I didn't sleep the night before my interview with the police. Instead, I huddled on the sofa in the den, a threadbare quilt tucked beneath my chin, the flickering light of the television almost hypnotic. The all-night Dolls by Design special on Shop Net drowned out Bree's snoring, the muted, angsty rock emanating from Alice's stereo, and the usual creaks and groans of our crotchety house settling in for the night. And with that chipper chatter in the background, I tried to figure out what I would say to Cal.

I showed up at the police station the next morning grouchier but no wiser.

The interview room smelled like pine cleaner and burned coffee. When I shifted my weight, a faint scent of body odor rose from the warp and weft of the chair's coarse upholstery. I tried to stay still, but I couldn't seem to stop fidgeting.

Across a battered table, Cal McCormack tipped his chair back on two legs. He absently tapped a ballpoint pen against his blank legal pad, clicking it open and closed, open and closed. The rhythmic *snick*s ate away at my nerves until I thought I might scream.

"So I guess you know why you're here," Cal said. Between his lazy-lidded gaze and laconic drawl, strangers might have taken Cal for nothing more than a good ol' boy. Sure enough, he could turn on the aw-shucks, chicken-fried charm when it suited him. But behind his sleepy blue eyes lurked a whip-smart mind and a shrewd ambition.

"Actually, no," I said, clasping my hands together on the table. "I can't imagine how I could help you."

Cal cracked a crooked smile, startling white in his tanned face. "Now, that's mighty telling right there." He snapped the ballpoint against the table, then made a quick note on his pad.

"Let's talk a minute about the night before Brittanie Brinkman passed away."

"Sure."

"Seems a little strange you were at a party hosted by your ex-husband."

I sighed. "I wasn't a guest. I served dessert. Just business."

Cal thrust out his lower lip and nodded, considering. "Huh. That must've rankled."

"What?"

"To be working for your ex-husband. And his girlfriend."

I felt a slow burn creeping up my throat. "I wouldn't call it 'working for them.'"

Cal's eyebrows shot up. "Huh."

He made another note on his pad. I tried to crane my neck subtly to read what he'd written, but his penmanship was atrocious, nothing more than a scrawl. I sank back in defeat.

"Yeah," Cal continued, shaking his head at my sorry situation, "there you are working for your ex and his new girlfriend while your high school flame comes cruising back into town. That must have really chapped your hide."

I made a sound of dismissal. "Good heavens, what does Finn Harper have to do with anything?"

Cal tipped his head, considering. "I seem to recall you two were pretty hot and heavy in high school." Cal knew better than most how close Finn and I had been. He'd tried to break us up more times than I could count. "I just think it must be unsettling to have him back. Especially under the circumstances."

"That was a long time ago, Cal. Finn being back doesn't really affect my life one way or the other."

"Uh-huh." He made another note, and I couldn't hold back a huff of frustration.

"Now . . ." He cleared his throat. "Tell me about the fight you two had that night."

"'You two'?"

"You and Brittanie."

"I wouldn't call it a fight."

He flashed another smile. "Seems like we need a dictionary in here. Maybe look up *employee* and *fight*."

"It wasn't a fight, Cal; it was a misunderstanding."

"Mmm-hmm. And what exactly did you misunderstand?"

"I didn't misunderstand anything. Brittanie did. She got it in her head that Wayne and I were flirting."

He chuckled. "Any truth to that?"

"None."

"So what gave her the idea?"

I heaved a sigh. "I don't know. She was drunk."

Another note.

"What about later that night?"

His tone remained mild, but there was a subtle shift in the atmosphere, like the dip in barometric pressure right before a storm. I held my breath, waiting for the deluge.

Cal met my gaze and lifted one eyebrow in question. "What did you do after the party?"

"I dropped Kyle off at his folks'—"

"That would be Kyle Mason?"

"Right. I dropped Kyle off, and Alice and I went home."

"And?"

"And nothing. I took a shower, took some ibuprofen, and went to bed."

"You didn't see Wayne after the party?" All pretense of casualness disappeared. "He didn't come to your house?"

I looked away for an instant, centered myself by studying a crack in the cinder-block wall behind Cal. Someone had painted the wall recently, and a thin skin of latex covered the imperfection. But the light and shadow and texture of the wall betrayed the flaw beneath the surface.

I took a deep breath and met Cal's gaze again. "No. I didn't see Wayne after the party. Didn't see him again until Brittanie's funeral."

Cal studied me closely before jotting another note.

"Would it surprise you to learn that Wayne told me he went to your house after the party? That you two spent the night together?"

I considered lying, but I've never done it well. I could get away with little fibs, the sort that folks tell to smooth over social situations. But I didn't think I could withstand Cal's scrutiny. He was a professional lawman, after all, and once upon a time we'd been close friends.

"It wouldn't exactly surprise me, no."

"Mmm-hmm. But he's lying."

He didn't ask it like a question, so I didn't feel compelled to answer directly. "Wayne does foolish things sometimes. Rash, impulsive." I paused, to be sure Cal had given me his undivided attention, before I added, "But he's a good man, Cal. Deep down, he's a good man."

He had to be. I couldn't bring myself to believe I'd spent nearly half my life with a bad man, so he had to be good.

"Good men do bad things, Tally."

And that was what worried me most.

That evening, after a day of hemming and hawing and second-guessing my every thought, I stood on the front step of the Harpers' big Tudor house. The mullioned bay window to the right of the door glowed softly from the light of three fake jack-o'-lanterns on the window seat inside, and a skeleton festooned with purple fairy lights danced on the iron-banded front door. Finn's dad had died nearly a decade earlier, and, from what I had heard, Mrs. Harper was bedridden from her stroke, so the decorating must have been Finn's work. Still more evidence that the wild child I had dated had been domesticated.

The doorbell sounded the Texas A&M fight song, a melancholy reminder that Sonny Harper's ghost had never quite been laid to rest. Finn's older brother, Sonny, had played football for A&M for two years before a freak case of meningitis took his life just before he started his junior year. Sonny's death would have been tragic enough on its own, but it also killed the Harpers' marriage and Finn's relationship with his dad. Mr. Harper stayed with his family, but his tepid wife and rebellious younger son could never fill the hole left by his beautiful boy, so brave and bright.

A light winked on in the foyer, and a moment later the door opened wide.

"Well, if it isn't the woman of the hour," Finn said.

He gestured that I should enter. Stepping foot into the hallway was like taking a step back in time. The marine blue carpeting that covered the foyer and swept up the stairs, the cream-on-cream striped wallpaper, the colonial brass chandelier, were all just exactly as I remembered them. A brass console table rested against one wall, its glass surface nearly covered by a massive cream, blue, and maroon silk floral arrangement.

Above that table, like a shrine, hung a picture of the Harper family in happier days: Mrs. Harper's sandy curls framed a plain, patrician face, and her tan shirtwaist dress with the white collar and navy bow complemented her tasteful tortoiseshell glasses frames. Behind her, a big hand on either shoulder, stood Mr. Harper and Sonny, both thick necked, hale, and hearty. Sonny smiled more widely, and his hair was a lighter shade of brown, a little longer at the nape, but he was otherwise the spitting image of his dad. A young, lanky, sullen Finn crouched at his mother's feet, his elbow resting on her knee. He looked more like his mother than his father, with her long face and pronounced cheekbones, but the stubborn set of his jaw was all Harper.

I studied the portrait while Finn closed and latched the door behind me. It predated my relationship with Finn by a couple of years, and I felt a pang of tenderness for the boy in the photo, his mouth too wide for his face, his ears hidden beneath unfortunate wings of feathered hair, the spark of challenge in eyes that had only begun to glimpse the hard realities of life.

"So," Finn asked, startling me from my reverie, "did you cover for Wayne or not?"

"What do you think?"

"You told the truth," he said. But his sigh of relief spoke of the doubt he had harbored. "Want some tea?"

I smiled. "Absolutely."

Finn led me back to his mother's kitchen, still decorated in muted blues and mauves with country geese and cabbage roses ringing the room. I sat at the oak dinette table, fiddling with the ruffled edge of a checkered place mat, while Finn went through the ritual of tea making.

Finn's affinity for tea started in high school. I always suspected it was an affectation, a conscious effort to be different from the other "alternative" kids who gulped black coffee and smoked clove cigarettes. Yet he had apparently never outgrown it.

"Would you like Earl Grey, Irish breakfast, or chamomile?" He looked up from the boxes he grasped in his broad hands. "That's the only decaf option I have," he said apologetically.

"It may keep me up, but I could really go for the Irish breakfast," I said.

"Lemon and sugar, right?"

I smiled. "Yes."

He puttered about the kitchen, and I watched. Mrs. Harper had never been much of a cook, preferring to bring in elaborate precooked meals from the deli of a high-end supermarket: plastic tubs of minestrone and breaded breasts of chicken Kiev, ready to pop in the oven for thirty minutes. So I was surprised to see the ease with which Finn negotiated the kitchen, spooning loose tea leaves into a wire mesh ball and rinsing the teapot in hot tap water. I was even more surprised when he peeled the tinfoil from a cake pan and sliced up squares of clearly homemade gingerbread, redolent with spices and the sweet-tart snap of lemon glaze.

"You cook?"

He ducked his head and shrugged a shoulder. "If you don't ski or skate, you have to learn to do something to fill up the long Minneapolis winters. I'm no Julia Child, but I can keep body and soul together."

I sank my fork into the tender gingerbread and popped a piece in my mouth. It was fantastic, like a well-blended perfume: a sparkling top note of citrus over the piquant bite of ginger and the darker, more complex notes of molasses and clove. I closed my eyes and moaned a little. "God, this would be so great with a scoop of lemon ice cream," I muttered. I took another bite and moaned a little louder.

"Careful, Tally," Finn teased. "My mom might get the wrong idea about what we're doing down here."

My eyes popped open to find a steaming mug of

tea before me and Finn across the table, tucking into his own slice of cake.

"How is your mom?"

He shrugged. "As good as can be expected. The stroke was bad. She's lost the use of her right arm and her right leg, and her speech comes and goes. She sleeps most of the time." He cleared his throat. "There's a nurse here during the day, and two nights a week. I've been looking at care facilities. For now, though, she's comfortable."

I felt as though I ought to say something, but everything that came to mind sounded trite and empty. So I just let the silence stretch until finally Finn broke it.

"So you survived your conversation with Johnny Law?"

"I guess so," I said, poking at the cake with the tines of my fork. "The big question, of course, was whether Wayne spent that night with me. But Cal seemed mighty interested in how I felt about Brittanie and . . ."

"And what?"

I cleared my throat and looked down into the amber depths of my tea. "Well, he pointed out that you being back in town might have stirred things up a bit." I held up a hand to ward off any comment. "I told him that was silly, that you didn't have anything to do with my marriage or its demise, but you know how ornery Cal can be. Like a dog with a soup bone."

Finn was quiet a moment, chewing softly. "Tally,

I'm glad you didn't lie for Wayne. You have a real chance to start over without him, and I don't want to see you get dragged into his mess."

A short, humorless laugh escaped me. "I'm already waist deep in this mess. Which is why I think I need to knuckle down and grab a shovel."

Finn froze, fork midway to his mouth. "I know that look," he said. "That 'ain't nobody better stop me' look you get right before you go off on some wild hare. What are you thinking?"

I picked up my mug and blew gently across the surface of the tea, relishing its warmth in my hands. "Nothing much," I assured him. "I just want to do a little poking around. See what I can find out about Brittanie. Maybe figure out who might have wanted to see her dead."

His fork clattered to the plate. "You're going to investigate a murder? Is that what you're telling me?"

I clicked my tongue against my teeth. "I'm not going to do anything of the kind. Just make a few discreet inquiries."

"That sure sounds like an investigation to me."

"Well, it's not. I'm just worried that the police are going to focus all their attention on Wayne—and maybe a little on me—and they'll miss something big."

Finn spread his hands wide on the table, as if he were trying to stop the world from spinning just a bit. "Look, Tally, I don't think Cal's seriously considering you as a suspect. He knows you better than that. He's just yanking your chain a little. And as for Wayne, well, that's Wayne's problem. Not yours."

I took a cautious sip of my tea, and then, when it didn't scald me, another. "I just can't figure out why Wayne won't tell the police where he was that night."

"Has it occurred to you that he's sticking to this ridiculous story because the truth is worse? Because he actually poisoned his girlfriend and listened to her death throes and did nothing to help her?"

The image he painted was so ugly, I staggered as if he'd struck me physically. Hot tea spilled over my hand. "You don't know Wayne like I do. He's an ass, but he's not evil. I don't know why he keeps lying about what happened that night, but he didn't kill Brittanie. And I can't let him go to jail for something he didn't do. I just can't."

Finn leaned across the table. "Dammit, Tally," he said, his voice taut with frustration, "he screwed you over seven ways from Sunday. Why would you protect him?"

I looked away, fixing my gaze on a ceramic cookie jar shaped like a goose. "He was my husband."

"Was. He was your husband. Past tense."

"My name is still Jones."

"So change it. Go back to being Tally Decker. Hell, Tally Decker knew how to stand up for herself."

I flinched at the contempt in his voice but forced myself to meet his gaze again.

"Yeah, well, Tally Decker is long gone. I could

change my name, but I can't bring her back. I can't unravel all the choices I've made through my life, Finn. And the people in this town will always see me as Wayne's something: his wife, his ex, his doormat."

"Exactly," he said more gently. "This town is holding you back. Get out."

A wistful smile tugged at my lips, and I felt tears gathering in my eyes. "I'm not like you. I can't just pick up stakes and start over."

"Sure you can. You just go. Go someplace where no one has ever heard of Wayne Jones. Go someplace where you can just be you."

I sank my fork into the gingerbread, but then stopped and pushed the plate away. "I don't think you get it, Finn. There is no 'me' without this place. Without Bree and Alice and Kyle and, like it or not, without Wayne."

He didn't answer at first, just got up, cleared the cake plates, tucked them in the dishwasher. He futzed with the cake plate and the sliced lemons, tidying the kitchen. I got the sense that, more than anything, he was buying time to think.

Finally, he came back to the table with the teapot—as round and shiny and red as a perfect maraschino cherry—in one hand and a white knitted pot holder in the other. He refilled our tea mugs, set the pot on the pot holder on the table between us, and settled back onto the ladder-backed dining chair.

"So, what can I do to help?" he said.

I took a sip of tea and swallowed hard to hide the depth of my gratitude.

"For now, nothing. Brittanie's life seemed to have three hubs: Wayne's Weed and Seed, Zeta Eta Chi, and the Lady Shapers. I think I stand a better chance of worming my way into all three worlds than you do."

For an instant, Finn looked as though he wanted to add something, but then he frowned and shrugged, his attention focused on the mug in his hands.

"Finn?" He looked up at me through his lashes, his expression wary. I plucked up my courage and thanked him the best way I knew how. "I wouldn't be me without you, either."

chapter 10

I arrived at the Prickly Pear Café fifteen minutes early for my lunch with Honey Jillson because I didn't dare arrive a second late. A wispy hostess with a dull brown bob ushered me to a table in the solarium. The Prickly Pear occupied a building that had once housed a florist and greenhouse, and during the cooler months, diners could sit in a glass-enclosed solarium, soaking up sunlight beside potted ficuses and sprawling cacti.

I drummed my fingers against the chintz-covered tabletop and fidgeted with the saltshaker until Honey arrived at noon on the dot. She surveyed the restaurant from the foyer and waved away the hostess when she spotted me. Her rigid posture and regal bearing made me acutely aware of my own untidy slouch, and I squared my shoulders as I waited for her to settle into the seat across from me.

"Good afternoon, Tallulah." Honey slid the napkin ring off her silverware roll with trembling fingers, while an acne-riddled busboy filled her water glass.

We ordered our lunch, ladylike salads and water with lemon, and traded pleasantries until our food arrived. By the time the waitress set my Asian chicken salad in front of me, I had learned that Honey was planning a silent auction to benefit the North Texas Italian Greyhound Rescue, that she had just accepted a position on the board of the Friends of the Dalliance Library, and that she was coordinating an Adopt-a-Family Christmas drive for the League of Methodist Ladies. In short, I got a crash course on just how busy an unemployed woman could be.

"So, Tallulah," she said, spearing a grape tomato on the tines of her fork, "I would ask how you have been, but I am afraid your private business has been splashed across the front page of the *News-Letter* all week."

Heat burned my face and the sound of my own heart beating pounded in my ears. I was so rattled, I stabbed my grilled chicken breast with unnecessary force, and droplets of sesame dressing—cast off from my culinary crime—spattered across my chest.

Honey pursed her lips and fluttered her hand dismissively while I dabbed discreetly at my mess with my napkin. "You mustn't let it bother you, dear. It will all blow over."

I snorted. Hand to God, I sat across the table from Honey Jillson, the mayor's wife and the most prim and proper woman I knew, and snorted.

"You don't believe me?"

"No, ma'am," I stammered. "I mean, yes, ma'am, I believe you." I took a drink of my water. "I just worry it's going to blow over and take my good name with it."

"Don't be ridiculous," she scoffed. "Wayne Jones's name may be ruined, but not yours."

"Problem is," I said, "we have the same name. I'll be painted with the same brush."

A bemused smile teased the corners of Honey's coral pink lips. "Ah, I know *that* feeling. The feeling that everything you have, everything you *are*, is all wrapped up in a man and might fly out the door on his shirttails at any minute."

I must have looked skeptical, because she laughed sharply. She leaned across the table and raised one eyebrow. "You know, I wasn't born to money," she said.

"Really?" Everything about Honey Jillson screamed privilege, from the cut of her coat to the cut of her jaw. She didn't wear wealth like a costume. She *was* wealth, bones and blood and skin.

Her smile widened and became more wry. "I heard an expression at a Zeta luncheon last year. 'Fake it till you make it.' That's what I did." She leaned forward and her voice dropped to a conspiratorial whisper. "I went to Dickerson on a full-ride scholarship; wrote papers for football players to earn the money for fancy clothes and sorority dues." She uttered a short crack of mirthless laughter. "I even managed to catch Dub's eye and get a ring on my finger before I ever let him meet my mama and daddy."

"No way."

"As it happens, if you fake it long enough, you really do make it." She sighed mightily. "But when I was your age, I lived every day in fear that someone would realize it was all just an act. I would use the wrong fork, or some folksy adage would slip from my lips and expose me as some dustbowl Okie right out of a Steinbeck novel."

"Would that have been so bad?" I asked softly.

She exhaled with a sort of resolute finality. "At the time, it seemed like the worst thing in the world. I remember the fancy ladies my mama cleaned for giving me their children's cast-off clothing and toys, hiding their distaste behind tight smiles, careful not to touch me lest they soil their gloves. But when I married Dub, all those fancy women fell over themselves to invite me to lunch or to have me on their favorite charity committee. I couldn't imagine losing that."

"But why would you? Wherever you came from, being married to Dub Jillson guaranteed your place in society."

"Exactly. Everything I had, I had because I was Mrs. Dub Jillson. If I lost Dub, I lost it all. Without children to bind us together, it would be easy for Dub to walk away. He might even get the marriage annulled."

"I thought—" I stopped, aghast at what I'd almost said. I was in eighth grade the year a drunk driver struck and killed Miranda Jillson, a high school senior, as she walked home from a babysitting job.

I expected Honey to wilt, but instead her lips compressed into a thin line and her spine somehow became straighter. "Yes, we had a child. But I didn't have Miranda until I was thirty-six." She huffed, a short, humorless laugh. "I had friends knitting booties for their first grandchildren while I was painting Miranda's nursery.

"Until the moment I heard her draw her first breath, I spent every day holding on to my life by sheer force of will."

I poked at my chicken salad with my fork and swallowed back sudden and unexpected tears. "I guess maybe I just didn't hold on hard enough," I said.

Honey reached across the table to rest a knobby hand on one of mine. "My dear, if anything, you held on too hard for too long." She gave my hand a reassuring pat that didn't jibe with the firm certainty in her voice. "That Wayne Jones, he isn't worth your tears, believe you me."

"Wayne's not that bad," I protested.

She harrumphed. "Seems every time I see the man, he's drunk as a skunk."

Wayne had been drunk at the luau, but I couldn't think of any other time Honey would have seen Wayne loaded. After all, Dub Jillson was old money; Wayne was new. They didn't really run in the same social circles, and Wayne usually stayed sober at business-related events.

My confusion must have shown on my face, because Honey explained. "Last year, just after they broke ground on that new shopping center out on Farm Road 410, Dub and I had the board of directors for the chamber of commerce to our house for dinner."

Of course. I was supposed to attend with Wayne, but Bree's fifth husband gave her and Alice the boot that very day, and I had to beg off. Wayne had been hoppin' mad that I'd chosen Bree over him.

Honey wrinkled her nose, as though she'd caught a whiff of something foul. "Wayne Jones got completely sauced. His face turned the color of Texas red clay, and he started slurring his words."

She clucked in prim disapproval.

Before I had a chance to defend Wayne's honor, someone called Honey's name from across the dining room. I looked up to find Deena Silver bustling our way, layers of ocean-colored chiffon billowing in her wake.

Deena, the owner and creative genius behind Dalliance's most exclusive catering company, the Silver Spoon, embraced her artsy nature, playing up her quirkiness whenever she could. An earth mother with a bit of Texas gloss, she dressed her voluptuous body in flowing, ankle-length skirts and sumptuous sari-print tunics. Her wrists dripped with silver bangles, and earrings like delicate wind chimes dangled from her plump lobes. She might have passed for a true Bohemian if her clothes weren't quite so scrupulously new, if her makeup weren't quite so perfect and pink, and if her hair weren't set in stiff, Texas-sized curls.

She didn't slow her energetic, rolling gait until she practically tripped into Honey's lap. They managed to exchange welcoming embraces and busses on the cheeks without actually touching each other, their hands held so flat and stiff, their fingers bowed backward.

When she straightened, Deena hitched the strap of her leather satchel more securely on her shoulder. "I'm so glad I ran into you, Honey. I've got a menu for the November Zeta luncheon that will knock their socks off, but I always like to get your blessing first."

"Deena, dear, do you know Tallulah Jones?" Honey looked pointedly in my direction.

Deena laughed, a full-throated sound without a trace of artifice. "Oh, my, I got so carried away about my pumpkin-ginger soup, I completely forgot my manners." She thrust a hand in my direction, and I grasped it in greeting. The skin on her plump hand was fine and soft, the babylike skin of a woman who gets regular manicures, yet her nails were unpolished and close cut.

"It's nice to finally meet you in person," I said.

"Exactly. A face to the name and all that. I was sorry not to come talk to you at the luau, but it was such a zoo. Besides, when I serve pork, I have to supervise the preparation very closely. I don't want some stressed-out minimum-wage worker infecting half of Dalliance with trichinosis." She laughed at her own whimsy. Without breaking contact with me, Deena rested her left hand on Honey's shoulder. Honey flinched almost imperceptibly, but her polite smile never faltered. "How did the plating go?"

"Smooth as silk," I said. "I can't thank you enough for your advice. With all of the topping individually portioned ahead of time, the serving was a breeze."

Deena gave Honey's shoulder a gentle squeeze. "Tally here called me for advice before her big debut at the Weed and Seed luau. Always happy to help a member of the sisterhood of the traveling pots." She laughed again, and I found myself inordinately pleased to be included in her circle.

I looked at Honey. "Deena gave me the best suggestions. Wayne has allergies, and Deena's the one who suggested using a special colored container for the servings that were allergen free."

Deena blew out a dramatic breath of air. "That's a lesson learned the hard way," she said. "Nothing like having to stick a customer with an EpiPen because you gave them the wrong salad dressing. Now I always keep a stock of red containers." She patted Honey's shoulder. "Like for that girl Marlene, the one with the egg allergy." She leaned in close, as if she were sharing a trade secret with me. "I usually serve Caesar salad at the Zeta luncheons, because it's one of Honey's favorites, but I have to make separate dressing for Marlene."

I glanced at Honey and saw that her smile had stretched to a thin, tight line and she was looking off into the middle distance. I was sure we were boring her to tears.

Deena glanced at Honey, her lips trembling in amusement, before winking conspiratorially at me. She patted Honey's shoulder once again and gave my hand a gentle squeeze. "Well, I'll let you two lovely ladies get back to your lunch. Honey, I'll drop the menu off at the Zeta alumni office. And, Tally, we'll have to get together to trade secrets soon."

She turned and bustled away, heading in the general direction of the bar. I watched her go with a pang, fearing that Honey would want to talk about me and Wayne again.

I admit I was relieved when Honey glanced at her watch and then threw me an apologetic smile.

"Speaking of the alumni office," she said, "I hate to eat and run, but I have a meeting with the Zeta board at one. We have to revise the scholarship application. Every year we try to come up with a timely essay question, and every year the meeting gets ugly."

Our waitress must have seen Honey's check of the time, because she scurried over with the check.

"Ugly?" I asked, settling my hand on the bill and tugging it gently in my direction. "How so?"

She sighed. "The usual social violence that occurs when too many women try to work together. Last year, JoAnne Simms suggested an essay about loyalty and fidelity. She talked about the rash of political figures who stepped down after being caught cheating and became quite indignant about the whole thing. Completely ridiculous."

I hummed noncommittally. "I don't know," I ventured. "Loyalty seems like a pretty important issue."

Honey looked momentarily flustered. "Well, maybe not ridiculous. It just didn't seem appropriate to ask a bunch of seventeen- and eighteen-year-old girls to discuss marital infidelity. And Br—"

She paused, her mouth set in consternation. I felt a twinge of guilt. Apparently conversing with me was like tap-dancing in a minefield.

"Brittanie Brinkman said that we ought to pick a subject a little more relevant to a college student's life. It's what we were all thinking," Honey continued, "but JoAnne didn't take it well. She's always been a bit unstable, you know. She sulked and pouted and shot down every other suggestion."

"Sounds like fun," I said, trying to lighten the moment.

Honey smiled. "Fun or not, it must be done. As you might imagine, the Zeta scholarship program matters a great deal to me. For years now, Dub and I have been on the panel to select the Regents'

Scholarship, which is certainly more prestigious and more lucrative. But my cohort endowed the Zeta scholarship, and so it's quite sentimental to me."

She turned a full ninety degrees in her chair. Then, resting one hand on the table and one hand on the chair's back, she levered herself slowly to her feet. She tottered for an instant before steadying herself.

I scooched back my own seat, grabbed the bill and my purse, and scrambled around the table to lend her my arm, but she declined my offer with a curt shake of her head. Together we walked out to the brick-floored entryway.

I handed our ticket to the hostess and began digging in my purse for my wallet. I expected Honey to make at least a show of offering to pay, but she didn't even glance at the check. Instead, she clutched her pocketbook to her chest and stared out the front window of the restaurant.

The hostess ran my debit card, and I made a mental note to shift a little cash from my pitiful savings account to my more-pitiful checking account the minute I got home.

I held the door for Honey. As she passed, I couldn't help but notice that she seemed somehow diminished, less starched and stalwart than she had when she arrived. It was almost as if she had aged during the hour we'd spent together. I hoped my mention of her daughter hadn't thrown her into a funk.

"Miz Jillson, thank you for joining me today," I

said when we reached her pristine white Lincoln Town Car.

"The pleasure was all mine, dear. Let's do it again soon." I held my breath as she wrestled open the car door. She paused before she climbed inside. "Tallulah, I would not presume to mother you, but I hope you will take the advice of someone older and more experienced than yourself. Don't waste another second worrying about Wayne Jones." She narrowed her eyes and looked at me hard. "Cut him loose before he drags you down with him."

chapter 11

"So, how was lunch at the grown-up table?" Bree dunked a dirty scoop into a well of warm water on the counter behind the display freezers as I pulled an apron over my head.

"Scary."

Alice slouched at the cash register, ringing up the waffle cones her mother had just prepared. Whatever weekday lunch traffic we had had was winding down. Soon Alice would take off for class, and Bree and I would spend the afternoon cleaning.

Bree laughed. "Come on, it couldn't have been that bad." She leaned back against the counter, propped on her hands, one ankle crossed over the other. "Spill it. What happened?"

"Well, let's see." I began ticking off gaffes on my

fingers. "I snorted, I cried, and I dribbled dressing on my shirt."

"Wow. Way to go."

"Oh, and I accidentally brought up the woman's dead daughter."

Bree sucked in a pained breath through her teeth. "Boy, I remember that. It was horrible."

Bree was two years ahead of me in school, so she would have been a sophomore the year Miranda Jillson died.

"What was horrible?" Alice asked as she sidled up to her mother and neatly picked her pocket.

"When Miranda Jillson, the mayor's daughter, was killed by a drunk driver." Bree snatched her wallet out of her daughter's hands, selected a couple of bills for Alice, and tucked the rest into her front pocket.

"She had been nominated to homecoming court just the week before," Bree continued. "The student council decided not to elect a queen that year, to just set the crown on an empty throne in her memory." She shuddered theatrically. "And everyone wore black mums to the dance. It was all very creepy, if you ask me."

Homecoming mums are a peculiar Texas tradition. Instead of wearing a simple, tasteful corsage, Lonestar high schoolers wear elaborate arrangements of silk mums, ribbons, plastic doodads, and even little stuffed animals, some nearly a foot in diameter with a lush trail of ribbons that hang almost to the floor. When it comes to these miracles of crafting architecture, bigger is always better. Mums can cost more than the party dress they're pinned to. I tried to imagine a herd of girls in hairspray-lacquered updos and pastel eveningwear, with explosions of black ribbon on their chests. Bree was right: creepy.

I grabbed a box of paper-wrapped drinking straws and began shoving handfuls of them into metal milk-shake tumblers.

"Creepy, horrible, awful, and sad," I agreed. "And I brought it up over plates of chicken salad."

"You have to cut yourself some slack," Bree said. "You've been having a tough week. Your etiquette engine may not be firing on all cylinders."

"My 'etiquette engine'? Is that another self-helpism?"

"No, smarty-pants, that's a Breeism."

Alice made a sound of disgust. "Mom, you're such a dork." Still, she pecked a quick kiss on her mother's cheek before tugging the straps of her backpack over her arms and heading for the door. "I'll be home for dinner," she called over her shoulder.

"Speaking of my tough week," I said as the door drifted shut behind Alice, "Honey said something at lunch that got me thinking."

Bree bent down to open one of the oak cabinets that lined the wall behind the counter and pulled out a bottle of Irish cream. "First, I'm making myself an adult milk shake. I was working my hiney off while you were lunching with the mayor's wife."

She started scooping dark chocolate ice cream into a silver tumbler. "Care for one? Or are you too snooty now for a Black Irish in the afternoon?"

"Are you kidding? Make mine a double."

She grinned as she added more ice cream to the tumbler and actually chuckled as she eyeballed a few ounces of Irish cream on top. While the milk-shake machine whined, I got two glasses, spoons, and straws, and set them out on a café table. The customers Bree had been serving when I came in had taken their cones to go, so we had the place to ourselves for the moment.

When Bree poured our shakes and settled into her chair, I explained. "Honey was off to a meeting with other Zeta alums, to discuss this year's essay topic for the alumni scholarship. She said that last year, JoAnne Simms and Brittanie got into a tiff after JoAnne suggested loyalty and fidelity as a topic. Sounded like JoAnne had more than an academic interest in the subject."

Bree took a long pull of her milk shake, then lifted the straw and licked it clean. "So?"

"Well, it reminded me that the night of the luau, Finn was giving me the skinny on what was going on at the party. He said JoAnne Simms called Brittanie a little whore."

Bree swirled her straw in her shake. "Do you think Brittanie had an affair with Garrett Simms?"

"I don't know. Maybe."

"That's sort of gross." Bree scrunched up her nose. "Garrett Simms is kind of gross."

I winced at the mental image of Brittanie with Garrett Simms, an oddly pear-shaped man with a wild thatch of curly red hair that crept down his neck and peeped up all the way around his shirt collar, like an Elizabethan ruff. I hated to be unkind, but the man was a yeti.

"Gross or not, he's JoAnne's husband. And JoAnne is the alpha-bitch of the Junior League set." Her parents had run the jewelry store on Dalliance's downtown square for years, and they left their lucrative business to their only daughter. JoAnne had grown up privileged, was still filthy rich, and unlike most of the women in her circle, she held the purse strings in her family.

"I imagine JoAnne is used to getting her own way," I added, "and it sounds like she didn't take kindly to some little chippie poaching her husband." I spooned up a little Black Irish. It slid down my throat like frozen silk, the alcohol leaving a glowing warmth in its wake.

Bree propped an elbow on the table and rested her chin in her hand. Her eyes sparkled with wicked mischief. "Oh, my," she purred. "You know, I've been to a mess of Wayne's Weed and Seed picnics, and they were never any fun at all. Then this year, you leave me to mind the store, and all hell breaks loose. I can't believe I missed it."

I licked my spoon clean. "I promise you, it's only interesting in retrospect. That night, it was just the usual petty bickering. Boring. It only seems exciting now because of, well, what happened after."

Bree waggled her fingers and made spooky *woo-woo* noises. "Because it was Brittanie Brinkman's last night on earth," she said in a deep midnight-movie voice.

I covered my face with my hands and groaned. "Yes," I said through my fingers. "But let's show a little respect for the dead."

Bree chuckled humorously. "Why? It's starting to sound like Brittanie didn't show a whole lot of respect for the sanctity of holy matrimony. Like maybe her relationship with Wayne wasn't a fluke."

And, I thought, like maybe JoAnne Simms had a motive for murder.

"Hey, Bree," I said, "any chance you could open the store tomorrow morning?"

She narrowed her eyes suspiciously. "I suppose so. Why?"

"Because tomorrow I'm going to dig that free pass to the Lady Shapers gym out of the pile of junk mail and use my sweatpants for their God-given purpose."

While most strip malls are as socially stratified as high school lunchrooms, Lantana Plaza offered a hodgepodge of businesses that ran the gamut from designer to discount. One of Wayne's associates once described the shopping center as "in transition," though it hadn't grown noticeably more upscale or downscale in a good fifteen years. Lantana Plaza seemed stranded in some sort of retail limbo.

The Lady Shapers Fitness Center, Lantana Plaza's

most recent newcomer, nestled between the rich people's Albertson's grocery store, which sold individually shrink-wrapped onions and boasted an olive bar, and a giant Hobby Lobby, filled with wood-burning kits and scrapbooking supplies. I had shopped at both the Albertson's and the Hobby Lobby, but I'd never braved the Lady Shapers.

Tinted film emblazoned with the Lady Shapers logo—a curvy goddesslike silhouette with a tape measure draped around her impossibly narrow waist—covered the shop-front windows, providing privacy to the center's customers. The privileged women of Dalliance didn't pay more than a thousand dollars a year in membership fees to let other people watch them sweat.

I hitched my duffel bag up on my shoulder and took a steadying breath before pulling open the glass door and entering the plush, carpeted lounge. Inside, fiber-art wall hangings in shades of gray and rose softened the stark white walls behind the chrome-and-glass reception desk. The high-end-hippie scent of aromatherapy massage oils almost completely masked the smell of fried chicken from the Albertson's deli.

Were it not for the zippy instrumental version of a Motown hit blaring over the speakers and competing with the rhythmic squeak of churning elliptical machines, I might have thought I'd stepped into a spa rather than a gym.

"Welcome to Lady Shapers. May I help you?" The perky girl behind the reception desk was torqued a little too tight to be a spa employee. She sat ram-rod straight, her taut body thrumming with barely leashed energy. The blond ponytail high on her crown bounced as she stood, clipboard in hand, ready to tackle whatever I threw her way.

"I have a coupon for a free trial membership."

"Awesome! Did that come in the mail or in the Sunday supplement of the *News-Letter*?"

"The mail," I answered, handing her the post-card.

"Awesome! I just need you to fill out these little forms here and have you sign the liability waiver, and then we'll get you set up." She clipped a sheaf of papers to the clipboard and handed it to me. "Just fill out what you can and sign by all the yellow sticky flags. I'm Ashley, if you need anything!"

By the time I got done releasing Lady Shapers and FitFab, Inc., from responsibility for everything from heart attack to fungal infections to something called "body dysmorphic disorder," Ashley had donned a telephone headset and was chirping animatedly to someone named Heather.

"Uh-huh, uh-huh, awesome! Yeah. Uh-huh, uh-huh. Yeah. Awesome! Oh, totally!" She scrunched up her nose and held up a finger to let me know she'd be just a moment.

While I pretended to study a flyer about personal trainers to avoid the appearance of eavesdropping, I sent up a silent thank-you to whatever divine force had spared me and Bree from a bubblehead like Ashley. Alice Anders might be a raging mass of

angst and anxiety, with a smart mouth and a stubborn streak wider than a mile, but at least she could
carry on an adult conversation. If I had to listen to
syrupy proclamations of awesomeness all the live-
long day, I would have to kill myself.

"Awesome. Yeah, last weekend was lame. There
was *nothing* going on. I spent all weekend updating
my profile. Superboring."

I had no idea what sort of profile she might be
updating, and I made a mental note to ask Alice.
But I knew all about boring, and a "superboring"
weekend sounded like pure heaven.

"So let's totally do something for Halloween.
Awesome. I gotta go. Awesome. Bye."

The peppy receptionist slipped her headset off
and took the clipboard from my hands. She flipped
through the papers before smiling up at me. "Well,
Mrs. Jones, welcome to Lady Shapers. Let me show
you around."

She sprang up from her chair and trotted ahead
of me. I followed at a more sedate pace, marveling
at the bare legs extending from the bottoms of her
tiny Lycra shorts. Muscles popped from her calves
with startling definition. Her legs were sculpted,
rounded with muscle, but without an ounce of
spare flesh on them. Never in all my born days had
I had legs that perfect.

As we moved into the first room full of exercise
equipment, I caught a glance of my own pudgy
form in the mirrors that lined the walls. I tugged my

fleece hoodie closer around my body and crossed my arms over my chest.

"So, Mrs. Jones, what can Lady Shapers do for you?"

I shrugged. "I guess I'd like to get a little more fit. You know, just get in shape."

"Awesome! No matter where you start, we can help you achieve your goals. And at Lady Shapers, we always say it's never too late to get in shape."

Apparently the Lady Shapers staff didn't emphasize tact in their staff training. I might have kissed my twenties good-bye when Ashley was still in grade school, but I was hardly old. And I was certainly younger than a lot of the carefully pruned and processed ladies I saw huffing away on the bikes and stair-steppers that lined the perimeter of the room.

In fact, there was one knot of women—JoAnne Simms, Jackie Conway, whose husband owned the big Chrysler-Pontiac-Jeep dealership off the interstate, and Trish Paolino, a wealthy widow who moved home to Dalliance after her octogenarian husband passed—who were in their thirties or early forties, but the handful of other women huffing and puffing were significantly older.

"As you can see, this is our cardio room. We have the very latest machines, with digital readouts of your heart rate, calories burned, the works." She paused so I could adequately appreciate all the gym had to offer.

"We strongly encourage our clients to stay hydrated while they exercise," she continued. "You can bring water, of course, but we recommend Vigor, our own house brand of sports drink. It comes in a bunch of flavors, it's got zero calories, and it's loaded with electrolytes and vitamins. We have a vending machine"—she waved in the direction of a brightly lit machine filled with bottles in all the colors of the rainbow—"and our members can order it by the case for home consumption. You can't buy it in stores, so that's a real perk of membership."

I didn't see how the opportunity to give Lady Shapers even more money was a perk. But apparently the women who joined did, including Brittanie Brinkman. Finn had told me that Wayne had given Brittanie a bottle of electric green Vigor the night she died, and it sounded as though that might have been how she drank the poison.

If the cases of Vigor were distributed through the Lady Shapers, that meant that the staff, and maybe the members, would have access to the stuff. Any of them could have poisoned Brittanie's bottles.

I looked over at JoAnne Simms. She wore a body-hugging dark green tracksuit, and her shiny mahogany hair, held away from her face with tiny jeweled clips, looked freshly set despite the sheen of perspiration she was blotting from her face. Her tiny hips swung from side to side as she strode purposefully on the treadmill, her arms pumping vigorously, as she listened to Trish Paolino gabbing away from the machine next to her.

As I watched, JoAnne reached out to pluck a bottle of electric green Vigor from the cup holder on her treadmill, twisted off the cap, and took a deep drink.

JoAnne Simms. Motive? Check. Means? Check. Opportunity? Maybe. But a strong maybe.

chapter 12

"Let's go check out our strength-training equipment," Ashley said, breaking me from my study of JoAnne Simms. She bounced up a short flight of stairs, and I trudged along behind her. "I saw you checking out the personal trainer information. Our trainers are the best," she gushed. "You should really think about setting up some sessions. They can help you with your form, and you'll get results a lot faster."

"Yeah, I'll do that." *About the same time I strut through the streets of Dalliance buck naked*, I thought.

"Oh, geez. How many times . . ." Ashley stomped over to a mess of huge inflatable rubber balls littering the floor between the massive white weight machines. With a dramatic sigh, she picked one up and racked it on two low parallel bars that ran the length of one wall. "Sorry about this. Clients and staff are supposed to rack the ab balls after they use them. It's not usually so messy in here."

"Don't worry about it. Let me help."

As Ashley and I both bent down to pick up balls, I caught a glimpse of something shiny at her throat. A pendant on a delicate gold chain. Three Greek letters stacked one atop another.

I didn't go to college, but I lived in a college town most of my life, and I recognized that particular trio of letters. Zeta Eta Chi, Brittanie's sorority.

Before I had a chance to talk myself out of it, I pounced. "Are you a Zeta?" I asked.

Ashley looked up at me with wide, vacuous eyes. "Huh? Oh, yeah." She smiled, the first genuine expression I'd seen from her. "Are you a Zeta, too?"

"Me? No. But one of my friends was. If you're a student here at Dickerson, you might have known her. Brittanie Brinkman?"

I held my breath as I waited for her reaction.

One thing I can tell you, Little Miss Ashley from the Lady Shapers shouldn't play poker. A series of emotions flitted across her face in rapid succession, each one as clear as the October sky.

Her eyes widened to the point you could see the whites all around her irises. Then her brows came crashing back down, and her upper lip twitched, before her mouth flattened and widened. Ashley knew Brittanie, but she didn't like her very much. And she felt guilty for thinking ill of the dead.

And then it was gone. The real Ashley disappeared again behind a bland mask of polite, professional concern.

"Yeah. Miss Brinkman was a member here and really active in Zeta alum events." She racked another ball. "But she was a few years ahead of me, so I didn't know her well. She was totally awesome. It's a real tragedy."

Right. Maybe Ashley would make a better poker player than I thought, because she told the lie like a champ. Brittanie wasn't just a distant sorority sister. According to my intel, Brittanie spent hours every day at the Lady Shapers. Ashley had to know her.

Rather than call her on the lie, though, I decided to play along.

"No, I suppose you wouldn't have known her well. I was trying to think if I'd seen you at the funeral, but I couldn't place you."

Ashley grimaced at me over the top of a massive fuchsia orb. "No. I wanted to go, of course. We're all sisters in Zeta Eta Chi. But I had a big family thing last weekend."

Except I had just heard Ashley tell the mysterious Heather that she'd been "superbored" and spent the whole weekend "updating her profile."

"Ashley, honey, leave one of those big ol' balls out for me."

Ashley and I both yelped in surprise.

Deena Silver, resplendent in a turquoise jogging suit and blinding white athletic shoes, her voluminous auburn curls held away from her face with bejeweled hair clips, stood by an elaborate weight-lifting contraption. A hot pink MP3 player no bigger than a book of matches was clipped to the collar of her jacket and the leads for a tiny pair of ear buds hung around her neck. She braced her hands against the machine and stretched up on her tippy toes, loosening her leg muscles.

"Sure thing, Miz Silver," Ashley said. She chuckled nervously. "You gave me quite a start."

"Sorry, sugar. I just finished suiting up." Deena jerked her thumb over her shoulder in the direction of another doorway, where the durable indoor-outdoor carpeting and grass-cloth wall coverings gave way to antiseptic white tile on the walls and floors.

"Hey, Tally." Deena raised one elbow up near her ear, twisted the other arm behind her, and waggled the fingers of her two hands as though she were trying to get them to meet up in the middle of her back. "I didn't know you were a member," she said through a grimace of effort.

"I'm not," I answered. "I'm just checking the place out. Ashley was showing me around."

Deena relaxed and gave me a big smile. "Well, why don't I finish the tour, and we can let Ashley get back to business."

I smothered a sigh of frustration. I wanted to learn more about Brittanie, and Ashley—who knew her and was lying about it—seemed like a good lead. But I could hardly decline Deena's offer. "Sounds great," I said.

"You heard the woman, Ashley. Scoot!" Deena playfully waved the younger woman away.

Ashley narrowed her eyes and looked back and forth between us. She looked as though she thought we might be tricking her somehow. But finally she flashed us a tight smile. "Let me know if you need anything, Miz Jones. Enjoy your workout."

Deena watched Ashley go, then strolled over to a stretch of floor mat. With a groan, she lowered herself to the ground. "Ooof. Hope you don't mind being saved." She waved me toward a padded weight bench, where I took a seat, letting my duffel bag fall by my feet. "Ashley's welcome tours usually end with sweat and calipers." She gave me a saucy wink. "You don't look like the caliper type."

I shuddered. "No, I'm definitely not. Thanks."

She stretched out flat on her back. "No reason you can't learn from my mistakes." She closed her eyes and sighed. "I hate it here."

"So why did you join?" I asked.

One lushly lashed eye popped open. "My husband gave me the membership as an anniversary gift last summer. Sweet, huh? He said that he'd take me to Cabo for our anniversary next year if I spent an hour at the gym three days a week." She grunted. "He's a real ass sometimes, but I do love the beach."

She heaved herself onto her side and pulled the last remaining ab ball toward herself, then flopped back into a supine position. "I come like clockwork, three days every week. But I lay here with an ab ball between my knees and just chill. If someone comes through, I make a show of raising the ball with my knees."

I found myself liking Deena Silver more and more. "Don't you get bored?"

She chuckled. "Sometimes I fall asleep. We call that 'meditating in a corpse pose.' I'm very spiritual, after all." She raised her hands and used the fingers of her right hand to point out a piece of red yarn tied around her left wrist. I'd seen something about that in one of Bree's fashion magazines. Lots of stars wore them as mystical lucky charms.

She fixed me with a penetrating gaze. "You won't tell, will you?"

I held up my right hand in a three-fingered salute. "Your secret's safe with me."

She laughed again, a sound as rich as warm dulce de leche. "Something tells me you were never a scout, Tally Jones."

"Nah. No one gave me merit badges for sewing my clothes or cooking my food. Besides, my mama didn't raise any fools. I wasn't going to sell anything door-to-door unless I got a cut."

Deena stared at me wide-eyed for a moment, and I thought maybe I'd gone too far. After all, I barely knew the woman. Heck, for all I knew, she'd been a scout her whole life and had a keepsake album full of merit badges. But then a deep, rolling wave of laughter sputtered to the surface, and pretty soon, we were both howling.

"You ladies all right?" Ashley's ponytail preceded her, popping into view at the far end of the weight room before her tiny face did. She looked mightily annoyed.

"We're fine, Ashley," Deena hollered. "Just sharing some exercise tips."

When Ashley disappeared again, Deena grumbled. "Toxic little creature."

"Who, Ashley?" I shrugged. "She seems okay. Just young."

Deena sat up and patted the floor beside her, indicating I should move in closer. "Oh, I suppose you're right. She got on my bad side early on, and I tend to hold a grudge."

"The calipers?" I guessed, slipping off the weight bench and settling on the floor mat. We were like a couple of schoolgirls sprawled on a bedroom floor. All we needed were a couple of Barbie dolls or some paste and glitter.

"That, too. Actually, before we even got to the calipers, she'd ticked me off. I made the mistake of saying I wanted to get in shape for the trip to Cabo, so I'd look nice on the beach. She asked where Cabo was and did young people go there. I sniped back that, no, it was really more of an adult vacation spot. She said, 'Oh, so then it doesn't *really* matter what you look like, huh?'" Deena finished off in a singsongy falsetto, a truly remarkable impression of the perky Ashley.

"She didn't," I breathed.

"She did. I wanted to shake her. Just because I'm not stupid enough to starve myself, it doesn't mean I don't want to look nice." She skimmed her hands down the front of her stylish jogging suit. I would never dream of sweating in anything so fancy. It looked as though it might be dry-clean only. "Skinny isn't the only beautiful."

"Amen," I said, leaning out to give Deena a high five.

"I suppose it wouldn't kill me to lose a few pounds. My daughter, Crystal, is getting married in the spring, and I'll have to have my picture taken in some hopelessly frumpy mother-of-the-bride dress. But I just can't bring myself to care too much."

"You don't look old enough to have a daughter who's getting married." I wasn't just blowing smoke. It was the God's honest truth.

"Bless your heart for saying so." She smiled. "I was a child bride, you know. And my mama always said, you can keep your figure or your face. I chose my face. Anyway, Crystal just graduated from Dickerson last year. She was helping serve at the luau. . . . Maybe you met her?"

"Crystal Silver," I mused, trying to recall whether our paths had crossed.

Deena laughed. "Heavens, no, I wouldn't name my child Crystal Silver. Tom Silver is my second husband. We'll have been married five years next summer. Crystal's last name is Tompkins."

"Well, I don't think I met her that night. But we were so busy, it's all a blur. I'd love to meet her sometime, though. My niece is a freshman at Dickerson. Maybe Crystal could give her some pointers."

"We'll make that happen." Deena propped herself on her hands and narrowed her eyes, searching my face for something. My face flamed beneath her scrutiny. "So why are you here?"

I patted my saddlebags and struggled to sound nonchalant. "I thought it was about time I got in shape. Been eating too much ice cream lately."

"Bullshit," Deena said. "You've got a new business and personal problems out the yin-yang. No way you just decided, oh, hey, maybe I'll test-drive an expensive gym membership. Why are you *really* here?"

"I got a coupon in the mail for a free week," I insisted.

"Mmm-hmm. And it's just a coincidence that Brittanie Brinkman, the dead girl who was sleeping with your husband, was a regular member here. Right."

The very same straight talk that made me like Deena so much had a downside. She wasn't about to let me off the hook.

I sighed, then glanced around to be sure we were alone.

"I'm trying to learn what I can about Brittanie. I want to understand why she died, and I think the only way to do that is to understand how she lived."

Deena's mouth turned up in a self-congratulatory smirk. "I knew it. That's fabulous. Very Nancy Drew of you."

"Don't get carried away. I'm no girl detective.

Just trying to get a handle on whether Brittanie had any enemies, people the police ought to be looking at more closely."

"Enemies, huh? Well, I can't imagine you'll get anyone here to gossip about her. Not to you, anyway. But there are definitely some people at this gym who didn't like the girl. Heck, I never knew a body who could piss off more people than Brittanie Brinkman."

"Did you know her well?"

Deena raised her hands in mock surrender. "Thank the Lord, no, I did not. But between my 'workout sessions'"—she made little quote marks in the air with her fingers—"and all the Zeta luncheons I've catered, I've had plenty of opportunity to see the girl in action. She's quite a piece of work."

"How so?"

"Let me count the ways," she responded with a laugh.

Suddenly she sobered, and we waited while Trish Paolino, clad in a dove gray jogging bra and yoga pants slung low on impossibly narrow hips, mounted the stairs and sashayed through the weight room on the way to the lockers. As she passed, she glanced at the two of us, lolling on the mats like a couple of slugs, and her lip curled in contempt.

"Busted," Deena said. "By one of the Furies, no less."

"The Furies?"

"Trish, Jackie, and JoAnne. They're here every

damned day, from nine to eleven, passing judgment on us lesser mortals." She made a face. "Do you want to blow this pop stand?" she asked. "There's a coffee shop two doors down."

We helped each other up and made our way to the front door. Ashley, chattering away on her hands-free phone, looked at me expectantly as we passed. I mouthed an assurance that I'd be back.

Five minutes later, Deena and I sat cloistered in an upholstered nook of the Java Jive, nursing ceramic mugs of hot chocolate topped with ruffles of whipped cream. A cinnamon scone rested on a napkin on the table between us, and we took turns breaking off little nibbles. It occurred to me that a Mexican chocolate ice cream—perfumed with cinnamon, vanilla, and maybe just a hint of hazelnut— would make a great winter flavor for Remember the A-la-mode, and I made a mental note to start experimenting soon.

"So," Deena said, pulling my mind back to more pressing matters, "Brittanie Brinkman had catty down to an art form. Take our mutual friend Ashley back there." Deena waved in the general direction of the Lady Shapers. "About a month ago, I overheard Brittanie telling Ashley about her new suede boots. She said some of the other styles came in special sizes for plus-size girls with chunky calves, so maybe Ashley should check them out."

"What? Ashley's not chunky. Just athletic. Poor kid."

Deena raised her eyebrows as she popped a chunk of scone into her mouth. She swallowed before continuing. "Don't feel too bad for Ashley. She gave as good as she got."

"Yeah?"

"Mmm-hmm," she hummed. "Ashley made a crack about how at least her breath didn't stink of sick." She shrugged one shoulder. "It's not exactly Oscar Wilde, but it certainly hit the mark."

"I don't get it."

Deena patted my hand. "Bless your heart. Where have you been the last decade?"

"Right here in Dalliance."

"Yes, well, even right here in Dalliance, some girls throw up to stay skinny."

"Oh." Of course. I'd seen the talk shows and made-for-TV movies about bulimia. I'd even seen brochures in my doctor's waiting room. But I'd never known anyone with bulimia. Or, at least, I'd never *known* I'd known anyone with bulimia. "Are you sure Brittanie was bulimic?"

"If you're asking if I ever saw the girl stick her finger down her throat, the answer is no. But she basically never ate anything at the Zeta luncheons, yet I caught her stuffing a piece of cake into her face in the bathroom once. And all that crazy exercising— hours and hours a day—it certainly fits."

I couldn't see how Brittanie's eating disorder could possibly help explain her death, but it made me feel unexpected pity for the woman who all but stole my husband. I couldn't imagine hating yourself so much that you couldn't allow yourself the simple pleasure of food.

How empty she must have felt.

And I wondered what sort of mischief she might have done to fill up the hole. I now had at least two women—Ashley and JoAnne—who couldn't stand Brittanie, and I had the feeling I'd only scratched the surface.

chapter 13

"Hey, Aunt Tally. How was the gym? You all buff now?"

I wanted to smack the smug off Alice's face but settled for flipping her the most ladylike bird I could manage.

"How was that physiology midterm?" I asked her.

She gave me the one-fingered salute right back. No doubt about it, Bree and I were raising one classy young lady.

I'd spent the afternoon working the counter at the A-la-mode, scooping sundaes while my brain worked over the bits and pieces of information I'd acquired. Now, during the dinner-hour lull, Bree and I had staked out a table to look at paint chips in the hopes of finding something the historic district would find more appealing than the allegedly purple gray I'd chosen over the summer. Alice had picked up burgers at Erma's Fry by Night and was peeking inside the take-out containers to figure out whose was whose.

"What do you think of this?" I asked Bree, holding out a strip of paper and pointing to one square of color. "Sort of a warm brown."

Bree sighed and blinked her eyes in exasperation. "Tally, honey, that's pink."

"It is not," I said, pulling the chip back to study it again.

She snatched the chip away from me and read the color name off the back. "Rosy dawn. Sounds like pink to me."

I shoved the stack of chips across the table. "I give up. You pick. At this point, I honestly don't care. I just want to make them happy so I can stop paying the fine."

Alice dipped a French fry in barbecue sauce and popped it in her mouth. "Why don't you meet with someone from the historic commission," she said around a mouthful of potato, "and have them help you pick out a color?"

Bree and I exchanged sheepish looks. "That's actually a good idea," Bree said.

Alice snorted. "I have good ideas, you know. You just don't listen to me enough."

"Don't push your luck, kiddo," Bree warned. "Tally, you know who's on the historic commission? Your new best friend, Honey Jillson."

"She's hardly my new best friend. Actually, after lunch yesterday, I'd be surprised if she ever spoke to me again."

Bree pulled the top bun off her sandwich and re-arranged the pickle slices, spreading them out to provide more even burger coverage. "What the heck? You may as well give her a call. It can't hurt."

I shrugged. "If it allows me to put off committing to a color for another twelve hours, I'm game. I'll call Honey in the morning."

The bell over the front door tinkled softly, and the three of us froze in the act of biting into our burgers. Thankfully, it wasn't a customer, but Finn.

He waved his hands as I started to get up. "No, don't mind me. I was just on my way home and thought I would stop in to see how your ill-advised investigation is going."

I gave him a squint-eyed look. "Is this Finn the reporter or Finn the friend asking?"

He smiled as he pulled a chair around and strad-dled it backward. "For now, Finn the friend. But if you get a real lead, I'm going to be in an awkward position."

"Well," I said, offering him a fry, "since I have nothing but rank speculation, you should be safe."

"I think it's more than speculation," Bree said.

"Maybe," I conceded.

Finn raised his eyebrows, chewed his French fry, and waited patiently.

I began ticking off the facts I'd learned on my fingers. "Brittanie managed to alienate just about everyone she met. In particular, she pissed off the teenybopper who mans the front desk at the Lady Shapers and who happens to be one of Brit's sorority sisters. And she maybe fooled around with JoAnne Simms's husband. JoAnne Simms, who is yet another sorority sister, who belongs to the Lady Shapers, and who thus has access to the sports drink that Brit drank the night she died."

I picked up my burger, slathered in cheddar cheese, mayo, and ketchup, in both hands. "Oh, and Brit was bulimic. Which doesn't have anything to do with anything, but it's sad as heck." I took a big bite of my sandwich and waited for Finn's response.

He reached for one of Bree's fries, but she slapped his hand away. "JoAnne Simms, huh?"

"Yeah, I know it's a stretch."

Finn shrugged. "I don't know. From what I remember, JoAnne Simms was bat-shit crazy and really possessive."

Bree bobbled her eyebrows and held out her fries as a peace offering. "Bat-shit crazy? Do tell," she purred.

"Well, it was a long time ago. But my brother, Sonny, was in her class in high school. JoAnne had decided that Sonny was the perfect boyfriend: popular, big-time athlete, good-looking."

"So the polar opposite of you," Bree teased.

Finn laughed. "Basically, yeah. Anyway, Sonny wasn't particularly interested in JoAnne. He always preferred blondes. He had the audacity to ask Miranda Jillson to the junior prom."

"Ooh," Alice breathed, a dribble of ketchup on her chin. "Did Mrs. Simms go all 'Carrie' on everyone?"

"Not exactly. Miranda Jillson turned Sonny down. She had a boyfriend at the time, and Sonny was being a dork to ask her at all. But word got out that he asked Miranda first, and JoAnne decided that was Miranda's fault instead of Sonny's. She launched a massive campaign against Miranda. Told everyone that Miranda was easy and had slept with half the football team. Even tried to convince some of Miranda's teachers that she had cheated."

"Wow. That's hard core," Alice said.

"No one believed any of the rumors JoAnne spread. But I know when Miranda was hit by that drunk driver, the scuttlebutt in the senior class was that JoAnne was driving and hit her on purpose."

"Really?" Alice was hooked like a fish on Finn's story.

He shrugged. "That's what Sonny told me. Of course, the police caught the guy who actually hit her. Three witnesses gave a description of the car, the guy had spent the whole night getting sauced at the Bar None, and they found Miranda's blood on his front bumper. But the point is that JoAnne's classmates thought she was just crazy enough to do something like kill a girl out of jealousy."

Bree snorted. "Teenagers will believe anything. Bottom line, JoAnne Simms didn't kill anyone. So she was a little bit of a stalker? Who hasn't been at one time or another?"

Alice raised her hand. "Me. I have never once been a stalker."

"Oh, zip it, Saint Alice. You're young. There's plenty of time for the crazy to come out. Besides, that was over twenty years ago. JoAnne Simms has led a perfectly respectable life since then."

Finn looked at his watch. "I gotta run." He stood up, snagged one last fry from my take-out tray, and began buttoning up his barn coat. "Listen; Bree's right. I seriously doubt JoAnne Simms is the same sort of psycho-bitch she was in high school. But do me a favor, Tally. Try to keep a little distance between you and JoAnne Simms. Just to be safe."

I nodded, but even then I was trying to think of how I could actually get closer to JoAnne and get her to talk about her relationship with Brittanie Brinkman.

"Tawny, let's go to the phones." The cold glow of the television washed the den in ethereal light, and I pulled the quilt up to my chin, willing myself to fall asleep. "If you're out there and you've experienced the Pocket Barber, give us a call and tell us what you think."

Tawny stroked the Pocket Barber with perfectly manicured fingers, a manic smile plastered on her face. "Bob, we've got Millie from Little Rock on the line," she purred.

Bob lit up like a kid on Christmas morning. "Hi, Millie!"

"Hi, Bob."

"Millie, have you ordered the Pocket Barber?"

"I bought two! One for my husband, for the hairs he gets in his ears and nose, and one for my son, for neck touch-ups between haircuts."

"And do you love it?" Tawny asked. She continued caressing the implement, an electric razor the size and shape of a fountain pen.

"Oh, my, yes." Millie from Little Rock sounded as though she were 106. "The swivel blade gets into all those hard-to-reach spots, and it cuts real close."

"Well, thanks, Millie." Bob—in a white turtleneck and red argyle sweater—looked like an extra from a Perry Como Christmas special, and he oozed an unctuous sort of charm.

"Tawny, I'm so excited we can offer the Pocket Barber at such a low price, because this will save people so much money. Touch-ups between haircuts, grooming eyebrows, even removing the pills from sweaters. It's like having your own personal valet."

I snuggled down beneath the quilt and closed my eyes, sighing softly. Nearly three in the morning, and sleep eluded me.

Bree said I didn't experience authentic emotions, and she may have been right about that. Maybe I wasn't good at feeling angry or sad or happy, but I was the reigning world champion at feeling anxious. All the stresses and strains of daily life followed me to bed, flitting around my brain and conjuring nasty nightmares about tornadoes and algebra tests and public nudity.

In the wee, wee hours of the night, when the stress got too bad to sleep, I dragged my pillow and blanket into the den and curled up on the sofa with the TV on. And that was when I watched home-shopping channels. I needed the chatter of the TV, something to drown out the sound of the nagging voices in my head, but if I put on some sort of show—a made-for-TV movie or a gritty crime drama or even a laugh-track sitcom—I ended up trying to follow the plot instead of drifting off to sleep. The home-shopping patter, though, was the entertainment equivalent of white noise.

I tried to slow my breathing and let Bob and Tawny's small-electronics sales pitch fill my head, forcing out the racing thoughts of infidelity, insolvency, and infamy.

"Folks, you know your Shop Net family loves to find you new and exciting items to improve your quality of life," Bob said. "We've got a brand-new offering, and you just can't beat this remarkable piece for value and functionality."

"That's right, Bob. The MiniAmp personal auditory enhancer will cancel out ambient noise and amplify conversation, so you never miss a word."

I remembered the fight Bree and I had on our hands when we tried to convince Grandma Peachy to get a hearing aid. I wondered if we'd have had more luck if we'd called it a "personal auditory enhancer."

"Just look at this," Tawny continued. "It's sleek, sharp, and so discreet. Just hook it over your ear like this—see how easy?—and it looks just like one of those hands-free cell-phone headsets."

I cracked open an eye, intrigued. Tawny didn't lie. The oval plastic doodad hanging on her ear looked like a cell phone earpiece. It wasn't tiny, like the hearing aids we showed to Grandma Peachy, but it was so prominent, so obvious, no one would ever guess what it was. The hearing aid that hid in plain sight. Brilliant.

I let my eye drift shut again. Sleep. I was supposed to be sleeping.

"Tawny," Bob cut in, "what I love about this product is its versatility. You can use this anytime you're trying to hear conversation in a big crowd—restaurants, parties, movie theaters, church. But you could also use this when you're hunting, so you can hear a twig snap or the faintest little rustle of leaves."

I didn't think that sounded fair. But, when you got right down to it, hunting wouldn't really be fair until we started arming the deer.

"Absolutely, Bob. And the MiniAmp can also help you keep tabs on your kids when they're playing in another room. You know how it gets real quiet when they're up to no good? Well, now you can hear exactly what they're doing."

Bob laughed, and his voice took on a sly, slippery tone. "You'll never miss anything, Tawny. You can hear what the neighbors are saying about your landscaping or what the good-looking guy across the room thinks of your new dress."

My eye popped back open and an idea started taking shape in my brain.

On the fuzzy screen of my twenty-year-old TV, Tawny tucked her loose auburn curls behind her ear, showing off the MiniAmp. "At only $26.98, this would be a great gift for an older relative, or even for a spouse. I know Carl would love to be able to watch television in bed after I go to sleep, and this would be such a great item for our household. Carl could keep the volume low enough for me to sleep, and yet he could hear his favorite shows. It might just save our marriage."

Bob laughed on cue. "Our viewers may have seen similar devices before, but the MiniAmp is special. See this little feature here?" The camera zoomed in on a dimpled bit of plastic on the front of the oval. "This is the very latest in digital directional microphone technology. Real cutting-edge stuff. By activating the directional mic, your MiniAmp will pick up on the sounds directly in front of you and minimize background noise."

Tawny oohed appreciatively.

"And the microphone rotates here"—Bob caressed the little mic and it swiveled around to the side—"so you can focus on sounds from the side rather than in front of you. This is great for conversations in the car."

I was fully alert by that point. With that little gizmo strapped to my head, I could hear the women at the Lady Shapers dish the dirt. I wouldn't need to worm my way into their sacred social circle. I could get the unfiltered, uncensored scoop from clear across the cardio room.

With my bed quilt trailing me like the train of a homespun wedding gown, I shuffled into the kitchen, felt around on the table until I found my purse, and rooted through it for my cell phone. Standing in the doorway of the den, I squinted at the TV as I punched in the number for Shop Net.

"Thank you for calling Shop Net. How can I help you?"

"Hi. I want a MiniAmp. And I need rush delivery."

chapter 14

Honey Jillson graciously agreed to discuss suitable exterior paint colors with me on the very morning after I called. Wednesdays were development days at the Zeta Eta Chi alumni house, so she needed to supervise the students and alumni putting together fund-raising packets. She assured me the job involved little more than collating, stuffing, and stamping, so it was no trouble at all for us to talk while the young women worked.

I don't know what I was expecting from the Zeta Eta Chi alumni house. Maybe a high-end spa environment, with trickling fountains and tropical aromas. Perhaps something akin to a French château, with gilded ceilings and damask-covered settees. Or even posh corporate offices with plush carpets and real oak wainscoting.

Whatever I was expecting, the Zeta Eta Chi alumni house was not it. In fact, the alumni house was nothing more than a converted garage behind the main house where the college girls slept and studied and partied. Neutral off-white paint coated the drywall, and posters from Zeta charity events hung in plain black metal frames, the kind you can pick up at any discount store. The furniture was clean but utterly utilitarian. And, on the day I visited, the interior was redolent of sausage pizza.

Honey greeted me with a weary smile. "The girls are upstairs in the multipurpose room, having lunch." Her smile tightened a fraction. "With any luck, they won't get sausage grease on the lovely new brochures we had printed up. The house depends on alumni contributions for so many of its activities. It's important that the solicitations look professional."

The notion of rich people asking for money from other rich people seemed odd to me, but I smiled and nodded.

"Why don't we take over that table?" she said, pointing the way to a worktable made from two short filing cabinets and an old door that dominated the center of the room. "That way we can spread out some."

She gathered up the scraps of paper and markers that littered the surface of the worktable and rested them on the corner of one of two more traditional desks set against the far wall of the room. One of the desks boasted a PC and a small ink-jet printer.

An open can of discount diet cola and a half-empty bag of tortilla chips suggested that someone had been doing homework there. The other desk was more orderly: stationery and mailing and packing supplies were arranged in tidy little boxes around an old IBM Selectric typewriter, its tan plastic cover just a tiny bit askew.

Honey and I sat at the newly decluttered work table.

"First," I said, handing her a silver insulated bag tied with a big white ribbon, "I brought you a little something to thank you for your help. I knew you liked butterscotch candies, so I went out on a limb and guessed you'd like butterscotch ice cream, too." She took the bag from me gingerly, her expression alarmed. "Don't worry; the insulated bag will keep it frozen for a good six hours."

"Well, thank you, dear. Dub and I will surely enjoy that." She set the bag next to her chair, and I began rooting around in my purse for the various paint chips I had brought—clipped together in groups of "maybe," "no way," and "no freakin' way."

"So," Honey said, "you need to choose new paint colors. Do you have the fan deck of approved shades from Tiburgh's Paints?"

My hand stilled in my purse and I looked up. "No. There's a set of preapproved colors?"

She nodded.

"So I didn't have to go through every color known to man at every single hardware store in the greater Dalliance metropolitan area?"

Honey chuckled. "Of course not, dear. It's refer-enced in the historic commission bylaws. Section five, subsection c; I believe it's paragraph four."

"You're kidding me."

Ridiculously, I felt tears welling in my eyes and a lump of misery gathering in my throat. Sudden-ly, it was just all too much. Too many rules, too many regulations, too many suspicions and social pitfalls, too much baggage. I had an impulse to get up and run—out the door, out of Dalliance, across the state line, and into the great unknown. I could picture myself bolting, running fast, and my body was already there: heart galloping, sweat beading on my burning face, breath coming in great heav-ing gasps.

Through a haze of completely irrational terror, I became aware of Honey Jillson patting my hand softly.

"Calm, dear, calm," she soothed. "Tallulah, I need you to breathe for me. Can you do that?"

I nodded, because I wanted to please Miz Jillson, but I really didn't think I could breathe at all.

"Hum." She closed her eyes, then opened them with a smile. "Let's hum 'The Yellow Rose of Texas.' I've always liked that song."

While half of my brain was already somewhere near Tulsa and an inky darkness flooded my peripheral vision, I clung to the sight of Honey Jillson's patri-cian features—her hair the color of unripe canta-loupe and her jaunty lilac neckerchief—and hummed along with her rendition of "The Yellow Rose of

Texas." I'm not gonna lie: the sounds I made were not songlike at all, but the act of humming seemed to slow my heart, and after a minute or two my breathing returned to normal.

"Oh, Miz Jillson, I'm so sorry," I choked out, terror replaced by mortification. "I don't know what came over me."

She smiled gently and patted my hand again. "It's called a panic attack, and you mustn't let it bother you." She waved her hand in the general direction of the ceiling. "Those girls up there get them when they get an A-minus or the polish on their nails doesn't match their lipstick. I think, under the circumstances, you're entitled to a momentary breakdown."

Her kindness itself threatened to bring back the tears, so I didn't dare say much. "Thank you," I managed.

"Now," she said, her tone brusque and no-nonsense, "let's pick a color for that lovely little house of yours. I have the Tiburgh's fan deck in my attaché, since we're having a historic commission meeting this evening and I didn't want to forget it." She paused in the act of rifling through her briefcase. "In fact, if we can settle on a color this morning, I'll make a motion to approve your choice as 'new business.' You won't even have to wait the two weeks to get it on the agenda."

A wave of relief washed through me, clearing away the last of the jitters. "Thank you so much, Miz Jillson. That would be great."

"Honey," she chided as she plopped a booklet of paint chips in front of me. "How do you feel about blue?"

With a limited selection to choose from and no fear that I'd get it wrong, it didn't take me long to settle on a misty, mossy green—nearly the color of Finn Harper's eyes—with accents of a deep terracotta and a lighter blush.

Honey was jotting down the names and numbers for the colors we'd chosen when a young woman in jeans and a yellow sweatshirt embroidered with a huge orange Z skipped down the stairs and into the front room.

"Miz Jillson," she said, "we ran out of the envelopes with the return address already printed on them. Do you want us to run off labels, or do we need to wait for more envelopes to get here?"

Honey sighed. "The labels look tacky, Lisa. I ordered more envelopes last week, and they should be here any day. Could you girls come back on Friday afternoon to finish up?"

Lisa's face tightened, and I had watched enough moods cross Alice's face to know that the young woman did not want to spend her Friday afternoon stuffing envelopes. But she forced a smile and said, "Yes, ma'am. No problem."

As she took the stairs two at a time to spread the word about the revised plans, Honey sighed. "It looks like I'm finishing up here earlier than I planned. Dub was going to drive me over to the historic commission meeting this evening, so I don't have my car. I hate to impose on you, but would you mind driving me home?"

"Not at all. It's the least I can do."

We made small talk on the ride to the Jillsons' house in the exclusive Ember Ridge neighborhood. The development, where Finn's parents lived, dated back to the 1960s and featured an eclectic mix of architectural styles nestled amid mature oak and pecan trees. While the Harpers' house was a Tudor, the Jillsons' Spanish colonial, just around the corner, had creamy stucco walls and a clay tile roof.

As I pulled into the driveway, I mentioned how much I'd always admired their house. "Every time I drove past, I thought how beautiful it was. In the summer, it looks so cool and inviting. I always wondered who lived here."

"Thank you, dear," Honey replied. She smiled as she gathered her satchel and her purse close. "I imagine we passed one another quite a lot back when you dated Finn Harper. But, of course, we wouldn't have had much reason to stop to talk."

I was stunned that Honey knew whom I'd dated in high school. My surprise must have shown on my face, because Honey chuckled.

"Tallulah, this is a small town, and an even smaller neighborhood. Ida Harper and I were close back then, what with her boy Sonny and my Miranda being the same age and all."

"Are you still friends?"

Her lips thinned and she looked out the windshield. "No. You would think that both of us losing children like we did would bring us closer together, but instead we drifted apart. I guess we were both so full up with sadness, we couldn't stand a drop more."

She gave herself a little shake. "But I heard about her troubles, and that she isn't doing well. I keep meaning to stop in to see her. Us old biddies need to stick together," she added with a wry smile.

"I'm sure she would appreciate that."

"And I understand Finn Harper has come home to take care of his mother. It certainly seems like that hellion has grown into a fine young man." She looked at me out of the corner of her eye, her expression heavy with significance.

"Yes, ma'am. He seems to have done well for himself. Maybe I made the wrong choice back in high school."

Her brow wrinkled and the corners of her mouth tightened. "Tallulah Jones, we all make choices we come to regret. Take it from this old lady. You can't dwell on the mistakes you've made in the past. You have to act in the here and now to make it right."

She wrapped one hand through the straps of her bags and put the other on the door handle.

"You're young and single. Finn Harper is young and single. Just make it right."

Before I could think to help her with the door, she climbed out of the car and began making her slow and careful way to her front door.

Just make it right, she said. It sounded so simple.

But I was pretty sure that nearly two decades be-

fore, when I chose security over the adventure of
Finn, I made a choice that couldn't ever be undone.

I wore a white sundress, as crisp as new money,
the night I broke Finn Harper's heart.

He picked me up in his dark green Scirocco,
Sonny's car before he died. For nearly an hour, we
cruised around town in a looping, baroque circuit
that brought us back again and again to the courthouse square. A mix tape—Nirvana, Pearl Jam, Nine
Inch Nails—blared from the stereo speakers, a raw
wound in the sultry summer evening.

I slipped out of my thin-soled sandals and
propped my feet on the dashboard, tugging my skirt
down over my bent knees so that only my toes, nails
painted a candy pink, peeped from beneath the ruffled hem. Finn slouched behind the wheel, the curve
of his body a physical echo of the desolate beat of
the music. His hand, tan and long fingered, draped
over the gearshift, but at stoplights he'd reach out to
brush my arm, just a whisper of a touch, as though
to reassure himself I was still there.

When the violet twilight deepened to a rich ame-
thyst, Finn pulled into the Tasty-Swirl parking lot,
the wheels of the Scirocco popping on the fine
gravel. The lot was full. A T-ball team in bright orange jerseys swarmed over two of the aluminum
picnic tables, while teenagers drifted from car to
car, wild-eyed and boisterous. The air smelled of
scorched chocolate and the sweet malt scent of waffle cones and the greasy tang of onion rings.

While Finn bought our ice cream, I staked out a table as far from the T-ballers as I could, a table halfway between the blue-white glow of the Tasty-Swirl's halogen lights and the velvet dusk beyond. I perched on the very edge of the metal bench, mindful of my bright new dress. Above me, bats swooped out of the night to feast on hapless insects. On the far side of the parking lot, a flock of grackles cloaked a small post oak in shifting shadows, chattering and squawking, and at odd intervals a glissando shriek pierced the air. I wrapped my arms around my waist and shivered.

"Tally." Finn's voice, liquid and low, startled me. He handed me a cone wrapped with a rough paper napkin. Already, pearly droplets of melting ice cream welled along the seam between the sugar cone and the waxy chocolate shell.

I tried to smile as I took it from him, but my mouth wouldn't seem to work right.

He frowned, accentuating the sulky fullness of his lower lip and the harsh geometry of his heavy brows. "What's wrong?"

"Cal McCormack told me yesterday that you turned down the scholarship to Southern Methodist."

He sat next to me, the origami folding of his lanky frame stirring the hot, heavy air.

"Cal McCormack needs to mind his own business. It just kills him that you turned him down for me."

"Forget Cal. Is it true? Did you turn down the scholarship?"

"I don't want to go to business school," he said.

"I know."

"But you don't understand."

It wasn't a question, so I didn't bother answering.

A rivulet of melted ice cream snaked across the back of his hand, but he didn't pay any attention.

"You ever seen cattle in a chute?" I nodded stiffly. I could see where this was going, and I didn't much like the idea of being nothing but an obstacle in Finn's life. "They take that first step and there's no going back. Each step after that, they can only go one way, one step after another until they're dead."

I looked away, off into the darkness. I knew all about putting one step in front of the other no matter where the path was leading. I didn't even get to choose that first step myself. My mama took it for me, when she threw away the handful of college brochures that came in the mail and the notice about signing up for the SAT.

Every part of me—my chest, my cheeks, even the palms of my hands—tightened, as if I'd been dipped in shellac that was beginning to harden and dry.

"Southern Methodist is hardly a slaughterhouse," I said.

He blew a stream of air through his nose and ran his free hand through his wind-tousled hair. "Dammit, Tally. You just don't understand."

He was right. I didn't understand. I didn't understand how someone could throw away a perfectly good chance to get a degree and make connections, the sort of connections that got you a steady job in an air-conditioned office. The kind of job where you could wear starched shirts and shiny shoes and go to the doctor without a dock in your pay.

"Tally, I don't want to end up in some miserable, soulless, dead-end job like my dad."

From what I'd seen, every job was miserable, soulless, and dead-end. Some just paid better than others.

"So what are you going to do?" I asked softly.

"I don't know," he said, all bluster and bravado. "I'm gonna be a screenwriter. But first, I'll travel some. See the country. Maybe go to Europe."

"Oh."

"You could go with me," he said.

I heard a boyish note of pleading in his voice, and that made me angry. We both knew I couldn't go with him. We both knew I had to watch after my mama. And besides, I didn't know how much it cost to fly to Europe, but it was surely more than I had saved up at the credit union. We both knew I couldn't go with him, but he asked anyway, so I would have to tell him no.

My face now so stiff that it felt like a mask, I shook my head.

"And I won't wait for you, either," I said, my voice sounding like that of a stranger. "I can't."

He stood up, hurled his dripping ice-cream cone into the nearest trash barrel, and loomed over me. I don't know where I found the courage, but I raised my chin and looked him in the eye.

"So that's it?" His words hung between us, as hard as flint.

I felt scooped out and hollow inside, the space Finn had occupied suddenly empty. The words I'd rehearsed all day turned to ash in my mouth, and I barely managed a nod.

He shoved his hands deep in his pockets and hunched his shoulders. "Dammit, Tally." I expected him to say more, to protest or rail against the unfairness of it all, but he didn't. Just cursed, then stalked off, leaving me alone in my new white sundress and thin-soled sandals.

From across the parking lot, I heard the roar of a revving engine, the angry sound surprising the other customers into a momentary silence. The Scirocco pealed out of the lot, spitting tiny pebbles in its wake.

I looked down in time to see a drop of ice cream mixed with chocolate coating slip from the edge of my hand and fall to my lap. With trembling hands, I threw the sad mess away and dabbed at the stain with a fresh napkin. My efforts only made the mark spread, and tears of frustration choked me.

I went home that night and soaked my dress in hot water and borax. The stain faded but never disappeared. And I didn't see Finn Harper again until he turned up on my porch that unseasonably warm October night.

And by then, I knew, it was far too late. The boy he was then, the woman I was now, were all but strangers.

chapter 15

The *mini* in MiniAmp suggested that the item was miniature. Relative to what, I couldn't say. During the Battle of the Hearing Aid, Bree, Grandma Peachy, and I looked at devices as tiny as my pinkie nail, and the MiniAmp looked huge by comparison. In reality it was only about the size of a cheap plastic cigarette lighter, but when it was hanging off the side of my head, it seemed enormous. As I casually strolled across the floor of the Lady Shapers, I felt like a Flintstones character, with a brontosaurus bone swinging from my ear.

As expected, the Furies—JoAnne Simms, Jackie Conway, and Trish Paolino—were lined up on a row of elliptical trainers, their legs churning and arms pumping in perfect sync with one another as they chatted, matching bottles of neon green Vigor in their cup holders. Until I walked in, they had the place to themselves. Simultaneously, without breaking stride, they fell silent and pivoted their heads to watch me enter. I threw them a nonchalant little wave and headed for the piece of equipment farthest away from them—a clunky, outdated cross-country ski machine.

I didn't have a clue how to use the ski machine, but I needed to be far enough away that the three women would feel comfortable resuming their conversation. So I turned on the MiniAmp, flipped the switch to use the directional mic, and adjusted the mic from its front to its side orientation. Then I carefully clambered up onto the narrow wooden skids, trying to snug the toes of my cross-trainers into the cupped metal toe caps.

But as soon as I got one foot in place and shifted my weight to that leg, the pressure sent the ski sliding backward. With my weight balanced precariously on one leg, the unexpected movement pitched me forward, and I clotheslined myself across the metal railing wrapped around the front of the machine.

In my MiniAmped ear, I heard a chorus of chuckles and snorts.

I gathered my dignity as best I could and, with all the grace of a vaudevillian doing a pratfall, managed to heave myself into position on the ski machine. My legs shook, and the skis slid back and forth by fractions of an inch until I got my balance. Tentatively, I grabbed the simulated ski poles and began shuffling my feet forward and back. After a few hesitant repetitions, I found an awkward rhythm.

Once I felt sure I wouldn't go flying off the back of the machine, I turned my attention to JoAnne, Jackie, and Trish.

Following Alice's advice, I closed my eyes and began moving my mouth slightly, occasionally nodding, as though I were having a deep conversation with someone on my cell phone. I felt like a lunatic, but after a few beats of quiet, nothing but the faint squeak of one elliptical trainer and the soft whisper of their gym clothes rustling, my ruse paid off as the three women began to converse in stage whispers.

It took me a few seconds to find just the right angle for my head, so I heard their voices rather than just the ambient noise of the fans and cardio machines, but once I did, I could hear them speak with astonishing clarity.

"Can you believe she's here? I mean, how do you even go out in public after a scandal like she's been through? It's all so white trash." I knew for a fact that Jackie Conway dated her second cousin in high school, so I don't know who died and made her an arbiter of class.

"I feel bad for her." From the glee in her voice, it sounded as if Trish Paolino didn't feel a lick of sympathy for me.

"Honestly, it's hardly Tally's fault that her husband cheated on her." And that, without question, was JoAnne Simms.

"Of course it's not her fault that he cheated," Jackie said. She spoke slowly and with exaggerated emphasis, as if she were talking to a toddler. "I was talking about the murder."

"That's hardly her fault, either," JoAnne countered.

"I wouldn't be too sure," Jackie said. "Everyone's looking at the husband right now, but have you met the man? He doesn't have the good sense God gave little bitty bunnies. My money is on her." By which she presumably meant me.

Someone snorted. "I can think of a dozen people who wanted Brittanie Brinkman dead, just off the top of my head," Trish said.

"Wanting the girl dead and actually killing her are two very different things," Jackie noted. "I would need a pretty powerful motive to kill someone in cold blood like that."

"Or you'd need to be crazy," JoAnne added. A shiver went down my spine. *Bat-shit crazy*, I thought.

Jackie and Trish laughed, and then I heard deeper breathing and swallowing as the three women followed the Lady Shapers creed of hydration, hydration, hydration.

"Well," Jackie continued, "my cleaning lady plays canasta with Vonda Hudson, who works down at the police department, and she told me that Wayne and Tally are each others' alibis. He said he was with his ex-wife the night Brittanie died. That's mighty convenient, if you ask me."

Trish gasped, suitably shocked. "But I heard that

Wayne was in the house that night. He listened to Brittanie cry out for help but just ignored her."

JoAnne tutted softly. "You two need to stop listening to gossip. Wayne wasn't home that night, but he wasn't with Tallulah, either."

I was so intent on listening to the conversation behind me, I completely forgot about my cover. When the ladies grew suddenly silent, I realized I had, at some point, stopped moving my feet. I opened my eyes and saw my reflection in the mirrored wall, my mouth hanging open just slightly, my head cocked at an awkward angle, and my body frozen in midglide.

With a sinking sense of dread, I slid my eyes to the side and, one by one, met the gazes of JoAnne, Jackie, and Trish, who had also stopped in midrotation on their elliptical trainers. Jackie and Trish wore matching thin-lipped, arched-eyebrow expressions of high indignation . . . basically, exactly the expressions I would expect from hoity-toity ladies who caught someone shamelessly eavesdropping on their conversation.

But JoAnne's reaction puzzled me. Her mouth quirked in a wry smile, and her eyes danced with silent laughter.

Then she winked at me.

I hightailed it straight from the Lady Shapers to the Dalliance Police Department.

The brusque young officer at the front desk looked at me as if I were a criminal when I asked to speak to Cal, and while I waited in one of the rock-hard Naugahyde chairs, the young man kept shooting narrow-eyed looks my way, as if he were waiting to catch me red-handed, doing something illegal.

"Tally Jones," Cal said from the hallway that led to the back of the station. He braced his hands on the doorframe and leaned into the waiting room, rocking up on his toes. "What brings you down here this fine day?"

I scrambled to my feet. "I think I may have some information about Brittanie's murder."

I expected Cal to look shocked, for him to demand the information right away . . . some sort of excitement. But instead, Cal just smiled one of his stingy, enigmatic smiles. "Well, then," he said, "you better come back and fill me in."

This time we met in Cal's "office," which was really just a modular cubicle of tan fabric and beige laminate. A couple of trophies for marksmanship served as bookends holding a half dozen plastic binders upright on a little shelf. A coffee cup, emblazoned with a cartoon of a dog trying to trick a cat into climbing into a clothes dryer, held down a stack of papers. Otherwise, there wasn't anything personal about the desk at all.

"Can I get you a cup of coffee or a soda?" he asked as I sat on a hard plastic chair.

"No, thanks."

"Suit yourself." He sat in his desk chair, leaning back so far, it was clear the springs were shot, and took a sip from the coffee mug.

"Cal, I think JoAnne Simms might have killed Brittanie," I blurted.

One eyebrow cocked up. "Really. And what makes you think that?"

I explained to him about JoAnne calling Brittanie a slut and how maybe Brittanie had an affair with Garrett Simms. And I explained how JoAnne seemed dead certain that Wayne wasn't home the night Brittanie died—which both bolstered Wayne's story and raised the issue of how JoAnne knew who was in the house and who wasn't. And, finally, I explained how JoAnne had access to the sports drink that Brittanie used. She easily could have poisoned the Vigor before Brittanie brought it home from the Lady Shapers.

Throughout my whole story, Cal's expression never changed.

"Well, that's quite a tale, Tally. But I don't think it holds much water."

"Are you kidding me?"

"No, ma'am," he said with a wry smile. "I'm not much of a kidder."

"But JoAnne had means, motive, and opportunity," I insisted.

Cal shook his head. "I think you've been watching too much television. That's not really how we solve crimes. See, we look for evidence."

Maybe he wasn't a kidder, but he sure was a smart-ass.

"Besides," he said, "it sounds like half of Dalliance had motive, and *everyone* had means—antifreeze isn't exactly uncommon, especially with winter coming on. As for opportunity, well, that's a little tricky."

"How so? It had to be someone who had access to the Vigor, either before or after it got into Wayne and Brittanie's house."

"Nuh-uh." He shook his head, as though he was real sorry to be the one to break the news to me. "The state lab tested the empty bottle of Vigor from Brittanie's bedside table, and every other bottle in the house and in the recycling, and they couldn't find a trace of ethylene glycol."

"What do you mean?" I knew exactly what he meant, but I just couldn't quite believe it.

"I mean that however Ms. Brittanie Brinkman consumed a lethal dose of ethylene glycol, it was not through a poisoned sports drink. And, in fact, from what the ME has been able to piece together, it looks like she ingested the poison between seven and ten the night before she died."

"But that was . . ." A heavy sense of dread seeped through my limbs.

"Yes, ma'am. That was during the Weed and Seed luau." He took another sip of his coffee. "So that there creates a whole new mess of possibilities."

"I guess it does," I said, my voice barely a whisper.

"In fact, it's a funny thing you should stop in to see me, because I was fixin' to call you myself."

"Oh?" I fixed my gaze on one of Cal's trophies,

studying the gold plastic man, the places where the gold coating had chipped off, exposing some dark material beneath.

"Yes, ma'am. It was some mighty dirty work, but we managed to track down a bunch of the bags of trash from the luau and have started going through them looking for traces of antifreeze."

"Really?"

"Yep. It's a big job"—he smiled—"as you can imagine. So far, we've only turned up one little item with any antifreeze on it."

I heard him speaking, but his voice was garbled and distant, as if I were underwater.

"It was this little plastic cup. We asked around a bit, and some folks seem to recall you used those same little cups to serve the sauce for your ice cream."

I finally mustered the courage to look Cal in the eye. His tone had remained amiable throughout his monologue, but I saw then that his blue eyes were as hard and cold as diamonds.

"Funny, huh?" he asked.

It wasn't funny at all, but I figured he already knew that.

He shrugged. "Now, of course, it might just be a fluke. You know, there was a lot of trash all mixed up, so maybe some antifreeze—either the poison or just some random bit of refuse—came in contact with that little plastic cup. We call that 'transfer,' and it happens quite a bit. But we're looking for more of those little red cups now."

Red?

He set the coffee mug on his desk and drummed his fingers on the edge of his computer keyboard.

"While the lab folks are looking through all that trash, though, I thought I might chat with you a bit. See if maybe you had something to add."

I cleared my throat and framed my question very carefully. "Are you implying that I poisoned Brittanie? With an ice-cream sundae?"

Cal held up his hands. "Whoa. I'm not implying anything. But someone might get that impression, don't you think?"

I leaned forward, willing Cal to believe me. "Listen, I did not particularly care for Brittanie Brinkman. But I didn't wish her harm."

He just smiled that Sphinx-like smile.

"And even if I did," I said, "even if I wanted to kill her, I sure as heck wouldn't have done it by poisoning an ice-cream sundae."

"No?"

"No. First, poisoned ice cream—"

"Actually, I think it's the topping that's the issue."

"Whatever. Poisoned sundae topping makes me look pretty guilty. And I'm not that stupid. And second," I added, feeling a glimmer of hope that this might convince him of my innocence, "Brittanie had made it perfectly clear that she didn't like ice cream. She didn't like any sort of sweets, and said my ice cream, in particular, was too rich."

"Huh."

"Yeah, huh. So if I wanted to kill Brittanie Brinkman, why would I put the poison in the one thing I knew she would *not* eat?"

He cocked his head, as though he was considering my point.

"Oh," I added, "and you said you found the antifreeze in one of the red cups?" He nodded. "Well, those cups were special—without pineapple—just for Wayne."

"Another one of your all-time favorite people."

I shot him an evil look. "But Wayne didn't even get sick, so clearly there wasn't any poison in the sundae topping."

Cal drummed his fingers in a curious rhythm, then squared the corners of the papers on his desk. "Well, Tally Jones, you've sure given me something to chew on. Like I said, it may just be a big coincidence that the lab found that antifreeze on your plastic serving cup. I'll be sure to let you know if we need to see you back in here."

I nodded. But I couldn't quite leave things hanging the way they were.

I swallowed hard. "Am I a suspect?" I asked.

Cal leaned back in his chair and brushed invisible crumbs from his tie. "I wouldn't say 'suspect.'" For an instant I felt relief so strong I thought I might start to cry. But then he shrugged and added, "I would say 'person of interest.'"

chapter 16

"What's the difference?" Bree asked as she eyeballed a couple of jiggers of tequila into the blender.

I waited until the whine of the blender died. "I called Finn on the way home and asked him that very question. He said, basically, one's actionable; the other's not."

Bree expertly rimmed a margarita glass with salt. "What does that mean?"

"It means, if the police call me a suspect too early in the game, I could maybe sue them. But as long as I'm just a 'person of interest,' they can destroy my reputation with relative impunity."

"Great."

"Isn't it, though?"

Bree strolled over to the dining table and handed me my margarita, and we clinked glasses in a wry toast.

"What about me?" Alice asked.

"You want to be a suspect?" Bree quipped.

"No, I want a margarita." Alice sat at the far end of the table, surrounded by open books and note-pads. She tapped her government textbook with the eraser end of her pencil. "According to my book, the drinking age was raised to twenty-one in re-sponse to lobbying by special interests." She drew out the words *lobbying* and *special interests* to illus-trate their evilness. "Fight the power, Mom, and let me have a drink."

"Baby girl, around here, I *am* the power. And I say you can't partake of the demon spirits until you're much, much older." Bree sat down across from me and took another sip of her margarita, giv-ing her daughter a wide-eyed look over the rim of her glass.

"That's so unfair," Alice argued, raising her childlike chin in defiance.

"Life is unfair," Bree responded with a shrug. She picked up her reading glasses and her cross-stitch and set to work. "Just ask Miranda Jillson. Cut down in her prime because of—drum roll, please—alcohol."

"Aha," Alice said, narrowing her eyes as she prepared to make her closing argument. "But Mir-anda Jillson wasn't drunk. She was just an innocent bystander. Wrong place, wrong time. The irresponsible person who got drunk and drove his car was—how old?"

She looked at me for an answer. "I don't know," I said as I slit open the statement from the electric company. "Thirty-five? Forty? He had kids in middle school; I remember that."

Alice preened. "See, I rest my case."

Bree squinted as she threaded a tiny embroidery needle with butter yellow floss. "I don't know that you made much of a point at all, child of mine. But in any event, this wasn't a debate. No margaritas for you."

Alice blew out a frustrated breath through her nose and began tapping her eraser on her book again.

"It's weird," I said, hoping to diffuse the tension. "I haven't given a thought to Miranda Jillson in twenty years, and now, in the past few days, it seems like everyone has a story to tell about her." I scrawled my signature across the last check for October's household bills and tugged it out of the book.

"Oh, wow," Alice said. "Baader-Meinhof."

"Gesundheit," Bree quipped. She never took her eyes off the delicate needlework in her hands, one of a set of floral fingertip towels she planned to give to her mother, my aunt Jenny, for Christmas. My hell-raising cousin, with her sin-colored hair and skintight T-shirts, looked remarkably old-fashioned with her rhinestone reading glasses set low on her nose and her embroidery hoop held in one dainty hand. Of course, when she paused to take a sip of her cocktail, she pretty much ruined the image.

Alice groaned. "Very funny, Mom. Seriously, we learned about this in my psychology class a couple of weeks ago. It's called the Baader-Meinhof phenomenon. It's like when you learn a new word and then, in the space of a couple of days, you hear the word again and again."

"So is it some kind of woo-woo sign or something?" I asked as I stuffed the check and payment coupon into the envelope, fussing with it until the address for the municipal electric company was neatly centered in the plastic window.

"No. You hear the word because you know it. Like, you probably heard the word all the time before, but you didn't know what the word meant so your brain filtered it out. Now you know the word, so your brain pays attention."

I sealed and stamped the envelope, then tapped all the bills into a neat stack for the next day's mail. "But I've always known who Miranda Jillson was. She's not new to me."

Alice pondered that a minute, her delicate features scrunched up in thought. At that moment she looked exactly as she had when she was four years old and trying to puzzle through the words of her Dr. Seuss ABC book. I fought an overwhelming urge to hug her tight and never let her go.

She made a little clicking sound with her tongue and teeth. "Ah. You knew who Miranda Jillson was, but she didn't have any significance for you. But then you had lunch with Mrs. Jillson and talked about her daughter, and now it matters to you. Information only has meaning if you have a context for it."

She laughed mischievously. "It's like you probably always knew who Cheryl Ladd was, but you never noticed that the clerk at the post office is named Cheryl Ladd until after we watched that *Charlie's Angels* marathon last summer."

We both giggled at the memory of me making a total fool of myself at the post office, grinning like an idiot when I put two and two together and then asking the sixty-something-year-old clerk if she'd been named after the younger model.

"So it's not a sign, just a coincidence."

"Not even that," she said. "Just a fluke of what gets caught in your sievelike brain."

"Alice Anders! Respect for your elders," Bree chided, pausing in the act of drawing her needle up at the end of a stitch.

"It's not disrespectful. Everyone's brain is like a sieve."

"Let me guess. You learned about it in psychology class?"

"Yep."

"So that's what we pay for? To have some egghead professor teach you that folks ain't bright."

Alice sighed dramatically, just as the oven timer began to buzz. "That's wrong on so many levels. First, you don't pay for my tuition. I have a scholarship. Second, it's a lot more complicated than 'folks ain't bright.'"

"Oh, lighten up, Saint Alice. I understand. Your poor old mama isn't *that* backwoods."

I detected a note of real pain beneath Bree's teasing. In high school, Bree joked about blowing off papers and failing classes, but it was all an act. Beneath the big hair and cleavage, Bree was a smart girl. She got As in most of her classes and even started quietly gathering brochures from colleges, until a pregnancy scare led to a shotgun wedding her senior year. She lost the baby a week after the wedding and lost the husband six months later, but she never managed to revive the dream of college.

Bree didn't begrudge Alice the chance to shine academically, but I had to think she was a little green-eyed about it, too.

"Okay, you two. Enough already." I pushed back from the table, set the bills and my checkbook on the corner of the nearest counter, and slipped on my oven mitts. I pulled the pan of enchiladas out of the oven and set them on top of the stove. The narcotic scents of cumin, chilies, and chocolate—the secret ingredient in my enchilada sauce—filled the air and calmed the tempers of my prickly little family. For the next few minutes, we did the dinner *pas de trois*: Alice putting away her books and setting out the silver, Bree filling water glasses, and me dishing up the grub.

"Alice," I said as I settled into my seat and spread my napkin in my lap, "you may be right. I feel like

I'm getting bits and pieces of information about Brittanie Brinkman, but I don't have any context for most of it. It's like trying to put together a puzzle without having the picture on the box."

Bree opened her mouth to comment, but just then the doorbell sounded. After my conversation with Cal that afternoon, I was as nervous as a cat, but I steeled my spine and went to answer the door.

In the living room, I twitched aside the sheer curtain and peeked out the sidelight window. Wayne Jones stood on my front porch, as bold as brass.

I had to yank on the handle to pry open the heavy front door because the wood had swollen in the recent damp and it stuck something fierce.

That sturdy door, nearly as wide as it was tall, was one of my favorite parts of the house. Clary Jenkins, who lived next door and fancied herself the neighborhood historian, called my door a "coffin door," said they made it wide enough to carry in a coffin back when folks laid out their dead in their front parlors. Alice didn't like that morbid explanation and declared it a "Christmas door," wide enough to carry in a Christmas tree without losing any needles.

The door popped free of its frame with a soft *whump*.

"Hey, Wayne. Come on in."

He took a few halting steps into my living room, looking around curiously. Wayne attended the closing for the house and handed over the check to the harried soccer mom who had inherited the house from her dad when he passed, but he'd never actually been inside. From his expression, I could tell he didn't know quite what to make of the hap-hazard thrift-store furniture and the signs of recent construction—a cordless drill, a paint-spattered step-ladder, a pile of vinyl tile scraps—that littered the floor.

I shut the door behind him, and he started. "We were just sitting down to dinner," I said. "Want to join us?"

He inhaled deeply. His face went slack and his pupils dilated. Wayne loved enchiladas.

But then he closed his eyes and shook his head. "No, thanks," he said. "I really shouldn't."

"Don't worry about it. There's plenty."

A rueful smile teased the corners of his mouth. "That's the problem. I'm trying to cut back."

"On what?" I asked, genuinely puzzled.

He looked annoyed. "On food," he snapped.

"Really?" I had never known Wayne to deprive himself of anything in his life.

"Back when I went out with the crews myself, I could eat whatever I wanted. But now I'm just a desk jockey, and all the booze and desserts have caught up with me." He patted his gut like a favor-ite dog.

I sighed. "I know, Wayne. I bought your pants, remember? But you can't be too tough on yourself. Getting a little soft around the middle is just part of getting older."

He frowned. "Brit put me on a diet. Said I had to

drop a few if I was going to keep up with her. I've been taking special pains not to eat too much dessert, because you know that's my big weakness." He sighed. "Don't suppose there's much point in sticking with it, now she's gone. But I'm gonna try to make her proud."

I never expected to feel sympathy for Wayne, and it rattled me a bit. Unsure how to respond, I patted his arm in commiseration.

He looked away into the middle distance and pressed his lips together tight, then cleared his throat. "She made me a better person," he continued. "She helped me increase profits by almost five percent this year, when everyone else in the industry suffered a loss."

It was on the tip of my tongue to point out that being a better businessman was not the same thing as being a better person. But, for Wayne, the two were pretty darned close, so I just bit my lip and kept quiet.

"I loved her," he said, so low I almost didn't hear him. "I was going to marry her. Ordered the ring from Sinclair's last month."

That knocked me back a bit. I already knew he was infatuated with her, smitten, but marriage meant so much more. It meant Brittanie was at least as important to Wayne as I had once been. I had been well and truly replaced. I took a deep breath, held it till it burned, and let it out slowly.

"So that was the hinky credit card charge Brittanie was angry about? An engagement ring?"

His gaze slid sideways, met mine, and bounced away. "Yeah. That's right."

Uh-huh. Wayne might have bought Brittanie an engagement ring at Sinclair's, but something told me that wasn't all he bought. And the rest of his purchase he wanted kept private.

"I'm real sorry," I said. I meant it, too. For better or worse, my ex loved Brittanie Brinkman. To him, she was more than just arm candy.

A muscle running the length of his jawbone clenched and released. "I wanted to propose at the luau, in front of God and everyone, but then that night the time never seemed right. You know?"

I did know. A public proposal was always a dicey plan, but when both parties were wasted and the potential bride was pitching a jealous fit, it seemed particularly ill-advised.

"Now she'll never know how much she meant to me."

An uncomfortable silence stretched between us as I tried to look anywhere but at Wayne. Maybe I just wasn't grown-up enough, but I didn't really want to watch my ex get all schmaltzy about another woman.

"So, uh, if I can't interest you in dinner," I said, "you want to have a seat in here?"

Wayne sniffed and nodded his head deliberately. "Thanks."

He took a spot on the sofa, tugging his pants up at the knees as he lowered himself onto the faded patchwork quilt draped over the seventies-era upholstery. I settled into my favorite bentwood rocker and waited for Wayne to spill his guts.

But he didn't say a word.

"Listen," I said, hoping to bridge the gap. "I'm sorry if I caused you grief by telling Cal we weren't together the night Brittanie died. I hope you understand why I had to tell the truth."

He nodded.

"You should really come clean with Cal," I urged. "That old saw about honesty being the best policy? It really is the truth."

Wayne didn't look convinced. "I'm working on it," he said.

Figuring I wouldn't be able to get a more solid commitment from him, I got to the heart of the matter. "So, what's on your mind? What can I do for you?"

He sighed. "I just wanted to see you. I . . ." He trailed off, and he pooched out his lips as if he were chewing on something, deciding how to put it. "I miss her, Tally. I know she wasn't an easy person, but neither am I. And I liked having her around. She made me mad sometimes, but she also made me laugh. She was just so darned spunky."

"Wayne," I said carefully, "I'm not sure I'm the best person to reminisce with about Brittanie's good qualities."

His chin dropped to his chest. "I know. I'm real sorry about that. But I don't have anyone else I can talk to. Her parents never warmed up to me much, and her mom falls to pieces every time I say Brit's name. And everyone else thinks I killed her. It's . . . awkward."

No kidding.

I knew Bree would accuse me of being a martyr again, but I couldn't turn Wayne away. I could only imagine how lonely he must have been, forced to grieve publicly yet entirely alone. And besides, I told myself, it wasn't as if I still carried a torch for Wayne. After catching him in flagrante delicto with his secretary, how much could the details of his relationship with Brittanie really hurt me?

I mentally considered and rejected a half dozen possible questions in rapid succession before settling on the tried-and-true. "So, how did you two meet?"

A faint smile lit his face.

"She was interning in the mayor's office one summer when I was serving as the liaison between the city council and the chamber of commerce. She looked so cute in her little suits, her hair pinned up like a schoolteacher's. She didn't have to do much—hand out the agendas and fill up the water pitchers—but she took it all so serious."

I gritted my teeth and refrained from pointing out that Wayne and I had still been very much married that summer.

"Course, I didn't get to talk to her much at those meetings, what with her working and all. But then the end of the summer, the Jillsons had that dinner to celebrate the new shopping center on FM 410, and she was there. Since I was flying solo . . ."

Wayne looked up at me, all sheepish. I guess the penny had dropped, and he'd realized that he was basically admitting to starting his romance with Brittanie long before our divorce.

I smirked, but then waved my hand to indicate he should continue.

"Well, uh, since I was by myself, I got seated with Brit at dinner. We talked about her internship, and what she had planned for her senior year in college. What she wanted to do when she graduated. And she asked me all sorts of questions."

He cleared his throat. "I gotta say, it felt pretty good to have someone ask my advice about business. Like I was wise or something."

I felt a pang of guilt. I don't know that I ever loved Wayne in a sort of fairy-tale romance sort of way, but I had certainly had great affection for him, had been willing to build a life with him. But I couldn't say that I'd ever really respected him. I never thought I was a perfect wife, but at that moment, I saw with crystal clarity one way in which I had obviously let Wayne down.

And maybe it was that guilt—that sure evidence of my own contribution to the collapse of our marriage—that compelled me to get in a little dig at Wayne.

"You know, Honey and I were talking about that dinner just the other day," I said.

Wayne looked surprised. "Really? When?"

I shrugged one shoulder as though it were no big deal. "Oh, the other day when we had lunch together."

"You and Honey Jillson had lunch?" Now he looked—and sounded—disbelieving.

I bristled.

"As a matter of fact, we did. She mentioned the chamber of commerce dinner. Said you got drunk, made an ass out of yourself."

Even in the dim glow of the table lamps' forty-watt bulbs, I could see the flush blossom on Wayne's cheekbones.

"I did not get drunk."

"Honey says you did."

"Bullshit. How was I gonna get drunk when Honey Jillson won't let booze in her house? She's been a teetotaler ever since that drunk driver killed her daughter."

"Doesn't mean you didn't get ripped before you showed up," I countered.

"Dammit, Tally, I'm not stupid. I'm not gonna show up for an important dinner like that drunk."

"Then why were you slurring your words?"

"For your information, I had an allergic reaction. The caterer—that Deena Silver woman—used pineapple juice in the glaze for those stupid itty-bitty chickens she served. I told everyone what happened. Hell, don't you remember me coming home will my face all swoll up?"

Now that he mentioned it, I *did* remember the reaction. God help me, I think I laughed at him. I know I refused to go out to buy him antihistamines because I was too exhausted from Bree's drama. I'd treated him like a nuisance, and that must have been such a letdown after Brittanie had set him on a pedestal at dinner.

I felt like a total heel.

"I'm sorry, Wayne. You're right."

I planned to apologize further, not just for brushing him off the night of the chamber of commerce dinner but also for taking him for granted for so very long, but Bree popped her head into the living room.

"Hey, Wayne," she said, her tone frosty.

"Bree."

A look of mutual loathing passed between them.

"Everything okay in here?" she asked me. "Your dinner's getting cold."

"Everything's fine, Bree," I answered. "I'll be along in a few minutes."

"Nah," Wayne said, standing up and brushing his hands down his pant legs. "I need to be going. I don't want to keep you from dinner."

"You sure?" I asked, hating to have him go on such a sour note. Our marriage was over, but I truly didn't hate the man. And since he was all but friendless at the moment, it seemed especially cruel to let him walk away in the midst of an argument.

He thrust out his chest and thumped his stomach. "Yeah, I wanted to get in a workout before heading home, and I have an early meeting tomorrow."

I held the door for him, watched as he swaggered down the walkway with his chin held high, as though daring the world to knock him down.

"Wayne!" I called.

He stopped and turned back. A gust of wind ruffled his hair, and in the half-light of late evening he looked younger. Like the man I married.

"Be careful," I said.

He raised a hand in acknowledgment before continuing toward his car. I waited until he got in and pulled away from the curb before shutting the door and making my way back to the dinner table.

As I picked up my fork and poked at the congealed cheese on my enchilada, I resolved to be a better friend to Wayne than I had been a wife.

"So about that whole idea of getting some context for Brittanie? I think I better do that, and quick."

chapter 17

The archives of the *News-Letter* smelled like a hamster cage.

"Holy moly, what is that stench?"

Finn grimaced. "It's this cedar stuff the owner, Nate, bought to try to keep pests away from the paper files. I think he got if off of eBay or something."

"You still keep paper copies of the archives?" I shivered, anticipating spending the day thumbing through newspapers just a hairsbreadth away from mulch.

"We've got the last forty years on fiche or scanned into the computer. And last year, Nate got a grant from the state to transfer all the old editions to microfiche, so we have journalism majors from Dickerson working in here at all hours of the day and night. But, until it's complete, we have to put up with Nate's cedar vermin control." He coughed. "You get used to it."

He pulled out a chair in front of a computer terminal and waited for me to sit before taking a seat by my elbow.

"Thankfully," he said, "Brittanie is young enough that any record of her life will already be digital." He dropped his voice to a rumbling whisper. "Nate hasn't really kept up with technology, so the files are still on a local network instead of posted to a secure site on the Web, but at least it's searchable."

The difference between a local network and the Web was wasted on me. I could check my bank balance online, and I even had an e-mail account (though I thought to check it only every couple of weeks). But I had listened to Kyle and Alice chatting at the store enough to know when to nod and when to frown. At least, I thought I did.

"Searchable. Good."

Finn elbowed me gently. "You have no idea what I'm talking about, do you?"

I pulled a face. "Is it that obvious?"

"Don't you have a Web site for Remember the A-la-mode?"

"No." I felt my hackles starting to rise. "I sell ice cream. It's not like I can do that over the Internet."

Finn snorted. "Actually, there are lots of places that do sell ice cream online. But at a minimum, you want people to know you exist. It's like the phone book. You don't sell ice cream over the phone, but you still have an ad in the phonebook."

The tips of my ears burned like fire. I was such a rube. All those years I had spent working behind the scenes for the Weed and Seed, I'd always just done things the same way year after year. After all, it was Wayne's business, and I just helped out a little. I never bothered to figure out if there were new, slick ways to run the business, approaches that might save money or increase sales. No wonder Wayne had been so impressed with Brittanie and her business school talk of branding.

"I make really good ice cream," I snapped. "That ought to count for more than all that marketing mumbo jumbo."

Finn leaned in so close, I got a whiff of the astringent scent of his shaving soap and the earthy citrus of Earl Grey tea, and I suddenly didn't want to bicker anymore. "I just want to make sure you get the exposure you deserve," he said.

I narrowed my eyes and shot him a sidelong glance. "Are we still talking about Web sites?"

He laughed softly, a candlelight and down-pillow kind of sound. "Yes. Web sites. And as soon as we get through this whole murder thing, I'm going to make sure you get a site as delicious as your ice cream."

He shifted in his seat, putting a breath of air between us, and keyed in a password on the computer terminal, a series of letters and numbers that appeared on the screen as a row of identical stars. "Now, let's see what we can learn about Brittanie Brinkman."

Finn pulled up the stories in chronological order.

A twelve-year-old Brittanie, with pigtails and coltish legs, stood with the rest of the Redeemer Church of Christ youth group, all of the smiling kids holding up Bibles wrapped in the hand-sewn slipcovers they were selling to raise money for a trip to San Antonio.

Brittanie as a sophomore, junior, and senior on the Dalliance High homecoming court, her dresses— from pastel taffeta ruffles to plunging necklines and body-hugging satins—marking both the rapidly changing styles and her rapidly developing body.

Spring of Brittanie's senior year in high school, the *News-Letter* ran a photo of her in her cap and gown to honor her receipt of the Dickerson Regents' Scholarship, a highly competitive full-ride scholarship. In the picture, she towered above her parents, who stared at the camera with the same dazed expressions they'd worn at her funeral.

"Look at her folks," Finn said softly. "See how they're sort of huddled together and away from her, as though she's some sort of stranger and they don't know quite what to make of her."

"Have you met them?" He shook his head. "I only saw them briefly at Wayne's, just after the funeral. Obviously that wasn't the best situation in the world, but they seemed like small, quiet people. It must have been weird to have this bright, golden child so full of energy spring up into their world."

"Like she was one of those alien kids from *Village of the Damned*," Finn said.

I laughed. "Well, she might have scared the beje-sus out of them, but they raised her right. The Regents' Scholarship is really tough to get."

"Doesn't Alice have that scholarship?"

I smiled. "Yes, and she's brilliant. I rest my case."

Finn made a little sound in his throat. "Obviously, I didn't know Brittanie well, but from what I've seen, I didn't take her for much of a scholar."

"What did she do in high school?"

He got up and rummaged through a big oak cupboard before returning with the 2005 Dalliance High Catalogue. Together we began paging through the yearbook, looking for any sign of Brittanie. In fact, she was everywhere. Homecoming court, the pom squad, candids at pep rallies and rambunctious car washes. I couldn't find a single picture, or even a mention, of her doing anything academic, which seemed a little odd for the girl who went on to win a highly prized academic scholarship. Apparently even in high school, Brittanie wore a carefully constructed mask.

"Once we get to her college years," Finn said as he scrolled through the listing of stories from the *News-Letter* archives, "we see a lot more of her. Sorority functions, a debate on cigarette advertising hosted by the undergraduate business school fraternity"—he kept clicking through the stories, his fingers flying—"an internship in the mayor's office, some sort of apprenticeship program with Sinclair's Jewelry—"

"Whoa. Back up. Sinclair's?"

"Uh . . ." He hit the back button a couple of times, then pulled up a screen full of text. "Yeah."

We read together in silence. Brittanie and JoAnne Simms had been highlighted in a story about a partnership program between the Dickerson business school and the Dalliance Chamber of Commerce, matching college kids with businesspeople for mentoring. The story included a picture of Brittanie and JoAnne, both smiling their beauty queen smiles, looking like the best of friends.

"That could be how Brittanie got to know Garrett Simms," I said. "And if JoAnne actually mentored Brit, helped her out, it would have made the betrayal of the affair even worse."

Finn slouched back in his chair. "You really have it in for JoAnne Simms."

"No, I don't."

"Yes," he said. "Yes, you do."

"I just want to figure out who could have poisoned Brittanie. It's not my fault that all the signs point to JoAnne." I scooted around in my chair to face Finn and folded my arms across my chest.

He clicked his tongue against his teeth. "Seems to me you're being pretty selective about the signs you're looking at. What's your evidence that JoAnne did it?"

He began ticking off the elements of my flimsy case on his fingers.

"First, you've got this adultery motive. And I guess that's as good a motive as any to kill someone, but JoAnne is hardly the only woman in Dalliance to hold that particular grudge against Brittanie." He narrowed his eyes. "You, for example."

"But I'm not a possessive psycho-bitch like Jo-Anne," I argued.

"Well . . . ," Finn hedged.

"Finn Harper!"

He laughed. "I'm kidding. But you see what I mean? Brittanie might have had an affair with Jo-Anne's husband, but she outright stole yours. Who's got the better motive?"

I shrugged, silently conceding the point.

"And your point about JoAnne having opportunity made sense when we thought Brittanie was poisoned with her sports drink. But if she was poisoned at the luau, there are tons more suspects. And, once again, you had more opportunity than JoAnne did. You actually had access to the food during its preparation."

A ball of lead settled in my stomach.

"Finn," I said softly, "do you think I killed her?"

"No, of course not," he said, laying a hand on my arm. He snorted. "I still think it was Wayne."

I glared at him, and he shrugged unapologetically.

"My point," he continued, "is that you've lost perspective. I think you've been so anxious to find someone—anyone—to blame for what happened, that you've stopped seeing the big picture."

His words so closely echoed my own from the night before—about the importance of seeing things in their proper context—that I really couldn't argue with him.

"So what do I do, oh wise one?"

"Sit back and let the police do their job?" he asked hopefully.

"Right. At the rate they're going, I'll be wearing an orange jumpsuit by Christmas."

"Okay, fine," he said. "Start with what you know. You know Brittanie was poisoned at the luau. Talk to people who were there, who might have seen what she put in her mouth, and take it from there."

I chewed on my lip, thinking of who had been at the luau who might actually be willing to talk to me. The list was pretty short. But right at the top was my new friend Deena and her daughter, Crystal.

I had just pulled my cell phone from my purse and flipped it open, poised to call Deena and set up a lunch date, when a rumpled older man with a pair of reading glasses propped on his shiny bald pate slouched into the archive.

"Hey, Harper, guess what?" he said. Then his gaze settled on me and his eyes widened in surprise. "Oh, sorry; didn't know you had company."

"Hey, Mike," Finn said. "This is Tally Jones, an old friend. Tally, meet Mike Carberry."

Mike narrowed his eyes and pinched his lips, his expression shrewd and calculating. "Good to meet you, Tally," he drawled.

"What's up, Mike?"

Mike's lips curled in a sly smile. "I just got off the phone with one of my sources in the state crime lab. They're still sifting through trash, but they found another one of those little red plastic cups."

I felt the blood drain from my face.

"And this one had antifreeze on it, too," Mike said. "Any comment, Ms. Jones?"

chapter 18

"This is totally lame."

"I know, Alice," I said as I maneuvered the van into the Tasty-Swirl parking lot. "But I'm going to owe you big time. And maybe you and Crystal Tompkins will hit it off."

Alice rolled her eyes. "Aunt Tally, Crystal Tompkins is seven years older than I am."

Ah, to be sixteen, when a seven-year age difference seemed like an insurmountable obstacle to a friendship. "Miz Jillson is something like forty years older than I am, and we're still friends." If I used the term loosely.

"But you're old."

Touché, little girl. Touché.

"Well, even if you don't become good friends, she may have advice for you about Dickerson. Professors to take and ones to avoid, which clubs are worth joining. Stuff like that."

Alice did not look convinced.

"Look, I'll spring for double onion rings."

She gave a grudging nod, and I knew that was the best I could hope for.

Deena and Crystal were already squeezed into a booth in the Tasty-Swirl's tiny dining room, green plastic baskets lined with waxed paper on the table in front of them.

The red pleather booths and white Formica table-tops might have been kitschy cute if they hadn't been so dinged up and dingy. Thankfully, though, the residents of Dalliance didn't patronize the Tasty-Swirl because of its sparkling ambiance. In the summer they came for Sno-Kones and soft serve, and in the winter they came for gooey grilled cheese on Texas toast and greasy burgers on buttered buns.

I had been surprised when Deena had chosen to meet there, since I figured her tastes would be a little more upscale. But as I watched her pop an onion ring in her mouth and then lick the grease from her fingers, I felt a pang of kinship.

She smiled as we approached. "Hope you don't mind that we went ahead and ordered. Crystal has a dress fitting at one, and I missed breakfast."

I handed Alice a ten and sent her to order our food while I slid into the booth. "No problem."

"Crystal, honey, this is Mrs. Jones. Tally, Crystal."

Crystal Tompkins had her mama's curvy figure and auburn hair, but she wore it cut short in a sleek bob. She wore a smart, fitted jacket over a crisp white shirt, a stark contrast to her mother's flowing chiffon tunic. Huge caramel brown eyes fringed with lush lashes dominated her cherubic face, and when she reached across the table to shake my hand, those eyes flashed with intelligence.

"Nice to meet you, Mrs. Jones."

"Please, call me Tally. And this," I added as Alice scooted in next to me, "is my niece, Alice Anders. Alice is a freshman at Dickerson. Your mom said you graduated last spring. Congratulations."

"Thanks," Crystal said. "Now I just need to get a job."

Deena clucked softly. "You need to apply to law school."

"Mom." I smothered a smile at the exasperation in Crystal's voice. Deena opened her mouth to argue, but Crystal waved her off. "Alice, what are you studying?"

My niece squirmed. She hated being the center of attention almost as much as Bree craved it.

"I don't know yet. I was thinking about psychology and I really like the class I'm taking now, but I also like my comparative literature class, and I'm going to do research for my professor next semester."

I knew Alice hated me bragging on her to folks, but I couldn't resist. "Alice got a full-ride scholarship," I said. "She'll get to do research with her professors every semester and even over the summers."

Alice sucked in a breath of mortification and

nudged my knee under the table. I nudged her right back. It was my prerogative to tell everyone how great she was, whether she liked it or not.

"Oh, did you get the Regents' Scholarship?" Deena asked. Alice nodded glumly. "That's wonderful! Especially given the tuition at Dickerson. Thankfully, I married my sugar daddy right about the time Crystal started."

"Mom!" Crystal and Alice exchanged a long-suffering look. The difference between their ages proved not nearly so vast as their contempt for their elders.

Deena laughed her rich, dark-chocolate laugh. "Crystal doesn't like me mentioning the fact that Tom Silver raised our standard of living considerably. But, truth is, he footed the bill for her education."

Crystal's sunny face clouded over, and she began fidgeting with the straw in her soda cup. "If I'd gotten the Regents' Scholarship, we wouldn't have needed Tom's money."

Deena swayed toward her daughter so their shoulders bumped. "Aw, baby. How many times do I have to tell you? I didn't marry Tom Silver so you could go to college. He may be a pain in the patoot sometimes, but I do love the man. Like my mother always said, you can love a rich man as well as a poor one. And he may grumble about the size of my ass, but he loves me back."

"Whatever."

Deena met my gaze and rolled her eyes. "Crystal

is still young enough to believe the whole world revolves around her. She just can't believe that I would fall head over heels for a balding horse rancher, and that his willingness to pay her exorbitant college tuition was just icing on the cake."

"Mom, can we drop this now?"

Alice squirmed uncomfortably beside me. I felt awful for inadvertently raising such a painful subject. Worse, I was worried I had alienated Crystal before I even got around to asking her about the luau.

"I'm sorry I mentioned the scholarship," I said.

Alice sucked in a horrified gasp; her adolescent logic dictated that apologizing for something only drew more attention to it and made it worse. But Crystal offered me a shy smile. "Don't worry about it. You couldn't possibly know that I lost the scholarship, and just about everything else I ever wanted, to my nemesis."

I almost laughed at the idea of this sweet-faced girl having a nemesis, but I noticed that Deena had tensed up, her smile frozen, the knuckles of her folded hands stark beneath the skin.

Crystal, blithely unaware of her mother's discomfort, gave a rueful chuckle. "I guess I'm going to hell for calling her my nemesis now that she's dead. But, honestly, she beat me out for every scholarship and internship I applied for."

And that was when it hit me that Crystal and Brittanie would have been in the same class. Brittanie got the Regents' Scholarship instead of Crystal, and Crystal must have applied for at least one of the internships that Brittanie had—either the one at Sinclair's, or the one at the mayor's office, or both.

"I, uh, I hear you're getting married," I said, trying awkwardly to steer the conversation to more neutral territory. I didn't want Deena to think I was trying to trick them into incriminating themselves.

Crystal's face lit up like a Roman candle. "Yes, the wedding's in July. Jason's a second-year law student at Texas Tech."

"And you're thinking of law school, too?"

"Yeah. I'm going to wait until next year to apply, though. That way, Jason will be graduated and can support us while I get my degree."

"That sounds like a good plan," I said.

"Ha. Tell that to my mom." Crystal jerked her chin in Deena's direction.

Deena's smile softened. "I just don't want you waiting in line to live your life. Why should you waste time sitting on the sidelines?"

"I'm not wasting time," Crystal insisted. She began ticking off her activities on her fingers. "I'm studying for the LSAT, and I'm going to intern at the DA's office in the spring, and I'm making money to pay for the wedding—"

"Making money doing menial labor," Deena interrupted. "You're too smart to be waiting tables and babysitting."

"Yeah," I said, "your mom told me you were waiting tables at the Weed and Seed luau." Out of the corner of my eye, I saw Deena stiffen again. "I can't imagine you want to spend much more of your life wearing a stupid grass skirt."

Crystal grimaced and inhaled a hissing breath through her teeth. "True, that was not exactly 'fun.' But it was money. And it honestly wouldn't have been so bad if everyone hadn't been so drunk."

"Really? Alice and I stayed pretty close to our van, so we didn't get to see much of the action."

She shook her head in disgust. "Half the guests were drunk when they got there, and I swear they might as well have slapped nipples on the margarita machine. Both Mrs. Paolino and Mrs. Jillson brought their own flasks—like no one would notice," she added with a smirk. "And the mayor put his hand on my ass. I don't think it was an accident."

Beside me, Alice snorted. "That's gross. And they say kids can't hold their booze."

Crystal and Alice exchanged a high five across the table.

"I'm sorry I missed all the fun." I shot an apologetic glance at Deena, who was glaring back at me. She'd clearly caught on that I was milking her daughter for information, and she was none too happy about it. I hated testing the limits of our new friendship like this, but I really wanted to know what Crystal saw at the luau. "I heard JoAnne Simms got wasted, too, and started calling people names."

Crystal took a long pull on her drink, then used the straw to break up the crushed ice in the bottom of the cup. Her lips twitched in a wicked little smile. "I only heard her talking trash about Brittanie. And I don't think that was the liquor talking."

"No?"

"Oh, no. JoAnne Simms was sober as a judge. Flat-out called Brittanie a slut." Her gentle features scrunched up in confusion. "Or maybe it was a bimbo?" She waved away her own question. "Whatever. She definitely thought Brittanie was a ho-bag."

That confirmed what Finn told me the night of the luau, but it didn't provide any new insights. And I was reluctant to push harder. After all, this was supposed to be a friendly conversation, not an inquisition.

Then Alice earned her double onion rings by asking, "Why? Do you think Brittanie was sleeping with Mr. Simms?"

Deena surprised me by laughing. "Brittanie with Garrett Simms? I don't think so."

"Why not?" I asked with a wry smile. "She seemed to like older men."

"Doesn't matter what Brittanie liked." Deena leaned in and dropped her voice to a stage whisper. "Garrett Simms is as queer as a three-dollar bill."

"No," I gasped.

Deena nodded, eyebrows raised. "My friend Simon says Garrett's always out at Maudie McGee's chatting up the college boys."

Alice appeared both fascinated and confused. If I had been a better aunt, I would have sent her to the counter to buy dessert instead of letting her listen to such adult gossip. But with Bree as her mother, Alice hadn't led a particularly sheltered life, so I figured, what the hey? "I thought Maudie McGee's was a bowling alley," she said.

Crystal pursed her lips, clearly eager to demonstrate how worldly she was. "It is a bowling alley. And it's also a gay bar."

"Huh," Alice said.

"So why would JoAnne think Brittanie was a slut?" I asked.

"Maybe because she *was* a slut?" Crystal offered.

"Crystal Louise Tompkins," her mother chided.

"Come on, Mom. She totally was a slut."

Deena drew herself up and pressed her lips together, her expression as prim and disapproving as a schoolmarm's. "There are many unpleasant truths in this world, young lady, but you do not have to call attention to all of them."

"Yes, but Mrs. Jones asked."

I felt the heat of a blush spread across my face. "I was just curious," I said meekly.

Deena reached across the table and patted my hand. "Of course you were, dear," she said. "But if I had to hazard a guess, I'd say JoAnne was angry about Brittanie and Wayne."

I shook my head. "JoAnne Simms and I barely know each other. Why would she care if Brittanie was romantic with Wayne? Unless . . . oh."

"What?" Alice asked impatiently.

"Unless . . ." I cleared my throat. "Unless JoAnne had an affair with Wayne, too."

Deena pulled a face. "I suppose anything is possible," she said. "But I was thinking more of JoAnne and Brittanie."

Alice giggled. "This is twisted."

"Seriously," Crystal said. "Doesn't anyone in this town have any morals? It sounds like everybody is sleeping with everybody."

"Not me," Alice said glumly, and she and Crystal giggled like little girls.

Deena ignored them. "I've catered enough Zeta luncheons to know that JoAnne, well, she appreciates women. But she comes from old Dalliance money, and her parents expected her to take over the family business, so it's not like she could move someplace more accepting of alternative lifestyles." She shrugged. "I guess she and Garrett Simms have a pretty good arrangement."

Our little group grew silent. I shifted in my seat, trying to figure out how to get more information without being obvious about my intentions. Finally, Deena took pity on me.

"Listen, Tally, I know you're trying to figure out who poisoned Brittanie." Crystal sat up straight, her eyes as wide as the Texas prairie, mouth a comical little O of surprise. "So why don't we cut through the bullshit and you ask what you want to ask?"

"Really?" Crystal breathed. "You're investigating a murder?"

Beside me, Alice leaned back and nodded. "Cool, huh?"

"Totally!" Crystal leaned forward, resting her elbows on the table, all business. "Do you think I can help?"

"I don't know," I said. "Were you working the table where Wayne and Brittanie were sitting? Did you see what Brittanie ate?"

Crystal shook her head. "Laura Ortiz worked that table. But Brittanie never ate anything. At least, not in public."

Deena rolled her eyes and pantomimed sticking her finger down her throat.

"What about the ice cream and the sundae topping?" I asked. "Did you see Laura serve Wayne his red cups of dessert sauce?"

Crystal thought for a moment. "Actually, yeah. That was sort of weird. I was in the staging area, and I saw a tray with two dishes of ice cream and four of the red cups just sitting on a tray stand, and then Laura skulked around from behind the Porta-Johns to pick it up. I snapped at her about leaving the ice cream just sitting there, because it would melt."

She looked over at her mom. "She said she needed a cigarette. That she couldn't handle all the drunken assholes without some nicotine."

Deena's nostrils pinched tight. "My servers are not supposed to smoke during their shifts," she said to me.

Crystal shrugged. "Anyway, she said Mr. Jones wouldn't care if the ice cream was melted because he was so drunk. He'd been throwing back margaritas all night." She cocked her head to one side. "Then I saw Laura again, not ten minutes later, with another tray of desserts including three or four more of the red cups. I got a little short with her, said apparently Mr. Jones did care about the melty ice cream. But she said, no, he already ate the first batch and wanted more.

"Laura said Mr. Jones was sort of a pig." She threw a sheepish grimace my way. "No offense."

"None taken, dear."

Crystal's story didn't shed much light on how Brittanie might have died, but it confirmed my assertion that my sundaes were not the vehicle for the poison. After all, if Wayne ate seven or eight portions of the topping and didn't get sick, then clearly it was perfectly fine.

"This is a pretty vague question," I said, "but did you see anyone acting weird that night? Maybe loitering near Brittanie's margaritas?"

"Oh, no," Crystal said, "Brittanie wasn't drinking. She never drinks alcohol. Too many calories."

"Never?" Alice asked, a thoughtful frown wrinkling her broad brow.

"Never," Crystal confirmed with an emphatic shake of her head.

"Okay. How about anyone just hanging around looking out of place?"

The young woman scrunched up her face in thought. "No. Not really. Just that one guy."

"What guy?" Deena and I asked simultaneously.

Crystal shrugged. "I don't know his name. He's just this guy. Skinny, kind of skeevy looking, black hair. Looks like a stoner, but he's old."

Deena's face lit with recognition. "Eddie Collins. Creepy little guy."

Crystal glanced down at the trim silver watch adorning her wrist. "Oh, crap, I have to run. All my maids are meeting me for the fitting, so I don't want to be late." She looked up at me with soulful, earnest eyes. "I'm sorry I couldn't be more help, Mrs. Jones. I didn't like Brittanie very much, but I hope they figure out who killed her. That wasn't cool at all."

"You helped more than you know," I said, even though I didn't mean it, as Deena and Crystal scooted out of the booth. "We'll have to do this again sometime."

"Next time, without the felonies," Deena said, then winked at me to soften the retort.

As I watched them leave, and Alice ordered a couple of chocolate-dipped cones to go, I felt as though I had taken one step forward and two steps back. Eddie Collins, Wayne's newest competitor in the lawn-care business, might have had a beef with Wayne—though Eddie's organic lawn-care alternative seemed to be pretty popular and he had just gotten into the business the summer before, so it was hard to imagine too much bad blood between the men—but I hadn't gotten even a whiff of a connection between Brittanie and Eddie.

Apparently, I still had some digging to do.

chapter 19

Driving with an ice-cream cone is no easy feat, and it's dang near impossible to juggle a cone, a minivan, and a cell phone all at the same time. So when my cell rang as I merged onto FM 410, I handed Alice my ice cream with a stern "lick that and die" glare.

"It'll drip," Alice complained.

"Fine. Then see if you can get the phone to do that speaker thing."

Alice made a sound of sheer disgust at my technological ignorance, but she pulled my phone out of my purse, flipped it open, and pressed some button so that I could hear the open line from across the car.

"Hello?" I said.

"Hello, Tallulah Jones."

Jesus Christ on a crutch, not again.

"Hey, Cal."

"Listen, Tally, I think you need to come back in and have a chat with me. See, the lab boys have now found four red plastic containers and six red plastic lids, all with antifreeze on them. And, well, we haven't found any antifreeze anywhere else in that whole big mountain of trash." He paused a beat to let that information sink in. I glanced over at Alice and saw that she'd gone as pale as fresh cream, her mouth hanging open.

"Tally," Cal said, "we've crossed the line from co-incidence to highly suspicious, wouldn't you say?"

I had a hard time saying anything, since I couldn't quite catch my breath. Finally I choked out a reply. "That's real interesting, Cal."

There was another beat of silence, nothing but the faint hiss of my tires on the road and the empty ether of the phone line.

"Tally? We go way back." All the teasing and in-nuendo had disappeared from Cal's voice, and he sounded deadly serious. "If you have something to say, it might be good to say it on your terms. But bring a lawyer with you."

"Okay," I said softly, ashamed at the tremor in my voice.

"Take my advice, Tally. Because you're no longer a person of interest. You're a full-on suspect now."

"Thanks for letting me know, Cal." I meant it. I didn't know much about law enforcement, but I suspected Cal was going out on a limb to warn me about how the investigation was progressing. We'd never dated in high school, and I think he flirted with me then more to annoy Finn than because he was really interested, but clearly that bond meant something to him, and I was grateful.

The line went dead, and Alice flipped the phone closed.

Neither one of us said anything for a few minutes. I was trying to figure out how to downplay what she'd just heard, make her feel secure, but all the lipstick in the world couldn't gussy up that pig.

"Aunt Tally?"

"Yeah, baby."

"I'm writing a paper about Brittanie's death."

I jerked so hard that my ice cream went flying, a big blob of white goo landing right in my lap.

"You're what?" I asked, certain I hadn't heard her correctly. I pulled over to the side of the road, while the drivers flying past honked and flipped me the bird. No way could I drive under those circumstances.

Alice fished around on the floor for a plastic grocery bag, dumped her half-eaten cone inside, and held it open so I could dump mine. Then she handed me a handful of paper napkins from inside the glove compartment.

As I cleaned up my pants, she explained.

"We have to write a term paper in physiology. I decided to do my paper on ethylene glycol poisoning and how it affects the metabolic processes. Professor Carter said it was a great topic." She lifted one shoulder. "Of course, he doesn't know why I picked it, but, oh, well."

"That sounds interesting," I said, not sure where this little revelation was heading.

"I've learned a lot about how antifreeze kills people."

I shuddered, at both the gruesome nature of my baby girl's research and the utter calm with which she described it.

"Crystal said that Laura Ortiz gave Uncle Wayne, like, six or seven servings of the sundae topping. But you said Uncle Wayne was on a diet, and really trying to cut back on his desserts. So that doesn't really make sense."

I smiled. "Uncle Wayne wouldn't be the first person to cheat on his diet."

Alice's expression remained perfectly serious. "No, you're right. Maybe he cheated and ate all that ice cream. Or maybe Brittanie—who pretended she never ate dessert but binged in private—maybe she took a bunch of Uncle Wayne's dessert, and that's why he had to ask for more. And if Laura Ortiz left her trays sitting around while she went off to smoke, anyone could have monkeyed with the cups."

"But I still don't see how it could have been the sundaes. Uncle Wayne definitely ate some of the ice cream—he told me later how much he liked it—but he didn't get sick."

Alice nodded slowly. "Well, see, here's the thing. Ethylene glycol itself isn't lethal. But in the body, it breaks down into different chemicals that are lethal. They create a condition called metabolic acidosis. Which basically just means your blood is too acidic. And that's what causes your whole body to shut down.

"From what I've read, Brittanie Brinkman already had a bunch of strikes against her. There are other reasons your blood can be too acidic. One, called lactic acidosis, you can get from crazy amounts of exercise. And another, ketoacidosis, you get when your body starts to break down its own muscles because you don't eat enough."

Wow. "So if Brittanie had a severe eating disorder and was starving herself and overexercising, her blood was already wonky," I said.

Alice smiled faintly and held open the plastic bag so I could dump my dirty napkins.

"Exactly," she said. "Plus, drinking alcohol—like real booze—actually blocks the effects of antifreeze poisoning."

"Okay." I nodded, trying to keep up with her nimble mind.

"Brittanie acted like she was drunk at the luau, but Crystal said Brittanie never drank alcohol. I'm guessing she was actually drunk on the antifreeze. The early symptoms include slurring and stumbling, just like you're loaded."

Alice closed her eyes. Her face seemed lit from within, the power of her concentration almost spooky in its intensity.

"But Uncle Wayne, he was definitely drinking alcohol. So maybe he *did* consume some of the ethylene glycol, but the margaritas kept it from making him real sick."

Alice turned to me, her wide aqua eyes luminescent. "And that would mean that whoever poisoned the ice-cream sundaes either knew Brittanie would eat Uncle Wayne's ice cream or planned to kill Uncle Wayne all along."

"Alice Marie Anders," I said, "where the heck did you get that big ol' brain of yours?"

She giggled, the mischievous smile transforming her into a child again. "You and Mom are pretty smart, yourselves. I just have the book learnin'," she teased, making fun of our down-home Texas slang.

I laughed along with her, overcome with amazement that such a brilliant mind could possibly be related to me.

Another car flew past, honking, and I realized we needed to get moving. Always a cautious driver, I flicked on my turn signal and eased back into traffic.

As we made our way home, I considered all the implications of Alice's analysis. On the one hand, if Cal got ahold of the information, it spelled my doom. My defense so far had been that it didn't make any sense for me to try to kill Brittanie with poisoned ice cream that she wasn't likely to eat. But if Cal had a plausible explanation for how I might have really been trying to kill Wayne, and poor Brittanie just got caught in the cross fire, no amount of sentiment or warm feelings would keep Cal from slapping a pair of cuffs on me.

On the other hand, the possibility of Wayne as the real target meant a whole new list of possible suspects.

And as I scanned that mental list, I put a little gold star right next to Eddie Collins's name.

chapter 20

Eddie Collins worked out of his house, a Victorian monstrosity on the very edge of the historic district, just beyond the greedy grasp of the Dalliance Historic Landmark Commission. One block closer to downtown, and Eddie would have been subject to the same restrictions on the exterior of his home as I was. As it was, though, Eddie had free reign.

Eddie had painted his house a mellow oceanic teal, with every layer of gingerbread trim boasting a different seaside color, from the indigo of the deep to the creamy yellow on the crests of waves. Shards of brilliant pottery and broken glass formed a mosaic on the skirting of his wraparound porch and on the risers of the steps. An explosion of red and fuchsia roses littered his yard and climbed a trellis archway over his front walk. In honor of the season, a cluster of goofy-faced jack-o'-lanterns guarded the door. Eddie's house looked as though it had been designed by a gifted five-year-old girl.

Early Monday afternoon, I knocked on his cobalt blue front door and, when I got no response, rang the bell. I could hear the buzzing tone through the door, abrasive and ugly, followed by shuffling and muttering. Finally the door swung open to reveal Eddie in a pair of dirty jeans that sagged at the knees and a rough-woven cotton pullover, the type you could buy on vacation in Mexico.

He blinked at me from behind round-lensed rimless glasses, like a cave dweller creeping into the light. His stark coloring—skin like skim milk beneath hair the matte black of old tires—added to the impression. How he managed to stay so pale doing a job that kept him out beneath the merciless Texas sun was beyond me. All the SPF in the world couldn't completely neutralize the summer sun, and wide-brimmed hats could do only so much. I didn't think Eddie had an actual full-time staff like Wayne did, so he must have been using cheap day laborers— the men who milled around the parking lot of the abandoned SnoShack, swarming every truck or van that even looked as if it was slowing down—to save himself the actual physical work.

And clearly the day laborers worked well without supervision. It was well after noon, yet Eddie looked as though he'd just gotten up from a nap. His thick curls were pressed flat on one side of his head, springing wildly on the other, and his pale blue irises swam in a slurry of watery pink.

"Hey, yeah. Can I help you?" His laconic drawl softened his consonants and stretched his vowels, like a record played at the wrong speed. I struggled to separate the words and had an irrational image of trying to pull a bully's chewing gum from Alice's hair.

"Hello, Mr. Collins. I'm Tally Jones." A spark of recognition animated his face. "I called about your lawn-care services."

"Sure, sure. Come on in." He shuffled back, opening the door and his arms wide in invitation.

The inside of Eddie's house was as dim as the outside was bright. Tea-dyed gauze curtains covered the windows, and the sepia light cast by a handful of table lamps didn't reach the corners of the high-ceilinged room.

Despite the dark, Eddie's living room felt welcoming in a shabby, comfortable way. Worn velveteen in shades of umber and ochre, russet and moss, upholstered the low, tatty sofas and chairs. Threadbare carpets softened the scarred oak-plank floors. Plants grew everywhere: jade plants and African violets filled chipped earthenware bowls, while golden pothos and spider plants streamed from macramé hanging baskets. The scent of their loamy soil provided a sharp counterpoint for the cloying musk of old incense.

"Sit anywhere," Eddie offered.

I chose a faded green armchair with a massive marmalade tomcat draped over one arm, snoring softly.

Eddie flopped onto the sofa, drawing one knee up to his chest and resting that foot on the sofa cushion. His bare feet were unkempt, the nails long and yellowed, a smattering of black hairs curling from his big toes.

He smiled, a sweet, wifty smile. "That's Jerry," he said.

"Like *Tom and Jerry*?"

"Nah. Like Jerry Garcia. He's a peaceful dude."

I reached out to scratch Jerry behind the ears, and his purr revved up a notch and he lifted his chin to lean into it. Beneath his meaty whisker biscuits, one little fang protruded. I decided he looked more like Elvis—fat Elvis, not skinny Elvis—than Jerry Garcia, but I wasn't going to quibble over Eddie's feline name choices.

"I always wanted a cat," I said.

Eddie cocked his head, a bemused smile wreathing his face. "So why don't you have one?"

I shrugged. "My mother didn't believe in keeping animals in the house, and my husband was allergic."

Eddie made a little sound in the back of his throat. "That explains why your mom and your husband don't have cats. But why don't you have one?"

I felt as though that was some sort of Zen riddle, like whether a tree falling in the forest made a sound if no one was around to hear it, so I didn't bother to answer. Instead, I let the silence stretch between us, broken only by Jerry's rattling, tubercular purr, until Eddie decided to get down to business.

"So what can I do ya for?"

"Well, like I said, my name is Tally Jones, and—"

"Right," Eddie interrupted. "You make the ice cream." A beatific smile spread across his face.

I smiled back.

"Fantastic," he said.

"Thanks. I was married to Wayne Jones."

Eddie's gentle expression clouded over, as though I had hurt him somehow. "Your husband does lawn care." He sounded puzzled, as though he knew he was the butt of some cosmic joke but he couldn't get the punch line.

"Wayne and I are divorced," I said.

Eddie closed his eyes and nodded sagely. "That's tough. But, listen, green is the way to go. Good for your soul, good for the planet, and good for your yard." He smiled. "I know I haven't been around that long, but two of my clients are in the Master Gardeners group, and they even invited me to give a talk at one of their meetings. You can trust your little corner of the planet to me."

Bless his heart, Eddie had about as much edge as a bowl of mashed potatoes. It was tough to imagine him summoning up the rage—or the nerve— to murder someone. But then, I thought, committing murder by poison was like dumping someone on their answering machine: as nonconfrontational as the interaction could possibly be.

"Listen, I'm sorry, but I lied about why I wanted to talk to you."

"You don't need help with your lawn?"

"Actually, I could use a lot of help. But that's not why I'm here. I wanted to ask you some questions about the Weed and Seed luau."

"Aw, man, that's uncool," Eddie protested weakly.

While I dug the groovy, laid-back ambience of Eddie's house, his hippie patois grated on my nerves. I didn't know Eddie when he was a kid, because he was five years and at least one tax bracket ahead of me. But he hailed from Dalliance, same as me, a child of the go-go eighties. Maybe he spent some time in Haight-Ashbury during his college years— I'd heard he went to Berkeley—but he was laying it on a little thick.

"Look, I'm sorry, but I didn't know whether you'd talk to me any other way. I want to know what you were doing at the luau."

"It was a party," he said with a shrug.

"Right. A party for Wayne's friends and clients."

"So?"

"So someone slipped poison in Wayne's dessert at the luau, and Brittanie Brinkman died because of it." Eddie's eyes widened and his breath hitched audibly. "And it just seems a little strange to me that you were there at all, since you're one of Wayne's competitors."

Eddie squinted shrewdly, and I saw a glimmer of the intelligent man behind the stoner facade. "What were *you* doing at the luau?" he countered. "You're sort of his competitor now, too."

I hadn't really thought of my relationship with Wayne in those terms, but I could see his point. "I was working at the luau," I explained. "I was invited."

"So was I."

My hand stilled on Jerry's head, and he made a breathless sound of protest.

"What do you mean, you were invited?"

"I mean Wayne asked me to be there." Eddie began picking at a frayed spot on the knee of his jeans.

"Right. Why would Wayne want you to come to a party for his clients, where you could schmooze with his customers? Maybe even poach a few."

"You'd have to ask Wayne." Eddie met my gaze as he spoke, as bold as brass. But he worried the tear in his jeans with increased vigor, and his pale pink tongue slipped out to moisten his lips.

I decided to go for broke. "You still have the letter?"

He paused just a heartbeat too long before saying, "I don't think so."

"Eddie, come on. You're not a very good liar. If you have the letter, let me see it. Prove to me you were invited."

He set his mouth in a mutinous pout, but I could see him weighing his options. Finally, he unfolded himself from the sofa and slouched over to a vaguely Asian sideboard littered with papers and a half dozen ceramic Buddha figures. He rooted around in toppling stacks of paper, until he finally grunted and pulled a single sheet out. He brought it to me, grasping it by two fingers and carrying it away from his body, as if he were worried about contagion.

"See, I was invited."

I took the letter, a single typed sheet of Weed and Seed company letterhead, and skimmed through it once quickly before reading it again closely. There wasn't much to it.

> *Eddie,*
> *I know your secret. Want me to keep it? Perhaps we can reach a mutually satisfactory arrangement. Friday the 9th at Lonestar Park, 7 p.m.*

There was no signature.

A few of the letters looked wonky, as though they weren't quite on the horizontal. I ran my fingers over the words and could feel the faint imprint of the letters. No doubt about it, the letter had been written on a typewriter rather than printed on a laser or ink-jet printer.

I waved the paper gently in Eddie's direction. "This doesn't sound like an invitation, Eddie. This sounds like someone was trying to blackmail you."

He didn't say anything, just picked up Jerry and cradled him against his chest. The cat kicked its feet as he was lifted, but then settled down against Eddie's shoulder, purring loudly and rubbing the top of his silky head against the underside of Eddie's chin.

"Why would someone try to blackmail you? What's the secret?"

Eddie shrugged, making Jerry squirm.

"Eddie, who sent this to you?"

He started and looked at me, his brow wrinkled in confusion. "Wayne Jones, of course."

I laughed. "No way." Eddie looked offended. "Aw, come on, Eddie. You've met Wayne. Does this sound like him?" I waved the paper in his direction.

"I don't know, Tally. I've never gotten a blackmail note before. It's sort of business related, so maybe Wayne thought he should use more formal terminology."

" 'Mutually satisfactory arrangement'? Trust me, I edited all of Wayne's business correspondence when we were married. Wayne Jones would never in a million years use a fancy-pants expression like that, even in a formal letter."

"You sure?"

"Positive."

Eddie sank back down on the sofa, and Jerry wriggled out of his grasp. The cat plopped onto the cushion next to Eddie, stuck one back leg straight in the air, and began casually grooming himself.

Eddie frowned. "If it wasn't Wayne, who was it?"

"Didn't anyone approach you at the luau?"

"No." Eddie fell silent. He absently stroked the curve of Jerry's back. "No," he repeated. "I thought it was weird that someone would want to . . . well, to have this kind of discussion in such a public place. And when Wayne basically ignored me, I figured he realized it was a bad idea."

I hesitated, not sure how much further I could push Eddie before he realized he could just throw me out of his house. When I spoke, I chose my words carefully and kept my tone as neutral as possible.

"You know, if Wayne wasn't the blackmailer, you could still be in trouble. Maybe it would help us figure out who sent you the note if you told me what the secret was."

"I told you. I. Don't. Know." He punctuated each word by jabbing his forefinger into his own leg. The sudden tension vibrating around him sent Jerry scrambling for safer ground.

"Eddie. You must have some idea. I mean, you went to the luau to talk to whoever sent the note. You must have had some clue what the threat was about if you bothered to respond."

He squinched his eyes closed and folded his arms across his chest, literally shutting me out. "I think you ought to leave now."

I stood and took a few steps toward the door, then turned to give it one more go. "Eddie, you do realize you basically just handed me a motive for you trying to kill Wayne, right?"

His eyes popped open in surprise, then narrowed in confusion.

I sighed. "You told me that you thought Wayne was trying to blackmail you. I don't know what sort of dirt you think Wayne has on you, but if you think he's about to expose some deep dark secret, you might want him dead."

Eddie shook his head vehemently. "No way, man. I didn't want to kill anyone. I just wanted to find out who was threatening me. I only thought it was Wayne because of the Weed and Seed paper."

"And you're telling me you don't have any idea why someone might blackmail you?"

He looked at his feet, his expression miserable. "I guess I can maybe think of a couple of reasons," he said softly. "Just like everybody else, I have a few secrets. But I wouldn't kill to keep any of them."

chapter 21

Wednesday nights were always a little slow at the A-la-mode, so Bree and I left Kyle and Alice in charge and invited Finn over to our house for drinks.

The mellow glow of the overhead fixture reflected off the warped glass of the kitchen window and bathed the room in soft, forgiving light. The cheap cupboards and stained linoleum floors, the hodgepodge of cereal boxes and generic canned goods that lined the exposed pantry shelves, all looked homey and comfortable instead of messy and depressing.

I stood by the island, carefully halving an avocado, prying out its stone with the tip of my knife, then scooping the tender meat from the leathery skin.

Bree, dressed in calf-length leggings, an over-sized Dickerson sweatshirt, and rainbow-striped socks, slipped a CD in the banged-up boom box on the kitchen counter. With a dramatic flourish, she pressed PLAY and Barry Gibbs's reedy falsetto filled the room. Bree shuffled from side to side, rolling her hands one over the other, then struck a pose, arms flung wide and head thrown back, before returning to her half-assed hustle.

I mashed the avocado in a bowl, unconsciously moving the fork to the beat of the Bee Gees. Bobbing my head, I pulled a lemon from a chipped porcelain bowl filled with citrus and tomatoes.

My knife broke the rind and sank into the soft flesh of the fruit, releasing a fine, pungent mist that burned its way like acid into my memory.

For an instant, I sat by the window in my Grandma Peachy's kitchen, perched on a wooden stool, its seat worn concave from generations of ample bottoms. A warm breeze blew through the fly screen, fluttering the flour-sack curtains and caressing my face as I grated the zest of lemons for homemade lemon ice cream. The astringent scent clung to my fingers like my own personal sunshine. Outside, I could hear Bree's throaty laughter as she traded sly jokes with the ranch hands. In the sitting room, Bree's mama, my aunt Jenny, played her 45s, practicing her disco dancing to Donna Summer and the Bee Gees, and Grandma's wooden spoon kept time as she stirred the custard at the stove.

I loved my Grandma Peachy's kitchen more than

anyplace else in the world. My mama scrubbed away her disappointment with Ajax and ammonia, leaving her kitchen as sterile as an operating room. In Mama's kitchen, I was clutter: messy, sticky, and as unwelcome as soda in her bourbon. But in the colorful chaos of Grandma Peachy's kitchen, I could spill the flour and lick my fingers and break off nibbles of pastry from the crust of just-baked pies.

I gave myself a little shake, reached for the wooden awl, and squeezed the lemon juice into the guacamole. I glanced at Bree to be sure she wasn't looking, then surreptitiously swiped my finger through the guacamole. I wondered whether Dalliance, Texas, was ready for avocado ice cream. Maybe with just a hint of lemon and chili. A sort of frozen guacamole.

I was sucking my finger clean when the doorbell rang. Before I could move, Bree sprinted to the door to welcome Finn inside.

Bree showed Finn around the house while I finished up the snacks and laid them out on the table; then Finn and I started munching while Bree worked her magic with the tequila and blender.

"So, is your mom with the home health aid tonight?"

Finn shook his head as he scooped up some guacamole on a tortilla chip. "The night nurse called in sick and the service couldn't get a sub. But Mrs. Jillson happened to call and asked to come visit Mom, so she's with her tonight."

He bit the chip and groaned. "God, these are fresh, aren't they?"

I smiled. "Bought them at the *tortilleria* this afternoon." I snagged a chip for myself. "I'm glad Honey touched base with your mom. We were just talking about the fact that they'd drifted apart, and she sounded so sad."

"Mmm-hmm. Honey mentioned that you two had talked. She seems pretty high on you."

I nearly choked on my chip. Surely Honey wasn't playing matchmaker?

Bree joined us, juggling three glasses of pale green frozen margarita, each finished with a float of blue curaçao. "Oh, Tally and Honey are the bestest friends now," she mocked.

"Hey, she helped us with the historic commission. Not only did they approve our colors—pampas grass, adobe, and sunset blush, which sounds like pink but isn't—but she also got them to suspend the fines for a month to give us time to get the house painted. So, yeah, I guess we are friends."

Finn chuckled and raised his glass. "Here's to Honey Jillson."

We all clinked glasses, then observed a moment of silence in appreciation of Bree's excellent bartending skills.

"So how's the murder investigation coming?" Finn asked. "Mike Carberry is beside himself with excitement about some new development, but he won't tell me what's going on."

I grimaced. "I tend to think that the official investigation and my own are going in very different directions."

I filled Finn in on all the latest. He seemed mildly intrigued that JoAnne Simms might bat for the other team, completely enthralled—and impressed—by Alice's armchair forensics, and absolutely aghast that I would actually go to Eddie Collins's house and basically accuse him of murder.

"Honestly," I assured him, "Eddie didn't seem particularly scary."

"Well, of course not," he said. "Unless Eddie Collins has changed dramatically in the last twenty years, he's about as scary as a newborn kitten."

I sat up a little straighter. "You knew Eddie back in high school?"

"Sure, I remember Eddie." Finn's face flamed.

"Uh-huh," I said. "And how exactly did you know him?"

"What do you mean?"

"I mean, your face is hotter than a habanero. Spill it."

He plucked a chip from the basket in the center of the table and began breaking tiny bits off of it, making a little pile of tortilla confetti. "I bought some weed off him a few times. He went to Berkeley, and he came home for vacations with a stash."

"Finn Harper," I chided.

"Listen, it was before we started dating." He smiled, that sideways smile that turned my knees to jelly. "I was a sinner, Tally. You knew that. It was part of my charm."

I snorted a little laugh. "Yeah, you're still a sinner. But it's not nearly as charming anymore."

He clutched his chest and lurched dramatically. "Oh," he gasped, "oh, cruel woman!"

I threw a chip at him. "Get serious, Finn."

He straightened, chuckling, and took another sip of his margarita.

"These are great, Bree."

"Uh-huh," she agreed. "But you're not changing the subject that easily."

Finn turned up his hands and shrugged.

"So," I said, "Eddie Collins was always a stoner, huh?"

"No, not really. From what the other guys said, Eddie was a real straight arrow in high school. Dated goody-two-shoes Miranda Jillson. Went to Berkeley on a scholarship, planned to be a doctor."

"But he came back a drug dealer?"

"I don't know that I would call him a dealer," Finn said. "He just always had a big stash, and he was willing to share."

"For money."

"Yeah, for money. But I guess my point is that I don't think he was trying to turn a profit."

"What about now?" I asked. "Could someone be blackmailing him because he's a drug dealer?"

Finn held up both hands. "Don't look at me," he said. "I've been gone a long time, and I don't do that crap anymore."

Bree heaved a mighty sigh and held out her hand. "Give me your cell phone." Finn obliged, and Bree dialed.

"Alice, honey, it's your mom. Is Kyle there?"

She rolled her eyes. "Yes, I love you and would be delighted to talk to you, but I have a question. . . . You sure as heck better not be able to answer this question. Just give the phone to Kyle."

Bree held her hand over the mouth of the receiver. "Sometimes I wish I'd dropped her on her head so she wouldn't be quite so smart.

"Kyle! Listen, kid. Don't freak out on me, but I need to know who's dealin' pot these days."

Bree started to giggle. "Kyle . . . Kyle . . . Kyle! Chill out. I'm not trying to get you in trouble. But you and I both know that if you wanted to score, you'd know where to go."

She held the phone away from her ear and stuck her tongue out at it. "No, you little dork. I'm not going to buy weed. I just need to know whether Eddie Collins deals. . . . You sure? . . . Okay, get back to work. And if you breathe a word of this conversation to my daughter, I'll string you up by your short and curlies."

Bree flipped the phone closed and handed it back to Finn.

"Eddie Collins gets high with the kids he hires as hourly workers, but he doesn't deal."

Finn and I stared at Bree in stunned silence.

"What?" she asked, popping a chip laden with guac in her mouth. "You both have your sources; I have mine."

"Fair enough," Finn said, a smile of grudging admiration spreading across his face. "But that eliminates one possible motive for blackmail."

"Are you kidding? Doing drugs with high school kids sounds pretty bad to me," I argued.

"It doesn't sound *great*," Finn conceded, "but it's not nearly as big a deal, crimewise, as dealing. It's still distribution, but a joint here and there instead of real quantities of drugs. I can't imagine Eddie murdering someone over it."

"Well, then, we're back to square one."

"Look," Bree said, "everyone agrees Eddie's a total pantywaist. So maybe the blackmail note has nothing to do with the murder at all."

I shook my head adamantly. "Two major felonies at one picnic? They have to be related."

Finn tutted softly. I knew what he was thinking, that I was making huge leaps of logic again. The blackmail and the murder didn't have to be related, and even then, on some level, I understood that. But I *needed* them to be related, because otherwise I was back to square one.

Again.

And I didn't know how much more time I had before Cal showed up with handcuffs and a warrant for my arrest. I had started this investigation trying to save Wayne, but now I was trying to save myself. And I wasn't doing such a hot job of it.

"So how can we find out about the skeletons that might be rattling around in Eddie Collins's closet?" I asked.

"He has a sister," Bree offered. "Her name is Shelley." She drained her drink and uttered a lady-like burp.

"And?" I prompted.

"And Shelley and her husband, Ted, are regulars at karaoke night at the Bar None. As am I."

"Do you think they'd talk about Eddie?" Finn asked.

"I don't know," Bree said. "But it's worth a shot. They're usually pretty drunk, and drunk people lack—what do you call it?"

"Discretion?" I offered.

"That's it," Bree said with a smile. "They lack discretion. So are you two game?"

I exchanged a look with Finn.

"Come on," Bree urged. "You'd get to hear me sing."

Finn raised one questioning eyebrow. "The night nurse promised she'd have someone there tomorrow night," he said.

I grabbed another chip, dunked it in the guacamole, and devoured it in one bite. "What the heck? Maybe we'll get lucky."

chapter 22

I don't sing. I'm beyond tone deaf and can't quite bring myself to inflict my off-key warbling on the world. As a result, karaoke night at the Bar None never held much appeal.

Bree, whose PG-13 Madonna covers made her a fan favorite, led the way to the bar, greeting her adoring public with smiles and waves and even the occasional blown kiss. Finn and I followed in her wake, exchanging more sedate greetings with a few familiar faces.

Bree braced her hands on the brass rail and greeted the bartender. "Hey, Andi."

Andi seemed an unlikely bar back. A cloud of tight gray curls covered her head, and she wore a glittery orange jack-o'-lantern sweatshirt. "Hey, Bree. Scarlet O'Hara?"

"What else? And these two," Bree said, waving in our direction, "will have beer."

Andi popped the tops off a couple of beers and thumped them down on little cocktail napkins, then bustled off to pour Bree's SoCo and cranberry. The bartender, a blocky, big-bosomed woman, moved with muscle-bound stiffness, graceless yet energetic, like a badger tunneling its way through the forest undergrowth.

While we waited for Bree's drink, we turned to survey the crowd. Finn took a sip of his beer and jerked his chin toward a table near the small raised stage. "There," he said, just loud enough for us to hear him. "Isn't that them?"

Bree, ever the soul of discretion, craned her neck to follow his line of sight. "Yep, Shelley and Ted Alrecht."

The couple sat across from each other, each with a two-handed grasp on a drink, as though the booze were a shield between them. Judging by the empty glasses littering their table, they were both well on their way to wasted.

Shelley had her brother's coloring, hair as black and oily as fresh asphalt, bisected by a brutally straight part, above a sharp, pixielike face and an elfin body to match. Ted Alrecht had a lean, rawhide-tough face, the spare build of a Depression-era field hand, and a head as round and bald as a cue ball.

Bree snagged her drink from Andi and asked her to start a tab, then wove her way toward the Alrechts.

"Shelley, Ted, you two gonna sing tonight?" They both looked up as Bree approached, looks of hunger flashing across their faces—Ted's a hunger for something he wanted, Shelley's a hunger for something she wanted to be—before their expressions resolved into polite smiles.

Shelley nodded in Ted's direction. "He's gonna do 'Achy Breaky Heart.' Me, I've got awful allergies." As if on cue, she sneezed violently into her cocktail napkin. "I'd sound like a sick cat. You?"

"Yeah. I thought I'd mix things up a little, do some Cyndi Lauper tonight. Mind if we join you?" Without waiting for an answer, Bree slid into an empty chair. "Shelley, Ted, this is my cousin Tally and her friend Finn Harper. I dragged them out to hear me sing."

Finn and Ted exchanged a grim-faced manly handshake before Finn fetched another chair, and we sat down.

"Harper?" Ted said, brow wrinkled in concentration. I held my breath, hoping Ted didn't place Finn as a reporter. I suspected we wouldn't get much information from Shelley and Ted if they realized they were talking to a reporter. "Didn't you play football for the Wildcatters? Woulda been 'eighty-four or 'eighty-five?"

I sighed in relief, even as Finn's smile tightened. "Nope, that was my brother, Sonny."

Ted nodded. "Sure. He was amazing, man. What's he up to these days? Didn't he go pro?"

"No. He played a couple of years for A&M, but

that's it." Finn didn't mention that Sonny didn't go pro because he never had a chance. He died after his second college season.

"Too bad," Ted said. "What did you play?"

I smiled at the casual assumption that Finn played something. That was what Texas boys did: played sports, drank beer, and chased skirts.

"Clarinet," Finn deadpanned.

I could almost see the wheels turning as Ted pieced it together, but then he laughed and clapped Finn on the back with his knobby hand.

A tipsy couple in crisp new cowboy hats and polished boots took the stage and began giggling their way through "Islands in the Stream." We all nursed our drinks and listened politely until they collapsed in a chortling heap and gave up about halfway through.

I turned to Shelley. "Aren't you Eddie Collins's sister?" She nodded, and I continued, hoping to draw her out. "I met him the other day. Seems like a good guy. Really knows his stuff, too."

Ted laughed contemptuously, a harsh bark of sound, and Shelley shot him a narrow-eyed glare.

"He's a great guy," she said, her words directed more at Ted than at me. "And he *is* smart. He was gonna be a doctor."

"'Gonna be,'" Ted mocked. "Hell, I was gonna be the starting QB for the Cowboys."

Shelley reached for a pack of cigarettes on the table and shook one into her hand. "The difference is, you didn't have no talent. Eddie, he's smart enough; he coulda been a doctor," she said around the cigarette, flicking her lighter. "Got a full ride to college." She inhaled deeply and held the flame to the paper.

"But then he flunked out and started dealing dope," Ted said.

She let the lighter go and exhaled, glaring at her husband through the steady stream of smoke.

"What do you know about it?" she snapped. "You have no idea what he went through."

I had completely lost control of the conversation. Ted and Shelley would get into a knock-down, drag-out fight, and I wouldn't get a lick of information, if I didn't separate them. I kicked Finn in the shin and, when he looked up in surprise, jerked my head toward the pool tables.

He sighed and leaned in close to whisper in my ear. "You're gonna owe me for this one." He shoved his chair back. "Hey, Ted. Looks like there's a table open. Wanna play a game?" Ted didn't budge. He stared hard at his wife, and you could see he was itching for a fight. "Come on, man," Finn cajoled. "Loser buys the next round."

The prospect of free booze jolted Ted out of his funk. "You're on."

Shelley watched her husband walk away, shooting daggers in his back as he went. When the guys were out of earshot, I tried to recapture her attention.

"A full-ride scholarship, huh? That's impressive."

"Yeah," she said, slowly bringing her focus back to me. "Like I said, Eddie's the smartest guy I know."

"More than smart, I bet. I mean, you have to be pretty driven to go to medical school."

Shelley scrunched up her face, as if she smelled some milk that had just gone off. "No," she admitted. "That was always Eddie's problem. Berkeley and med school—that was Daddy's idea. Daddy wanted Eddie to get the hell out of Dalliance and make something of himself, and he decided the best thing to be was a doctor. Eddie could have been a doctor, but that's not what he wanted."

"Huh. So what did Eddie want to do?"

She took a sip of her drink, something amber and bubbly, like a whiskey and ginger ale. A soft smile lit her face, and I thanked the booze for loosening her tongue. "He didn't want to do nothin' but hang out with his girlfriend and party. But he did what Daddy said. Eddie was a good boy."

I couldn't wrap my brain around what it would be like to have parents who pushed you to leave Dalliance, who wanted you to go to school instead of get a job. But I did know what it was like to live your life making up for someone else's regrets. After all, I broke up with hell-raiser Finn and, eventually, married into the financial security Wayne could provide, all so I wouldn't repeat the mistakes my mama made. And look how great that turned out.

I sighed, saddened by what I imagined to be the inevitable outcome of the story. "So once Eddie got to college and didn't have Daddy looking over his shoulder anymore, he started making bad choices, huh?"

She pursed her lips and shook her head, her eyes unfocused as though she were staring into the past. "No, he started unraveling even before he left for Berkeley. That summer, he became sullen and moody, would snap at us for no apparent reason. Started drinking."

She laughed a little at some private joke. "I mean, he drank some in high school. Everybody did," she said with a wry smile. "But that summer he started drinking heavy. Liquor instead of beer, like he was trying to get as drunk as he could as fast as he could. Then, when he went off to California, he had access to all sorts of drugs."

She sighed.

I shook my head in commiseration. "I wonder what happened."

She pressed her lips together. We'd come to a line that, even drunk, Shelley was unwilling to cross.

I caught Bree's gaze and willed her to keep quiet. The silence stretched out, awkward and begging to be filled. Shelley took another drink and shrugged.

"It about killed him when Miranda Jillson died."

"That's right," Bree said. "I forgot they dated."

Shelley glanced at Bree before nodding. "Yeah. They weren't dating when she died, of course. Broke up just before Eddie's high school graduation."

About the time Eddie's disposition took a turn for the worse, I thought. Maybe Miranda dumped

him, and he didn't take well to rejection. Was it possible that Brittanie and Eddie had dated and Eddie
had lashed out when he was thrown over for Wayne?
I couldn't imagine what Brittanie would see in Eddie. But then again I couldn't really imagine what
Brittanie saw in Wayne.

"Still," Shelley continued, "they might have
patched things up eventually, after Eddie finished
college and moved home. I mean, they were really
in love, you know? He never did get over her death.
Finally, he flunked out, started running drugs from
South America, got busted for selling dope, ended
up doing a little time."

"Eddie went to prison?" I asked. I couldn't imagine soft, wifty Eddie surviving in prison. Maybe
Eddie was tougher than I was giving him credit
for.

Shelley blushed, and her expression grew guarded.
"Yes. But that was a mistake, a long time ago. He's
grown up since then. Eddie's a successful businessman," she concluded, just as Finn and Ted returned to the table with a round of fresh drinks.

Ted laughed. "Right," he said, picking up the
thread of their fight as though he'd never left. "Snake-
oil salesman, more like."

"Oh, hush. You're just jealous."

"Dang it, Finn," I whispered as he handed me a
bottle of beer. "I give you one little job. . . ."

"I suck at pool," he whispered back.

"Jealous of what?" Ted was saying. "Eddie's new-age bullshit green lawn care?" Contempt dripped like venom from every word. "I sell a quality service for a reasonable price, don't charge a premium for a bunch of crap."

The temperature in the room dropped, and Shelley's face hardened into a mask of pure hate. "You shovel shit for a living."

"It was good enough for your daddy."

Shelley stubbed out her cigarette in the black plastic ashtray. By the look on her face, she would have rather put it out by cramming it in Ted's smug smile. "Leave Daddy out of this. He didn't even have a high school diploma, and look what he built for his family. And Eddie, he built up his lawn-care business from scratch. You never built a thing in your life, just waited around to pick up the scraps Daddy left behind."

"Bullshit. Frank Collins was a good man, and I was grateful to him for giving me a job. But I put my own stamp on Soil Systems after he passed. I'm the one who made the connections with the agricultural extension and started doing the soil and well-water testing. That's where we make our biggest profits. So don't tell me I just rode on your daddy's coattails."

Shelley tapped another cigarette from her pack and lit up. "Yeah, you just love sucking up to those rich bitches in the Master Gardeners, making sure the damn dirt is good enough for their precious roses."

"Now who's jealous?" Ted asked with a sly smile.

"Shut up," Shelley snapped, but a glimmer of a smile teased the corners of her mouth.

"Uh-huh," Ted said, "you know you want this." He stretched back and patted his own abs.

"I said, shut up." All the heat was gone from Shelley's voice now, and she gazed up at her husband through her eyelashes.

Bree, Finn, and I exchanged looks of disbelief. Five minutes before, I had thought they might come to blows, and now I was worried they'd have make-up sex right there on the table.

Bree cleared her throat. "I'm gonna sing," she announced, pushing back from the table and abandoning us.

Finn quickly followed her lead. "Tally, you wanna dance?"

I did not want to dance in the slightest, especially not with Finn Harper. But I didn't want to watch the bizarre mating ritual unfolding at the table.

"Sounds great," I said.

Onstage, Bree launched into Cyndi Lauper's "Time After Time." I caught a glimpse of her—clutching the mic in both hands, eyes closed, head thrown back in abandon—before Finn pulled me into his arms.

"That's the second time tonight I've saved your bacon," Finn said, his lips pressed close to my ear. "Your debt is mounting."

I tipped my chin to look him in the eye. "These

days I pay all my debts with ice cream. What's your favorite flavor?"

He tucked my head back into his shoulder and leaned in close. "Cherry," he murmured as he tugged me closer, molding me to his lean body.

It felt like coming home. His hands rested on the curve of my waist; my fingers brushed the soft fringe of his hair; my head fit just beneath his chin. We swayed gently as Bree's achingly clear voice sang of lost love and the hope of reunion.

"If you're lost, you can look and you will find me," she sang. But I wasn't lost at all. Finn had already found me. His scent—familiar beneath a new cologne, a different soap—and the slow, strong beat of his heart filled up an emptiness I hadn't even known I possessed.

We rocked, barely moving, until the melancholy melody faded away. And then, for just a breath of time, we stood still, bodies entangled.

The first tinny beats of "Girls Just Want to Have Fun" jolted us apart.

I laughed nervously. "Just like back in the high school gym, huh?"

Finn studied me like a puzzle. "Yeah," he said finally, "just like high school."

We made our way from the dance floor to the bar. Finn ordered another beer, and I switched to diet soda so I could drive us all home.

"Sorry I dragged you out here," I said before taking a sip from my drink, using the swizzle stick like a straw. "Made you sit through that freak show"—I waved in the general direction of Ted and Shelley's table—"and we didn't even learn anything particularly useful."

Finn lifted his chin just slightly. "Not so fast. Maybe *you* didn't learn anything useful, but I did."

I chucked him in the shoulder. "What? Were you holding out on me?"

He clutched his upper arm in mock pain. "No, of course not. But," he added, bending low to whisper in my ear, "I had to wait to get you alone."

My pulse kicked up a notch, and I felt my face blaze with heat.

"So? Spill it."

He crossed his arms over his chest, clearly proud of his investigative prowess. "Ted wasn't just blowing smoke about Eddie being a scam artist."

"What do you mean?"

"Apparently, Eddie's organic fertilizer and weed killer is nothing but the usual chemical stuff, mixed with some manure and repackaged."

I digested that nugget of information as we inched our way around the edge of the growing crowd, looking for a quiet nook in which to talk. We finally settled on a spot behind a stack of amplifiers that completely obliterated our view of the stage. That location had the added benefit of letting us snag Bree when she finished her karaoke set.

"Whoa," I said, settling one hip on the edge of the stage. "So all those people who are paying a premium for earth-friendly lawn care . . ."

"Are getting royally ripped off," Finn concluded with a nod.

"How does Ted know?"

Finn shrugged. "I asked him the same question, and that's when he clammed up. I don't think he meant to tell me about the scam at all. Just too drunk to stop himself."

"Mmm," I agreed, sipping through my tiny straw again. I caught Finn watching my mouth and quickly lowered my drink. "Shelley seems really protective of her brother. I don't think she'd be so quick to forgive Ted if he got Eddie arrested for fraud."

"Ted didn't tell me outright how he knew about Eddie's shenanigans, but my guess would be that he tested the stuff. From what he was saying, that's what Soil Systems does now. In addition to managing septic systems, they test soil and groundwater for chemicals."

I nodded. "That could be the secret that Eddie's blackmailer was threatening to expose. So the big question is whether Ted did the testing on his own or whether someone else sent him the samples."

Finn made a face. "I can't imagine shaking Eddie down would be any better for Ted's marriage than getting him thrown in jail."

"Good point. So that would seem to suggest that someone else sent the samples to Ted for testing. And maybe that's our blackmailer."

"My guess is Wayne," Finn said. "Eddie can't have much money, and who else has a motive to pull the rug out from under a helpless old stoner like him?"

I had to concede that Wayne was the obvious choice, but I wasn't convinced. "Wouldn't Wayne be better off exposing Eddie? Like you said, there's no indication Eddie has a lot of money stashed away to pay a blackmailer. If Wayne drove Eddie out of business, he would make more in the long run than he could through any blackmail scheme."

"That's what I love about you, Tally," Finn said, a dopey smile spreading across his face. "You're so honest, you assume everyone else is, too . . . even criminals. Wayne doesn't have to choose between blackmailing Eddie and running him out of business. He can do both."

I snorted. "Believe me, I know Wayne's not honest. But he's also not that subtle, you know?"

Finn laughed. "Yeah, I know. I've seen those neon green trucks."

"Exactly. No way Wayne could hatch such a convoluted plan. If he found out Eddie was scamming people, he'd want the world to know ASAP, and he'd want his picture next to every headline."

The only validation I got from Finn was a miserly nod. "Look," I huffed, as Bree skipped down the stage steps, spotted us, and headed our way, "if Ted did tests on a soil sample for Wayne, Wayne would have to have the results somewhere. He didn't like to bring work home, so let's just go through his office. If we find the results, then we have our answer."

"Great plan," Finn said, a note of sarcasm in his voice. "I'm sure Wayne will invite us right in and let us have a look around."

Bree, glowing from her triumphant onstage performance, clapped her hands together. "I don't know what you two are talking about, but it sounds like we get to break into Wayne's office. And you know I'm all about breaking and entering."

"Don't be ridiculous. No one is breaking into anything." I rummaged around in my purse, fishing out a bristling key ring that I held up high for all to see. "I have the key."

chapter 23

"Shh," Bree said, her finger to her lips, "be vewwy quiet. We're hunting wabbits!"

She and Finn, who had continued to drink their way through karaoke night while I sobered up to drive, fell all over each other giggling like little girls. We huddled together outside the low concrete office building of Wayne's Weed and Seed, doing our best to avoid the halogen lights that lit up the parking lot. The signature Wayne's Weed and Seed trucks were arrayed in neat rows, with the one closest to the main road decked out in giant magnetic letters that spelled BRIT, LOVE YOU 4-EVER BABE, W.

"Seriously," I snapped under my breath, "if you don't both keep it zipped, I will make you wait in the car."

After a round of shushing, they grew quiet for a

moment, and I was able to flip through my keys until I found the one with the bright green sticker on its bow. It slipped easily into the keyway.

From behind me, Finn whined, "Tally, Bree's touching me." The sputtering giggles started up again.

I swallowed a pissy comeback and turned the key in the lock, breathing a sigh of relief when I felt the tumbler give. I'd been a little worried that Wayne had had the locks changed after the divorce.

I had my hands braced on the door, ready to push, when Bree yelped, "Wait!"

"For the love of ... Bree, you about gave me a coronary. What is your problem?"

She pointed to a decal on the door, announcing that the building was protected by an alarm system.

"Nah," I said. "That's just for show. Wayne had a security system once, but he kept forgetting the code, and he racked up huge fees for false alarms."

I opened the door and slipped inside, with Finn and Bree tumbling after me. I led the way through what passed for a showroom, wincing when Bree crashed into a cardboard display for drought-resistant turf grass. Rather than risk someone breaking a leg—which would get us caught for sure—I flipped on the light in the plain-Jane hallway leading back to the offices, but I didn't want to leave it on for long: it was a straight shot down that hall to the front door and then to the street, and there was no way to hide that light from random passersby.

So as soon as we entered Wayne's personal office,

I turned on the office light, flipped off the hall light, and shut the office door.

I pointed to two armchairs upholstered in a dark green twill. "Sit."

My partners in crime dutifully settled into the chairs and began whispering to each other. I don't know what they were saying, but they both thought they were pretty funny. Meanwhile, I did my best to ignore them and get down to business.

At home, Wayne Jones was a messy man. He left his clothes wherever he removed them, so vast drifts of sweaty undershirts would amass beside his side of the bed, and stinky socks sometimes sat in the middle of the kitchen floor. I found dirty coffee mugs by the toilet, in the shower, and oddly, in the fireplace. Trying to right his messes wore me out.

But at the Weed and Seed office, he took pains to hide the chaos. His bookshelves were orderly, his wastebasket empty, and his computer monitor dust free. The smooth stretch of his oak desktop held a phone, a pencil cup stocked with sharpened number twos and blue ballpoints, and a single silver-framed picture of Brittanie.

I studied the picture. Brittanie's head was turned and tipped back, her mouth open in a toothy smile, as though she were laughing up at someone standing behind the photographer. Her hair blew wild about her freckled face, and the rosy-gold glow of late-afternoon sunlight drenched the scene, turning her usually pale blond hair to molten amber. I almost didn't recognize her. In that picture, Brittanie looked fresh and young and real. I imagined that she hated the picture, and I felt a stab of affection for Wayne for choosing that one shot for his desk.

Unfortunately, Wayne's obsessive tidiness in the office was purely superficial. Inside the drawers and filing cabinets, chaos ruled. Wayne could find just about any document, even the most insignificant scrap of paper, in an instant, but if there was some method to the madness of his filing, it had managed to escape me for the full seventeen years of our marriage.

I started with the big drawers on his desk, hoping Wayne would want to keep blackmail documents close at hand. In the first drawer, I found a dozen take-out menus, about three years' worth of utility bills, antacids, a half dozen brightly colored plastic poker chips, and an orange-haired miniature troll doll.

"I have to piddle," Bree announced.

"Good heavens, you two turn into such babies when you drink," I chided, opening the second drawer. "You're a big girl, Bree. You know where the bathroom is." I glanced up in time to catch her sticking her tongue out at me. She closed the door behind her on her way out of the office.

"Any luck?" Finn asked, as I began thumbing through the higgledy-piggledy mass of papers in the bottom drawer.

"Not yet."

Just below a half dozen customer invoices, I discovered a handful of nine-by-twelve-inch clasp en-

velopes held together by a binder clip. The first
thing I noticed as I flipped through them was that
they all had labels—JULY COUPONS, PRESS CLIPPINGS,
THANK-YOU CARDS—typed directly onto the envelopes rather than printed on adhesive labels. And I
mean *typed*: the printing had the same slightly off-
kilter look as Eddie's blackmail "invitation."

"Whoa," I said softly.

"What? Did you find something?" Instantly, Finn
sounded sober again.

"Maybe."

He came around the desk to look over my shoulder as I released the binder clip and fanned the envelopes out. The envelope second from the bottom
was different from the others, a paler shade of tan,
and it was labeled simply E.C.

Finn and I exchanged looks of incredulity. Could
Wayne really be so whacked-out that he would label his blackmail file?

When I opened the envelope, I glimpsed a single
sheet of paper with a blaze orange logo in the corner, a pair of intertwined *S*'s. I pulled the sheet free,
and, sure enough, it was from Soil Systems, Inc.,
Ted Alrecht's company. I skimmed through the
short introductory paragraph, about completing a
full-spectrum chemical analysis on the submitted
sample labeled COLLINS GREENCARE, but then I hit a
wall when I got to the list of results. "Benzo" this
and "4.5-dioxyethyl" that . . . I didn't know what
the laundry list of chemicals did, but they sure as
heck weren't organic.

Behind me, Finn whistled softly.

"What do you think?" I asked.

"That's not exactly a smoking gun," he whispered. "I mean, anyone could submit a sample and say it came from Eddie's service. But this would sure be enough to prompt a full-blown investigation."

"You think?"

"Oh, yeah. If someone sent this to me, as a reporter, I'd be on Eddie Collins like white on rice."

I pushed the results back in their envelope and was adjusting the clasp when Bree came scurrying back into the office.

"Oh, shit, oh, shit, oh, shit," she breathed. "Tally, I'm so sorry."

Before I could ask her what she was sorry for, Wayne appeared in the doorway to his office.

"Tally?" Wayne said, peering around uncertainly, as if he wasn't sure he was in the right place.

"Wayne. What are you doing here?" I gasped.

"I was driving by when I saw the light"—he waved over his shoulder, and that was when I realized the hallway light was back on—"and I thought I better check it out."

He lowered his brow in confusion. He pointed a finger at my chest. "Better question is what are *you* doing here? And with them," he added, waggling his finger to encompass Bree and Finn.

"Wayne, I'm real sorry. This probably isn't the best idea I've ever had."

Bree busted up laughing. "Oh, sorry," she said,

bent over at the waist and trying visibly to regain her composure. "It's not funny. I'm sorry."

I rolled my eyes. "Look, Wayne, now that it looks like you were the murderer's intended victim, we've been trying to figure out who would want you . . ." I paused, trying to think of a way to soften the blow. I couldn't. "We're trying to figure out who would want you dead."

"And so you broke into my office?"

"Maybe I should explain," Finn said, stepping to my side and placing a protective hand on my shoulder.

"Yes—," Wayne said.

"No—," I said at the same time.

"Oh, boy," Bree sighed, before she began giggling again.

I glared at both my inane cousin and my patronizing . . . well, I didn't know what to call Finn other than "patronizing."

I squared my shoulders, took a determined breath, and pulled the Soil Systems analysis out of its envelope again.

"This look familiar?" I asked Wayne.

He crossed the room in two long strides and plucked the paper from my fingers. As he read through the contents of the report, the wrinkles in his forehead grew deeper and deeper.

"What the *h-e*-double-toothpicks is this?"

"It's a chemical analysis of lawn-care products," I said, watching Wayne's expression closely.

He sighed in annoyance and shot me a disgruntled look. "I know *that*. I use these chemicals all the time. What does this have to do with the price of tea in China?"

Finn's hand on my shoulder tightened.

"Wayne," I explained, "that's an analysis of the crap Eddie Collins is putting on people's lawns. The stuff he's calling all-natural and organic."

Under different circumstances, I might have found Wayne's expression of wide-eyed surprise comical. Even under the present circumstances, Bree found it hilarious. She had to sit down, she was laughing so hard.

"No kidding," Wayne breathed, sinking slowly into one of the green armchairs. "No kidding," he repeated a little more forcefully.

And then he started to laugh, too. "That son of a bitch," he chuckled. "What a con man! Whoo-ee, I can't wait for this to get out."

A flash of realization brightened his features. "You," he said, pointing at Finn. "You're a reporter, right? You oughta run a story about this in the *News-Letter*. I'll give you quotes and everything. And I'm gonna call Channel Eight."

I interrupted his tirade before he could actually start drafting the press release. "Wayne, you didn't ever see this before? It was sitting right there in your desk drawer."

"Heck no, I never seen it before! I don't know who stuck it in the drawer, but if I had dirt on that little weasel, I sure as heck wouldn't keep it in my desk drawer. I'd be shouting it from the dang rooftops." He laughed and snapped his fingers. "I know: I'd put in on the side of all my trucks, just drive around Dalliance letting everybody know that Wayne's is still the best lawn-and-garden service in town."

I shot Finn an "I told you so" look, and he rewarded me with a wink of congratulations.

Still, if Wayne didn't put the test results in his own drawer, that raised the question of who did.

"How about these?" I held up the clasp envelopes, the ones with the typed labels.

"What?" Wayne squinted at the envelopes. "Those are just odds and ends. Coupons and such."

"Did you type up the labels?"

Wayne laughed again. "Come on, Tally. You ever know me to file anything in my whole life? I'm not one to label and organize."

He had a point.

"So if you didn't, who did?"

"What difference does it make?"

"Just answer the question."

I'd miscalculated, pushed too far. Wayne drew himself up and puffed out his chest. "Do I have to remind you that I found the three of you breaking into my office? I should call the cops on you. I certainly won't take orders from you."

Bree, whose giggle fit had subsided to a lopsided smile, stepped in to smooth the waters. "Aw, come on, Wayne. You gotta admit we pretty much made your day with that news about Eddie Collins. Maybe your week. You wouldn't call the cops on us after that."

Mollified, Wayne grumbled. "No, I don't suppose I would. But I'd still like to know what the Sam Hill is going on here. What difference does it make who did my filing?"

I couldn't see much point in trying to dance around the truth. "Someone was trying to blackmail Eddie Collins. Someone using Weed and Seed letterhead, and someone who typed the blackmail note on an actual typewriter. Just like someone typed these labels."

Wayne's expression grew closed, and I could tell he was chewing on something, trying to decide what to tell me and what to withhold. Finally, he looked at me, narrow eyed and considering. "Can we talk in private? Without them two," he added, indicating Finn and Bree.

I looked up at Finn. His lips were pressed tight and his brows were bold slashes above his soft green eyes. He did not want to leave. I wasn't sure whether he didn't want to miss the scoop or didn't want to leave me alone with Wayne. Loyalty and opportunity looked pretty much the same right then.

"Finn, could you take Bree out for some air?" I handed him my key ring. "You two can sit in the van and listen to the radio. I'll just be a minute."

"Come on, big fella," Bree purred. "Why don't you show a lady a good time?"

"What, you see a lady around here?" Finn quipped, hooking his arm through Bree's. They both laughed, tipping their heads together like old chums, and headed toward the door. But before they disappeared down the hallway, Finn looked back over his shoulder and raised his eyebrows meaningfully. Despite everything, I felt a smile tug at my lips. If I got in a jam, Finn had my back.

When the door clicked shut behind them, and Wayne and I were alone, he leaned forward, bracing his elbows on his knees and clasping his hands.

He blew out a long stream of air before he spoke. "Brittanie was getting me organized. She's the one who put together those files. She was going to do a bunch more, too. But that doesn't mean anything. Just because Brittanie typed up these files doesn't mean she typed up that note you're talking about."

His defense of Brittanie was touching. I wondered if he would have defended me like that. Probably. Wayne wasn't faithful, but he could be loyal to a fault. It was a distinction I was only then coming to appreciate.

"Wayne," I said softly, coming around the desk and perching on the other armchair so I could meet him face-to-face, "it's quite a coincidence, don't you think? That the blackmail letter and the folders were typed rather than printed, that the subject of the blackmail was in one of those typed envelopes . . ."

"Yeah. Guess so." He stared off into the corner

of the room, his face a picture of misery. "It just doesn't make any sense," he said. "Brittanie and I talked about Eddie. We talked about adding an earth-friendly line of products and services so we could take away his competitive advantage. You know, the service and reliability of Wayne's Weed and Seed but better for the environment." I could almost hear Brittanie's earnest voice uttering the words, the whole enterprise like one big business school class project.

"She was all set to take on the competition above-board," Wayne added. "Why would she blackmail him?" His Adam's apple slid up and down his throat, and his voice was tight with emotion. "Why wouldn't she tell me about it?"

"I don't know, Wayne." I rested a hand on his arm, patting and stroking it gently, as if I were soothing a fussy baby.

He sniffed. "And going all the way across town to the Zeta offices just to hide it from me? Dammit, Tally, didn't she trust me?"

My hand froze on Wayne's arm.

"What?"

"What do you mean, 'what'?" he said peevishly.

"What's this about the Zeta house?"

"That's where the typewriter is." He spoke slowly, as though I were some sort of half-wit. "We don't have a real typewriter anymore. Not since I got the computer system back in 'ninety-eight."

"She typed up your file folders at the Zeta office?"

He nodded, a "this isn't rocket science" look on his face.

"Didn't that seem a little weird to you, Wayne? Why not make the file labels right here?"

Wayne shrugged. "Brit has an ink-jet printer in her office." He jerked his thumb over his shoulder in the direction of the office door and the hallway beyond. "But it's older than dirt, and it can't handle much more than paper. The file labels she bought, and those big envelopes, they kept getting gummed up in the works. So she took them over to the Zeta alumni offices where they have an honest-to-God typewriter. She was over there all the time, anyway. It was no big deal."

My brain was racing a mile a minute. Wayne was absolutely right. This didn't make sense. I could see why Brittanie would use the Zeta typewriter for the labels and envelopes, but why would she haul letterhead across town to type a note that could easily be run through the printer? If she wanted to keep her activities secret, she risked far more exposure typing the letter around a gaggle of sorority sisters rather than printing it in the privacy of her office. And if she was more concerned with keeping the whole affair secret from Wayne, why would she label the blackmail file—however cryptically—and leave it in his desk drawer?

A convoluted theory started to form in my mind, one that seemed ridiculous but fit with all the bits and pieces too well to be dismissed out of hand.

What if someone wanted to kill Wayne, but

wanted to deflect suspicion away onto someone else? Maybe the real killer concocted this whole scheme to make it look as if Wayne were blackmailing Eddie . . . so when the cops found out about the fake shakedown, they would focus on Eddie as a suspect.

Crazy?

Heck, yeah. But I was starting to think that every last man, woman, and child in Dalliance, Texas, was crazier than a peach-orchard boar.

If I was right, that meant the killer had to be someone with access to the Zeta house and someone who was at the luau. Deena Silver spent a lot of time at the Zeta house planning their various events, and she could easily have tampered with Wayne's food at the luau. But she wasn't a Zeta, herself, and it would be strange for her to use the typewriter. Besides, she might have had a reason to knock off Brittanie, but I couldn't see any motive for her to kill Wayne.

The only other person I could think of was JoAnne Simms. The whole thing just kept coming back to her. Maybe, despite all her rage at Brit for taking up with Wayne, she still harbored hopes of rekindling her romance with the younger woman. And Wayne stood in the way.

Besides, JoAnne had inside information that very few people possessed. As the owner of Sinclair's, she would have known that Wayne bought an engagement ring. The possibility of an impending engagement might have been enough to push her over the edge.

As motives went, it still seemed a little weak, but it was all I had at the time. And I couldn't afford to dance with JoAnne Simms anymore. I needed to confront her fair and square.

"Tally?" Wayne was waving his hand in front of my face. "Lord, girl, you were a million miles away. What are you thinking?"

I jumped up, grabbed my purse, and headed out. "I was thinking, Wayne," I called back over my shoulder, "that you better watch your back."

chapter 24

I slipped into the softly padded hush of Sinclair's Jewelry like a sinner late for church. And like a rosary or a hymnal, my purse with the secret stash was clutched tight in my hands; it held the digital recorder Alice used to tape her lectures and the heaviest ice-cream spade we had lying around the A-la-mode. I wanted evidence—a confession, ideally—but I was prepared to defend myself if need be.

JoAnne Simms appeared to be the only person working that Friday afternoon, and she was busy waiting on a man in a rumpled suit. His pants needed hemming, and the attaché case at his feet was battered, but his hair was neatly combed and his shirt smartly pressed. He looked like an accountant or a lawyer, the kind of guy who has an office upstairs from an appliance repair store and who types his own letters. Professional, but not especially prosperous.

A slight shift in JoAnne's body language, nothing more than a straightening of her shoulders and a tip of her chin, let me know she was aware of my entrance, but she never let her attention waver from her customer.

Quite the contrary, from where I stood, she seemed to be completely entranced by him. And if Deena was right about JoAnne's sexual preferences, the woman was quite an actress. She gazed up at the man through demurely lowered lashes, as though she had a delicious secret to tell. She caressed the velvet tray with the very tips of her French-manicured fingers, long, languorous strokes. She laughed, a throaty shiver of sound, then lifted a glittering diamond tennis bracelet and draped it over her own delicate wrist. A small gesture, the spare, elegant move of a geisha, set the bracelet undulating, catching the light in a shower of sparks.

He nodded, and JoAnne sighed happily, a sated smile softening her mouth.

As he fished out a credit card to hand her, she caught my eye, raising her eyebrows in silent greeting, a flash of humor in her heavily lashed eyes. I felt like a voyeur, caught in the bushes with my binoculars in hand, but I managed a brief smile in response.

I watched as JoAnne wrote out a receipt in an old-fashioned carbon receipt book, ran the card

through the scanner, and stapled the merchant copy
from the card reader to the yellow page in her
receipt book. The man tucked his copies of the re-
ceipts and the oblong velvet box in his lapel pocket,
picked up his attaché case, and turned to go. He
stood straighter now, head high, a cocky swagger in
his step as though he were wearing Armani instead
of off-the-rack Men's Wearhouse.

When the glass door whooshed shut behind him,
I approached JoAnne. She was tiny—if I'd stood
close enough, her Texas-teased hair would have just
brushed the tip of my nose—and perfectly made-
up. Her delicate garnet cashmere sweater set off the
luminous pearls at her throat and her gardenia-
blossom skin, and the soft light of the store blended
away the fine lines that normally framed her eyes.

"Well, Tallulah Jones, as I live and breathe," she
gushed in an over-the-top Southern belle simper.

"Hey, JoAnne." I nodded toward the door.
"Who's your friend?"

She frowned, following my line of sight, then
laughed softly. "Oh, just a customer."

I must have looked skeptical, because she laughed
louder. "Really," she insisted.

I cocked my head. "Huh. Looked like you knew
each other pretty well."

She gave me a teasing wink. "Most of my customers are men, buying gifts. They don't care about
bracelets and earrings. They care about grateful
wives and girlfriends. So that's what I sell them. I
show them how wearing diamonds and gold makes

me feel and let them imagine their own sweethearts having the same reaction. Works like a charm."

She shrugged. "Sales are about seduction, right?"

"Guess so," I muttered.

Maybe that was what I'd been doing wrong with Remember the A-la-mode. I had been selling ice cream—or trying to—when maybe I should have been selling how ice cream made me feel.

I made a mental note to talk over a more seductive marketing strategy with Bree. If anyone knew how to sex it up, it would be Bree.

"So, Tally, I've been expecting you."

"Really?" I asked, genuinely surprised.

JoAnne waved her hand dismissively. "You've been sniffing around me like a lost pup for the last week. I figured, eventually, you'd come scratching at my door."

When I walked through the door, I knew my only advantages were surprise and sheer audacity. Now it appeared I had somehow played right into JoAnne's hands.

"Listen," she said, "why don't we sit. I'm exhausted, and I imagine this is going to take a while."

She gestured that I should follow her around the display cases and into the back of the store. As I rounded the big glass and brass box, I expected to see JoAnne wearing wildly impractical stiletto heels, but she actually wore pristine white crosstrainers.

I looked up to find her watching me. She shrugged. "This"—she indicated her perfect hair, perfect face, and perfect outfit—"is all people can see from that side of the counter. I may as well let my feet be comfortable."

As she led me through a short hallway lined with sleek black-and-white landscape photos, I started to get a little nervous. If I was right—if JoAnne had tried to kill Wayne to win back Brittanie—it might not be the smartest move ever to follow her down a deserted hallway. "Don't you need to stay out front?" I asked.

"No. The door has a sensor. If someone opens it, we'll hear a chime back in the office. Most afternoons, I can get all the paperwork taken care of and still have time to watch my soaps."

The office was as utilitarian as the showroom was posh. A simple aluminum desk and wooden banker's chair dominated the space, with a smaller table bearing a boxy monitor and CPU tower set at a ninety-degree angle. A couple of black filing cabinets, a bookshelf crammed with binders and a portable television, and two molded-plastic side chairs completed the office suite.

"Have a seat."

I settled myself into one of the plastic guest chairs while JoAnne slid behind the desk and folded her forearms on the desk blotter. Immediately I realized what she'd done. On the showroom floor, she was a diminutive employee, but now, in the office, the height differential had been erased and she was the one in a position of power.

Negotiating has never been my strong suit, but I

knew I needed to regain my footing, throw her off-kilter.

"JoAnne, did you try to kill Wayne at the Weed and Seed luau?"

Her facial muscles twitched and her eyebrows shot up to her hairline, and finally she started to laugh. "What? Of course not! Why on earth would I want to kill Wayne Jones?"

So much for the direct approach.

JoAnne eyed me shrewdly. "Are you recording our conversation?"

I shook my head, all wide-eyed innocence.

She clicked her tongue against her teeth. "Come on, I wasn't born yesterday. Hand it over." She held out her hand, palm up, and waited.

"I don't know what you're talking about," I bluffed.

She sighed. "Look, I'm not saying another word until you put a tape recorder in my hand."

I hesitated a moment longer, but she stared at me, unblinking, so I dug out the digital recorder and gave it to her.

She eyed it curiously. "Cute. They make these things smaller and smaller every year." She turned the recorder this way and that until she found the OFF button and clicked it.

"Now, what specifically can I help you with?"

"Well, for starters, at the gym the other day, you said you knew Wayne wasn't at the house when Brittanie died but that he definitely wasn't with me."

She grimaced. "Oh, that. Just a slip of the tongue.

Don't worry, Trish and Jackie don't have more than a half dozen gray cells between them. They won't remember what I said, and I assure you that I won't blow your alibi again."

"My alibi? I don't need an alibi!"

"Are you sure about that?" JoAnne asked slyly.

I pressed my lips together in consternation. In fact, it was looking more and more like I did need an alibi. "Regardless," I said, "I already told the police that Wayne wasn't with me that night."

JoAnne laughed, a soft, liquid sound like water at the bottom of a deep stone well. "That explains why Wayne has been pestering me about coming forward. Poor Wayne. First he wanted you to lie about being with him that night, and now he wants me to tell the truth about being with him that night . . . and neither of us is willing to oblige him."

Now I was totally confused. "So you *were* sleeping with Wayne? I was led to believe you'd, uh, been romantic with Brittanie."

An enigmatic smile touched JoAnne's face. "Actually, I've slept with them both. Not at the same time, though."

"What?" I felt as though the whole world had tilted on its axis. Crazily, it occurred to me that this must have been what it felt like for the people on the *Titanic*, when the ship suddenly tipped on end.

"Aw, poor, sweet, naive Tally Jones," JoAnne tutted. "You don't have a clue what goes on in this little town, do you? Why, we could put Peyton Place to shame."

"I don't understand," I insisted. "If you were sleeping with both Wayne and Brittanie, why did you call Brittanie a whore? I mean, how was she—" I stumbled to a halt, mortified by what I was about to say.

JoAnne didn't seem offended, though. "How was she any worse than me? She wasn't. But my affairs with both of them were long over. No, I've mended my ways. Celebrated two years of sobriety the first of this month."

"Sobriety?"

"From sex," she said matter-of-factly. "I joined Sex Addicts Anonymous. In fact, I joined just after things ended with Brittanie. Sleeping with a self-destructive college kid?" She pulled a face. "Not my finest moment."

"So you don't have sex anymore?"

She laughed that sultry laugh. "Heavens, no. I'm not abstinent. But I'm in a loving, monogamous relationship with a dear woman, who shall—for obvious reasons—remain nameless. It's about love for me now, not compulsion."

"Well," I said. "That's nice."

I wondered fleetingly if they made greeting cards to congratulate people on such things.

Just then, a gentle chime sounded, indicating someone had come through the front door, and JoAnne excused herself.

For a moment, I sat perfectly still, digesting what I'd just learned. The notion of JoAnne Simms, with her pearls and her cashmere sweaters and her perfect small-town pedigree, being an addict of any sort was troubling. But a sex addict? It was too much to process.

And JoAnne had basically admitted that she and Wayne were together the night Brittanie died. Yet, even though she claimed she wasn't having an illicit affair with Wayne any longer, she apparently wouldn't go on the record with his alibi—which wasn't really an alibi at all, now that the police had determined that Brittanie was poisoned at the luau.

It made my head hurt.

As I sat there, though, listening to the faint sounds of JoAnne conversing with someone in the front of the store, it occurred to me that I was in a prime position to answer at least one nagging question. What had Wayne purchased from Sinclair's other than Brittanie's engagement ring?

With a quick glance at the office door, I scooted around behind the desk. I had seen JoAnne write up her sale in a carbon-copy receipt book, so I started looking for similar books and in no time found a bunch of them stacked neatly on a shelf. I pulled one out and found that it bore a label on the front: August 09—2. If Brittanie had seen the jewelry store charge on Wayne's credit card statement near the first of October, then he'd probably made the purchase in September.

I found the three books for September and began thumbing through them.

From out front, I heard JoAnne laugh. I didn't have much time.

Near the middle of the second September receipt

book, I found one with "W. Jones" listed as the customer. My heart beat faster. It might not get me closer to solving the murder, but at least I might get an answer to *something*.

Sure enough, the receipt listed two purchases. But it didn't describe what he bought, only provided catalogue item numbers.

The first item, to be engraved "Always My Sugar," cost almost six grand. I couldn't help it. It cut me to the quick. I had been Wayne's "sugar." Me. It hadn't been carved in precious metal or celebrated with a diamond; it had simply been the name he gave me in the dark quiet of the night. And here he had spent a small fortune to erase all that and give the title to Brittanie.

I blinked away unexpected tears and looked at the other entry on the receipt. Again, the catalogue number didn't tell me much, but the price was more than eight hundred dollars and a note said the piece should be engraved "Step Twelve."

Step Twelve?

"Tsk, tsk, tsk."

I nearly jumped out of my skin. I'd been so absorbed in what I was doing that I hadn't heard the chime of the front door opening or JoAnne returning to the office.

"You're like a terrier, aren't you?" she said. "Well, did you find what you were looking for?"

I didn't see any point in beating around the bush. "Not really. What's this?" I pointed at the second item on the receipt.

JoAnne smiled. "Well, that's this," she said. She tugged on a delicate gold chain around her neck, one I hadn't noticed before, and pulled a pendant from beneath her sweater. It was gold, inlayed with diamond chips, and it was shaped like a poker chip.

"Step twelve," she said. "Carry the message of forgiveness to other sex addicts and live a life of healing. Wayne gave this to me to celebrate my second anniversary."

I must have looked as confused as I felt.

"Wayne is an addict, too. I'm his sponsor."

Suddenly, I remembered the handful of poker chips in Wayne's desk drawer. They must have been tokens, symbols of his milestones on the path to recovery.

"That's why I was so angry at Brittanie," JoAnne continued. "Because she knew he had a problem and took advantage of it to worm her way into his life. And because she was not supporting him in focusing on getting right with God and breaking his bad habits. She was pushing him to be more aggressive, more competitive, more materialistic. The exact opposite of what he needed to be doing."

She took the receipt book from my hands, closed it, and returned it to its shelf. Then she tucked the gold and diamond poker chip back under her sweater.

"And that's what Wayne and I were doing together the night Brittanie died. The stress of the proposal, seeing you at the luau, his fight with Brittanie . . . He was in real danger of relapsing. So he called me. We went to an all-night meeting in Dallas. Wayne was miles away when Brittanie lay dying, and I was right there holding his hand."

Her face grew hard then, her expression fierce. "But those meetings are private. Sacred. And if you tell a soul what I just said to you, I'll deny every word."

As I put the van in gear, my phone rang. I sighed as I answered, half expecting to hear Cal McCormack telling me that they'd found still more red plastic sundae cups tainted with antifreeze. But, instead, Finn Harper greeted me.

A little hiccough of pleasure rippled through me. "Hey, Finn."

"Tally." He pitched his voice low, as if he were afraid of being overheard, and his words were hard and tight with urgency. "Listen, Mike Carberry has been acting like the cat with the canary all damn week, and he finally let it slip what's going on."

"What?"

"I guess Cal turned over the forensic evidence from the state crime lab to the district attorney's office, and he took it to the grand jury."

I sat there with the van in gear, my foot on the brake, halfway out of my parking space. Behind me, an irate driver laid on his horn. But I couldn't move.

"Tally, honey," Finn said, "they indicted you for Brittanie's murder about twenty minutes ago."

chapter 25

A warm breeze, sharp with the scents of cedar mulch, rosemary, and chlorine, drifted through the screen door to the deck. The soft hum of the pool filter was almost hypnotic.

"I miss having a pool," I murmured. "Living close to downtown is great, and I don't really need a yard, but I wish we had room for a pool."

Finn's voice came from just over my shoulder, so close his breath stirred the fine hairs at my temple. "Do you want to go for a dip? Probably the last chance for a moonlight swim before next summer."

A hysterical giggle bubbled up inside me. It would probably be my last chance for a moonlight swim before I stood trial for killing Brittanie Brinkman.

The underwater lights glowed through the rippling water like the heart of a brilliant gemstone, beckoning, but I shook my head. "No, thanks. I don't have a suit."

"It's just the two of us."

I didn't answer.

"Haven't you ever been skinny-dipping?" His voice vibrated with silent laughter.

My face burned. "You know perfectly well I've been skinny-dipping in this very pool, Finn Harper."

"So?"

"No."

"Why not?"

"It's undignified."

He laughed. "Tally, baby, you're on the lam. Comparatively speaking, skinny-dipping is no big deal."

I shook my head.

"Coward."

"I'm not a coward." But I was.

I kept my gaze fixed firmly on the blue fire of the pool as I heard him moving away, then back.

"Come on," he said, draping a towel over my shoulder.

"Oh, I don't—"

"I dare you."

"What about your mother?"

"Doped to the gills on her pain meds and sound asleep upstairs. No one will see you."

"Except you."

"Except me." He let the words hang in the air, something between a challenge and an offer. I didn't respond, and he sighed. "It's a moonless night, Tally.

I'll turn off the pool lights, and your modesty will be safe."

Still, I hesitated.

"Promise," he whispered, as he tugged gently on a lock of my hair. "I'll meet you out there."

He slipped open the screen and padded across the deck to a breaker box on the side of the house. The backyard went dark. After a moment of rustling, I heard a splash and a loud whoop.

"Come on, Tally," Finn called from the inky night. "The water feels great."

I took a fortifying breath before shimmying out of my skirt and pulling my top over my head. I paused for an instant with my hands on my bra clasp.

Coward, Finn's voice echoed in my head.

In for a penny, in for a pound.

I slipped out of my skivvies, rolling them up inside my shirt and making a tidy stack of my clothes on the closest family room chair. I wrapped myself in the towel and crept across the deck, testing the ground with my toes until I found the concrete lip of the pool and the aluminum railing for the steps.

The soft lapping of the water gave away Finn's location. I waited until he drifted to the far side of the pool before dropping the towel to the ground and slinking into the water.

I gasped at the shock of the cold, then again as a hand closed around my ankle.

"Finn!"

He chuckled softly. "Sorry. Couldn't resist." He

drifted away again, and I allowed myself to relax into the embrace of the water, floating on my back, my ears filled with the sound of my own hollow breath.

We stayed like that for a while, alone together, gliding separately through the water. Occasionally floating close enough to brush a hand against a knee or a foot against a shoulder before ricocheting off in slow motion.

Eventually, Finn spoke. "You know, I always sorta figured we'd end up in this situation, but I thought I'd be the fugitive and you the one giving shelter."

The laughter welled up from deep inside me, unnaturally loud in the chill quiet. "If our roles were reversed, I'da called the cops on you by now," I teased.

"No, you wouldn't have," he replied, suddenly serious.

We slid past each other in the water, not touching, but I could feel the slip of the water, stirred by his passing, caress my skin.

"She did a lot of bad things," he said softly, "but she was too young to be a really bad person."

I didn't have to ask about whom he was talking.

"Imagine," he continued, "if all the world would ever know of you was what you did before you turned twenty-four. If you never had a chance to be anything more than a silly, selfish child."

I thought about that, fluttering my fingers through the heavy silk of the water. Once upon a time, I'd had a chance at adventure, a chance at life. And I'd sent it away, peeling out of the Tasty-Swirl parking lot in a cloud of road dust. By the time I was twenty-four, my die was cast: I was Mrs. Wayne Jones.

"I'd been married almost five years when I was her age," I murmured.

Finn, not following my train of thought, laughed softly, a devilish chuckle. "I don't think being married made you more experienced than Brittanie Brinkman. She got plenty of experience without having a ring around her finger."

"Finn Harper," I chided. "That's not kind."

He laughed again. "You always were my conscience, Tally." His tone sobered. "Lord knows I needed one."

After a beat of silence, he continued more casually. "For what it's worth, your, uh, troubles won't be the only big story in tomorrow's *News-Letter*. We'll be running a report that Cal had an affair with Brittanie."

I levered myself up and let my feet drift back to the bottom of the pool. Water sluiced from my head, and thick hanks of wet hair clung to my cheeks.

"Cal McCormack? Really?"

"Really."

"So maybe he killed her," I said.

"Tally, he wasn't even at the luau."

"No, he wasn't there. But all we have is Cal's say-so that Brittanie was poisoned by the luau sundaes."

"Cal's say-so and the say-so of the state crime lab."

"But the state crime lab analyzed evidence Cal collected. He could have slipped the antifreeze in Brittanie's sports drink or whatever, then manufactured evidence to make it look like she was poisoned at the luau. The sundae cups, Wayne . . . maybe they were all just red herrings to hide his crime."

Finn paddled closer. "You've been watching too much TV. Besides, why would Cal want to kill Brittanie?"

"I don't know. Maybe he was angry that she dumped him."

"That's a pretty big leap of logic."

"Not really," I said. I knew he was right, but I was grasping at straws. "They had an affair. Sex with a pretty young girl, that's heady stuff for a guy staring middle age in the face. Look what it did to Wayne."

Finn snorted. "If every guy she knocked boots with is a suspect, you're going to have to round up just about every Y chromosome in Lantana County. She slept with just about everyone."

"Not you."

His silence was as damning as a gavel.

"Oh, God. You slept with her?"

"Tally—"

"You *slept* with her?"

A few labored steps brought me close enough to grasp the stair rail with both hands. I began to pull myself up the steps when Finn shot around to my right and covered my hand with his own.

"Aw, Tally, don't be mad," he coaxed. "It was just

one night. Back when my mom had her first stroke. I went to the Bar None to get away from the hospital smells and the constant shadow of death. She came on to me. I was drunk, and she was so damned *alive*. But it didn't mean a thing."

"I bet it meant something to Brittanie," I hissed back.

"I doubt it." He'd got his back up, and his tone was none too friendly. "She hopped from my bed to Wayne's pretty darn quick. Much like someone else, who shall remain nameless."

I flinched as though he'd struck me.

"Don't you dare compare your one-night stand with Brittanie Brinkman to us." My chest felt tight, as if something deep inside me was about to explode. "I loved you," I gasped. "I loved you more than my own life."

"Apparently not," he snapped. "You sure as hell weren't willing to give up much to be with me, and you latched on to Wayne Jones practically before I crossed the county line."

His voice was hard and angry, and an ugly possibility began to form in my mind.

"I . . . I'm cold. I would like to get out of the pool now." I held my breath for his response.

He sighed heavily and let go of my hand. But rather than simply let me leave, he climbed out himself. In the faint ambient light, I could see his pale form rise out of the water, then hold open my towel for me.

"Come on. I don't want you catching chill."

Reluctantly, I pulled myself up and stepped close enough to let him wrap the towel around me. I couldn't hold back a shivery-sounding sigh of relief when he tucked the towel closed and moved away.

He flicked a wall switch to turn on the track lighting over the deck. I blinked at the sudden brightness, but not before I saw Finn drop the towel from his waist and step back into his shorts. I shivered, nothing but a scrap of terrycloth between me and the whole great big scary world.

When I grew used to the light, I found Finn facing me. "I'm sorry. Look, I'm not angry about you dumping me anymore. Hell, you did me a favor. God, Tally, I loved you like crazy, but if we'd stayed together . . . can you imagine what a disaster that would have been?"

His words nearly brought me to my knees.

I had told myself the same thing for years—that following Finn would have been nothing but a misery in the end—but to hear him say it, to know he was happier having lived without me, felt like a punch to the kidneys. Right at that moment, with my future prospects fading fast, losing the promise of the past, the bittersweet might-have-been possibilities, was more than I could bear.

"So I'm sorry I snapped at you, but don't you think you're overreacting?" He spoke in quiet, measured tones, as though he were still trying to keep his temper in check. "I'll admit sleeping with Brittanie was not my finest moment. But we were consenting adults—*single* consenting adults—who had a fling. It's not like I did anything illegal."

"Really?" I whispered.

"Of course, really. What do you—? Oh." He raised his hand in a placating gesture and took a step in my direction. I took a step back, to keep my distance, but I didn't have much room to maneuver without going back in the pool.

"You were at the luau that night," I said.

"Tally, you can't honestly believe I had anything to do with Brittanie's death."

"I don't know what to believe anymore."

Finn narrowed his eyes and held my gaze, the force of his will a solid thing between us.

"Believe *me*."

An elemental desire to throw myself into his arms, lose myself in him, nearly overwhelmed me. I couldn't speak, couldn't breathe.

"Tally," he murmured. "You can't be afraid of me."

But I was. Desperately afraid.

Even as I raised a trembling hand to ward him off, reason told me Finn Harper didn't kill Brittanie Brinkman. Yet he terrified me.

Because in the few weeks Finn Harper had been back in Dalliance, I'd started thinking that I could strip away the years of suburban hausfrau just like old varnish and get back to the fresh and vibrant girl I'd been. The girl full of promise and passion. The girl Finn Harper loved.

But in the instant he admitted to sleeping with Brittanie, I saw with dizzying clarity the great long time that had passed since Finn and I had last gone skinny-dipping in his mama's pool. Nearly half my life. Nearly half Finn's life. We'd both made and lost friends, loved other people, become other people.

We were strangers.

And Tally Jones could never be Tally Decker again.

A wave of adrenaline surged through my body. It felt just like the panic attack I'd had at the Zeta alumni house, but I couldn't get it together to hum my way through it.

Fight or flight.

Flight won.

Rapid, shallow breaths left me light-headed. My one rational thought, that my clothes were inside Finn's house, dissolved beneath the compulsion to put distance between us.

I spun on my heel, and I ran. Finn called my name, but that only made me move faster.

I didn't feel anything—the cold night air raising gooseflesh all over my body, the slice of the gravel walkway on the soles of my feet, or even a lick of shame—as I fled into the night, wearing nothing but a towel.

chapter 26

I slipped down the pitch-black tunnel between Mrs. Harper's house and her cedar privacy fence, stepping on a garden hose as I ran, yelping when the soft rubber gave way beneath my foot like a live thing, then stumbling through the small cluster of trash and recycling containers standing sentinel at the corner of the house, and lunging into the front yard like a sprinter falling on the finish line.

I staggered in one direction, then another, like a mime walking into an imaginary gale. The animal instinct to move grappled with my utter lack of a destination. Behind me, I could hear Finn, still calling for me in a tense stage whisper. He cursed softly, and something clattered against the side of Mrs. Harper's house.

Finn was following me.

Had I been the slightest bit rational, I would have stopped where I stood and waited for Finn to emerge into the ambient glow of the streetlights. I would have let him take me by the hand and lead me back inside his mother's house. I would have fetched my clothes from the family room and gotten dressed in the powder blue half bath, while Finn made me a cup of strong black tea in his cherry red teapot. I might have made some sheepish apology, which he would wave away, and he would have covered over the awkwardness with a goofy joke and a clumsy hug before driving me to the police station to deal with Cal.

But that night I was about as rational as a rabid raccoon.

I ducked around a thick stand of ornamental bamboo, then surveyed the street around me and took off in the direction of the only other familiar house in the neighborhood. Darting from hedgerow to hedgerow, cowering in the shadows of cherry laurels and nandinas, I made my furtive way to the home of Dub and Honey Jillson.

Their house was lit up like Christmas, every window blazing. I felt utterly exposed as I slunk up to the front door and rang the bell.

"Please, please, please," I muttered under my breath. Please be home. Please let Honey answer the door instead of Dub. Please don't be having a dinner party.

"Oh, thank you," I gasped, as the oak door

opened a crack and Honey Jillson, in a pink velour tracksuit, peered out.

"Tallulah Jones?"

"Hey, Miz Jillson. I hate to impose, but could I trouble you for . . ." I looked down at my own sorry self. "Well, for a robe and a phone?"

She opened the door wider. "Of course, dear. Do come in out of the cold."

Bless her heart, she didn't say a word about her neighbors seeing a naked lady on her porch or even the fact that it was nigh on midnight and not really an appropriate time to come calling. Just opened her door and invited me in like the gracious Southern hostess she was.

"Why don't we just go sit in the den? Dub lit a fire in the fireplace for me before he went out with his lodge brothers, so it's nice and toasty."

"That sounds like heaven," I said.

She ushered me into a spacious room with split beams running across the ceiling and wide-plank pine floors. Chocolate leather furniture dominated a space made softer by Southwestern-style textiles: throws, rugs, and wall hangings. A fire roared in the massive fireplace, and above the oak beam mantel hung the obligatory bronze Texas star.

"Let me just run upstairs and fetch you a robe," Honey said. "There's a phone right there on the end table."

I trotted over to the phone and quickly dialed home.

"Hello?"

"Bree! It's Tally. I'm at Honey Jillson's house, and I don't have any clothes, and I really, really need you to come pick me up."

"No, Grandma Peachy," Bree answered. "I'm not sure when Tallulah will be getting in tonight."

"Bree?"

"Yes," she continued, "I'd be happy to pick up your prescription, but Alice has my car. Right. I know that show you like about the *police* is on tonight, but right now, I'm stuck."

"Bree, are the police there?"

"Uh-huh."

"Oh, crap," I said.

I heard a tussle on the other end of the line, then Cal's voice. "Tally Jones, where the heck are you? You're in a pile of trouble, little girl. I've got a warrant for your arrest."

"Cal, I didn't do anything wrong."

He sighed. "I'm inclined to believe you. But the DA is in an all-fired hurry to close this case, and he got the indictment. It was out of my hands. The best thing for you to do right now is turn yourself in."

"No."

"Tally, you look guilty as sin by running. And where are you gonna go?"

I didn't have even the faintest idea how to answer him, so I hung up.

I pulled the towel closer around me and, in a daze, wandered around the room.

I was drawn immediately to a cluster of framed

family photos on a wrought-iron console table. They seemed so solid, so homely, an anchor of normalcy in a sea of crazy.

There was Honey with Dub on their wedding day, Dub standing ramrod straight in his narrow-lapelled suit and Honey radiant in a smartly tailored gown and fingertip veil. Another picture of Dub with two men who must be his brothers, all posed on sleek dark horses. Honey standing in a half circle of women in neat floral dresses and wide-brimmed hats, one crouching low with a sign that read DALLIANCE, TX, MASTER GARDENERS.

A picture of Honey in a plaid dress, her hair cut to her shoulders and flipped up at the ends, holding a towheaded baby. Miranda.

And, finally, a picture of a teenager, taken on a beach—Galveston, perhaps. Her tawny hair blew in a wild tangle around her suntanned face, and eyes the color of the twilight sky flashed with laughter.

For an instant, I saw nothing but those eyes, that halo of caramel hair, and I thought it was a copy of the picture of Brittanie that Wayne kept on his desk. But this girl's hair was darker, the nose longer, the mouth fuller. And the girl's outfit—a pink-and-green-striped rugby shirt over a golf shirt with the collar flipped up—dated the photo to the early to mid-1980s. Miranda.

"Here you go," Honey said.

I spun around and found her holding out a long terry robe. I took it with a smile.

"There's a powder room right there," she added,

and pointed me toward a door just to the left of the table of pictures.

I shut myself in the bathroom and slipped on the robe. I turned on the water and waited for it to get warm, all the while doing a little rudimentary math in my head. I washed the scent of chlorine from my hands and face with the freesia bathroom soap and felt quite a bit better about life.

When I emerged from the bathroom, I found Honey sitting on the big leather sofa, sipping tea from a delicate china cup. She patted the seat next to me, and when I dutifully sat she handed me my own steaming cup of chamomile tea with honey and lemon.

"Did you make your phone call, dear?"

I took a sip of the tea, but it scalded the tip of my tongue. "Yes, ma'am. I was hoping my cousin Bree could come pick me up, but she can't. If you don't mind me borrowing your robe, I'll just drive myself home." Of course, my car keys were in Finn's family room. And I didn't have any money for a cab. I figured I'd either have to hoof it home or hunker down in Honey's nandina bushes until morning.

"Don't worry about that," Honey soothed. "You just sit here and have a nice cup of tea with me. Keep me company."

"I, uh, was admiring your family photos," I said. "Miranda was a really beautiful girl."

Honey smiled. "Yes, she was. She was all the best of me and Dub."

"You know, I met a man the other day named

Eddie Collins. I think he went to the junior prom with Miranda."

She stiffened, and her eyes narrowed just a touch. "You must be mistaken. Miranda didn't go to her junior prom. She had mono that year. She missed nearly her entire spring semester."

Bingo.

I'd lived in a small Southern town my whole life. I knew that "having mono" was code for "being pregnant." And the timing was just right. Miranda Jillson, with the golden hair and striking violet eyes, had "mono" just a few months before Brittanie Brinkman, with the golden hair and striking violet eyes, was born. There was a reason Brittanie looked nothing like Fred and Linda Brinkman: they weren't her biological parents.

No wonder Brittanie seemed to lead such a charmed life. She had a real-live fairy godmother— Honey Jillson—who sat on the board that awarded the Regents' Scholarship and made sure Brittanie got the plum internships with Sinclair's and in the mayor's own office.

I blew gently across the surface of my tea, thinking about the fact that stoner Eddie Collins was probably Brittanie's father. I wondered if he knew.

"So, Tallulah, I understand you're in a bit of a bind."

"Yes, ma'am?" I was in several binds at the moment, and I wasn't sure which one Honey was talking about.

"Dub mentioned when he got home that city hall

was abuzz with the news that you'd been indicted for murder."

She said it calmly, as though she were commenting on a particularly mild winter or the rising price of fresh produce.

"Miz Jillson—"

"Honey."

"Honey, I promise you I didn't do anything wrong."

"Oh, I know that, dear. Anyone can tell you're not a criminal. But, on the other hand, I certainly can see how the authorities would be suspicious of you. After all, not only did Wayne run around on you like a randy hound dog, but the ink was barely dry on your divorce papers when he proposed to another woman."

"Wayne actually hadn't proposed yet. Just bought the ring," I said softly.

Honey looked mildly baffled for an instant. "Oh. Of course. JoAnne Simms mentioned that Wayne bought an engagement ring. I guess I just assumed he'd gone ahead and proposed."

"Honey," I said, "this tea is wonderful. Very soothing. But under the circumstances, could I bother you for a little tipple of something stronger? Just to settle my nerves."

"I'm afraid we don't keep alcohol in the house," she said. She lifted one shoulder. "Personally, I never partake. Makes people reckless. Foolish. Like at that picnic your ex-husband threw, everyone behaving in such an undignified manner."

That statement jarred something loose in my mind: Crystal Tompkins mentioning that Honey Jillson was carrying a flask the night of the luau. But if the flask didn't contain alcohol, what was in it?

Honey Jillson and I sat quietly together, sipping our tea, while I figured out how she had accidentally murdered her own grandchild.

Honey knew about Eddie's sham organic gardening products because he'd practically invited the master gardeners to test his wares. And she had access to the typewriter on which she wrote the blackmail note. Since Brittanie was doing Weed and Seed work at the Zeta alumni house, Honey would have had the opportunity to steal some letterhead from Brittanie's papers and slip the blackmail evidence in the stack of files Brittanie typed up for Wayne.

Although Honey had accused Wayne of being drunk at the chamber of commerce dinner, Wayne had insisted he had explained his behavior to Honey by telling her about his pineapple allergy, and she knew—thanks to her long business relationship with Deena Silver—how to identify which cups were the allergen-free cups for Wayne.

She just didn't count on Brittanie stealing Wayne's dessert and bingeing on it, or on the fragility of Brittanie's body chemistry.

"Honey?"

"Yes, Tallulah?"

"Why would you want to kill Wayne?"

She sighed heavily but didn't seem at all surprised that I'd figured out what happened. "You of all people must understand that. I let my Miranda throw away her life on that good-for-nothing Eddie Collins. He wouldn't even stay in Dalliance to marry her after he got her pregnant." She clicked her tongue against her teeth in disgust. "Wayne Jones is no better. Ill-mannered and boorish, can't keep his fly buttoned to save his life. He would have ruined Brittanie's life just as surely as he ruined yours."

A faint smile brushed her lips. "It would have been particularly sweet if the authorities had blamed Eddie. Finally, a little justice for my precious baby girl."

Her teacup rattled against the saucer, and tea splashed out onto the pants of her tracksuit. She set the cup and saucer on the side table, picked up a cloth cocktail napkin, and began dabbing at the spot.

That was when I noticed the prescription bottle on the side table.

Honey reached for her teacup, but her hand drifted right past the cup and her sleeve knocked it to the floor.

"Miz Jillson? Honey? What did you do?"

She settled against the back of the sofa and let her eyes drift closed. "I made my baby girl give up her child to maintain appearances. And I let my grandchild grow up a stranger to me for the same reason. I—" Her breath hitched, and she made a smacking sound with her lips, as if her mouth were too dry to speak. "I gave up *everything* for my good name, and I'm not about to lose it now."

"Oh, Honey, don't do this," I pleaded, letting my own cup fall to the floor as I leaned over her, prying her eyes open. They were glassy and unfocused, but her pupils contracted with the light.

"You're about her age," she slurred softly. "My Miranda would have been just about your age."

I grabbed the bottle off the side table. The prescription was for Ida Harper, amitriptyline tablets for pain. It had been filled just two days before, on Wednesday, the day Honey spent the evening at Ida's bedside.

The bottle was empty.

I grabbed the phone and dialed 911.

"I need an ambulance, right away."

"Address?"

"What? Crap. Honey, what's your address?" She didn't respond. "I don't know. It's the mayor's house. Mayor Jillson."

"And what's the nature of the emergency?"

"She took a lot of pills. A lot of pills. Please hurry. Please."

"Please hold with me—"

I threw down the receiver and ran for the front door, the terry robe flapping around my knees and sagging open around my chest.

I ripped open the door, ran to the lawn, and yelled with all my might, "Finn! Finn, hurry!"

From somewhere in the distance, I heard an answering cry. "Tally?"

"Finn, I'm with Honey Jillson. Hurry!"

I dashed back inside, leaving the door wide-open, and picked up the phone again.

"Is someone coming?" I yelled, even as I grabbed Honey's wrist and felt for a pulse.

"An ambulance has been dispatched," the operator said, her voice reassuringly calm.

My breath caught on a sob when I felt a flutter beneath Honey's paper-thin skin.

Then Finn was beside me, his hair in wild disarray, his face flushed from running.

"Help," I said, and felt the tears begin to slide down my face.

He took in the scene quickly, and gently lifted Honey from the sofa and rested her on the floor, arranging her long, bony limbs as carefully as if they were made of glass. And then, as I looked on in teary wonder, my ne'er-do-well high school boyfriend began doing CPR on the mayor's wife.

As he tilted back her head and blew gently into her nose and mouth, the front door crashed open.

I looked up, expecting the EMTs, but instead saw Cal McCormack and Bree.

"How did . . . ?"

Cal shot me an irritated glare. "I know the dang mayor's phone number, Tally. It didn't take a genius to figure out where you were." Behind him, Bree shrugged apologetically.

"What the holy heck is going on here?" Cal asked.

His question prompted my tears to flow harder.

"It's Honey. She tried to kill Wayne and accidently killed Brittanie and now she's taken a bunch of pills."

Cal shook his head in disbelief, then snapped, "Did you call an ambulance?"

"Of course!" I snapped back. "I'm not stupid."

Finn, softly counting chest compressions, looked up. "Little help?" he muttered.

Cal was across the room in a flash. With remarkable grace, he took over the gentle pressure on Honey's chest, while Finn scooted up toward her head to continue mouth-to-mouth.

Feeling useless, I trotted back to the front door, grabbing Bree's hand and dragging her after me. We stood on the lawn together, holding hands like little girls, waiting solemnly for help to arrive.

chapter 27

Alice locked the door behind the last of the evening's ghosts and goblins. She turned and slid down the glass until she was seated on the linoleum and buried her head in her pinafore.

Halloween business had boomed at Remember the A-la-mode. Bree's brilliant idea to give free jack-o'-lantern sundaes to all the children cost us quite a bit of sherbet, but the banana splits and malts their parents bought more than made up for it. And the *News-Letter*'s dramatic front-page story—that somehow made it seem as if I busted Honey Jillson for murder and saved her life all in one night—assured everyone it was safe to eat ice cream again.

But now, the witching hour approached, and all

the trick-or-treaters were well on their way to a sugar crash. Alice, in her blue dress and white pinafore, looked ready to crawl down the nearest rabbit hole, and Kyle, his hair plastered into an impressive Mohawk, wasn't doing much better.

"Come on, kids, how about a scoop for the road. We can clean up tomorrow," I offered.

"No," Kyle moaned.

"Bed," Alice said.

Bree, dolled up as an Old West saloon girl, complete with zillions of red tulle petticoats and a feather in her sausage-curled hair, helped pull her daughter upright and wrapped her in a smothering hug. "You two have been troopers," she told the kids. "Go home and get some sleep."

Bree unlocked the door to let Kyle and Alice out and found Finn Harper standing outside on the sidewalk, a cardboard banker's box in his arms.

"Hey, little boy. Want some candy?" she quipped.

"Mmm. Depends on what you got."

She laughed as she held the door for him.

"Hey, Tally. Nice getup."

In honor of my store's name, I had dressed as Davy Crocket. By the time Finn showed up, I'd lost the coonskin hat, my hair was sticking up seven ways from Sunday, I had smears of ice cream all over my faux-suede coat, and I was practically sprawled across one of the iron café tables. If Santa Anna laid siege to the store, I would have simply handed him the keys.

"You know me. Always dressed to the nines." I waved him in. "Bree and I were going to have some ice cream to celebrate the end of the worst month ever. Care to join us?"

"For your ice cream? Absolutely."

"I'm scooping," Bree offered. She slipped behind the counter. "Pick your poison."

Finn and I groaned in unison.

"Sorry. Poor choice of words."

"I'll have butter pecan with hot fudge," I said. "And I believe Finn will have cherry."

He nodded as he took a seat across from me. "You remembered," he said, a wicked smile curling his lips.

My face burned, and I sat up a little straighter. I didn't really know where I stood with Finn. We hadn't talked about my little freak-out in his back-yard. But I knew I'd made an important realization that night by the pool. Being with Finn reminded me of the girl I'd once been, a girl we'd both loved. But all the slow dancing and hand holding in the world couldn't unwind the last eighteen years. We had both changed irrevocably.

I would always be Tally Decker, but I'd also al-ways be Tally Jones, and I didn't know how Finn Harper felt about Tally Jones. Heck, I didn't even really know Finn Harper at all.

"How's Honey?" I asked, hoping to find more neutral territory.

His smile faded. "They pumped her stomach. She's still weak, but she'll be all right. She's sticking by what she said in her note, so the DA will have to decide how to proceed when she's a little stronger."

While I was on the phone with Bree that night at the Jillsons' house, Honey had been upstairs taking the amitriptyline and finishing a note, explaining how she had tried—and failed—to kill Wayne.

"So what's in the box?" I asked.

Finn winked. "I went to talk to Eddie Collins today."

I cringed.

"Yeah, he's not doing so hot. Between Wayne trashing his business with that letter to the editor in the *News-Letter* and then finding out about Brittanie, he's had a rough week. He didn't have any comment for the paper. But . . ."

He leaned down to set the box on the ground and nudged it closer to me with his toe.

"He said this showed up at his house, and he's pretty sure it's yours."

I half expected the box to explode. But with Finn smiling encouragement, I opened it carefully. Inside, curled up on a stained and threadbare towel, slept a tiny marmalade-colored kitten.

I sucked in a breath.

"What is it?" Bree asked, setting a tray laden with three sundae dishes on the table.

She peeked in.

"Aw, cutey-patootie."

"Eddie said anyone who wanted a cat should have a cat. Because, and I quote, 'they're all about love. Groovy.' "

Bree snorted. "He did *not* say 'groovy.'"

"Oh, yes, he did." He nudged me under the table with his foot. "What are you going to name him?"

Tentatively, I reached out to stroke the kitten's silky little head. He didn't even open his eyes, just scooted over onto his back to show me his tummy.

"Sherbet," I said. "He's the color of sherbet."

"I'll be damned," Bree said as she spooned up a luscious dollop of French vanilla oozing with warm caramel. "Miss Color Blind got it right this time." She turned on her dim-witted toddler voice. "Yes, Tally, the puddy-tat is orange."

"Bite me, Bree. The puddy-tat is also probably a health-code violation."

Finn laughed. "I think we can keep the health in-spectors at bay long enough for you to eat your ice cream. You should hurry up, before it melts."

"Mmm," Bree moaned around another spoonful of sundae. "That's the problem with ice cream. It melts."

I dipped my spoon in my ice cream and popped it in my mouth. It was cool and warm, salty and sweet. I savored the weight and texture of it on my tongue before swallowing.

I met Finn's eyes across the table, their soft hazel green as familiar as my own reflection, even though the man before me was all but a stranger.

I licked a drip of fudge from the back of my spoon. "Actually," I said, "that's what I like about ice cream. It melts, but it's still absolutely delicious."

Tally's Tropical Sundaes

You can make Tally's luscious tropical sundaes, even if you don't have her Tahitian vanilla bean ice cream. Serves 4, generously.

2 pints ice cream*

4 cups finely diced tropical fruit (a mix of mango and pineapple is great, but feel free to add kiwi, papaya, or others you like)

½ cup toasted coconut flakes (optional)

½ cup toasted chopped macadamia nuts (optional)

Tropical Coconut Dessert Sauce (recipe below)

*Vanilla ice cream (homemade or store-bought) is great, but don't use French vanilla, because the additional egg yolks in French vanilla ice cream are a poor fit for the brighter notes of the tropical fruit. You could also use mango or banana ice cream or a tropical sorbet.

For each sundae, start with 1 cup of ice cream or sorbet. Top with 1 cup of fruit, then ⅓ cup of Tropical Coconut Dessert Sauce and 2 tablespoons each of the optional coconut and/or nuts.

Tropical Coconut Dessert Sauce

This silky-smooth sauce, brightened by the kick of lime and ginger, tastes like sin on a spoon (sweet but with a hint of heat). It's great on ice cream and sorbets, but it's equally good drizzled over fresh fruit or served alongside carrot or spice cake. Best served chilled or at room temperature. Yields 2⅔ cups.

1 heaping tablespoon arrowroot powder

1 14½-ounce can lite coconut milk

⅔ cup sugar

Zest of 1 medium or 2 small limes

3 tablespoons lime juice

3–4 tablespoons grated fresh ginger with juice*

Mix the arrowroot with a quarter cup of the coconut milk to make a slurry, and set aside. Combine the remaining ingredients in a small saucepan. Gently bring to a boil, then remove from heat and allow to steep for about 15 minutes. Strain the sauce to remove the zest and ginger, and return to the saucepan. Bring the sauce back to a slow boil, whisk in the arrowroot slurry, and, as soon as the sauce starts to bubble, remove from the heat and allow to cool.

*For a more mild ginger experience, you can substitute 1½ ounces of crystallized ginger, sliced thin, for the fresh. If you use crystallized ginger, which has sugar on it, reduce the sugar in the recipe from ⅔ cup to ½ cup. If you want even more ginger heat, make the sauce the day before you serve it and refrigerate overnight.

Read on for a sneak peek at
Wendy Lyn Watson's next
Mystery à la Mode,
coming from Obsidian in July 2010.

"I can't even believe that woman is related to me."

"Alice, honey, I hate to tell you, but you and your mama are like two kits in a litter. Hardheaded, tenderhearted, and too smart for your own good." I ran a hand through my hair and sighed. "Too smart for *my* own good."

Alice folded her arms across her chest and cocked a skinny hip. She still looked more like a child than a woman, and I had a tough time remembering that she was finishing up her first year at Dickerson College. "That is so not true, Aunt Tally. I would never in a million years show up at a formal event looking like a ho-bag."

I studied my cousin, Alice's mama, trying to see her through her precocious teenage daughter's eyes. Bree Michaels wore a vibrant pink tank dress that

clung to every luscious curve of her statuesque
form. A beam of late-afternoon sunlight filtered
through the atrium windows of Sinclair Hall, bright-
ening her bouffant updo to a glossy maraschino-
cherry red. And when she threw her head back and
laughed at one of her admirers' quips, her abundant
décolletage frothed like freshly whipped cream until
I thought she might overflow her D cups. She looked
like a sexy strawberry sundae, and the men surrounding her—from adolescents to octogenarians—
practically drooled on her three-inch spike heels.

Out of the corner of my eye, I caught Alice tugging on the cuffs of her prim white cotton dress
shirt, and I smothered a chuckle.

"In your mama's defense, the invitation called
this shindig a 'reception,' and they're serving barbecue and ice cream. Not exactly black tie and
tails."

"You know what I mean," Alice huffed. "You
dressed appropriately."

I glanced down at my own outfit, a knee-length
black skirt and French blue wrap shirt. "I look like a
waitress," I muttered.

"Better a waitress than a call girl."

"Show a little respect, Alice. And cut your mama
some slack. She's terrified she's going to embarrass
you today."

Alice snorted.

"Seriously. Bree was a hot mess this morning. She
tried on three different outfits and spent an hour on
her hair, and she was still shaking so bad I thought

she'd collapse the minute we walked in here and saw all the posters and displays."

My niece nibbled on her lower lip, and I could see the wheels turning behind eyes as wide and blue as the prairie sky. "Mom's no shrinking violet," she insisted.

"You're right. Bree's cocky as heck when she's on her own turf. When she's singing karaoke at the Bar None or scooping cones at Remember the A-la-mode. But Honors Day on a college campus? Scares the piddle out of her." I wrapped an arm around Alice's scrawny shoulders and pressed a kiss to the silky hair at her temple. "Your mother is so freakin' proud of you, little girl. Just turned seventeen and you're presenting a research project at a prestigious private university? When she was your age, your mama had just gotten hitched to husband number one and was living in a camper in her in-laws' side yard. She doesn't want to hold you back, kiddo."

Alice leaned in to me, and I gave her a little squeeze. Underneath the eighty-pound attitude, she was a great kid.

Before we could get any gooier, a smartly dressed woman emerged from the curtained platform that ran along one side of the atrium and made a beeline for us. I put her somewhere in her early to mid-thirties. Her caramel-colored hair fell just past her angular jaw in a chic asymmetrical bob, and funky tortoiseshell glasses rested on her aquiline nose. As she strode closer, I could see the nubby weave of her ankle-length gray dress and eggplant jacket, maybe linen or hemp. The name tag pinned to her breast read DR. EMILY CLOWPER, DEPARTMENT OF ENGLISH.

"Alice, have you seen Bryan?" she snapped. Like a pit viper on speed, she vibrated with barely controlled energy.

"No, Dr. C.," Alice said. "Reggie said he was still running off programs."

Emily glanced at her watch, clearly irritated. "Figures. Go find him, will you? It's time to get this show on the road."

Alice slipped from under my arm and trotted off without a backward glance.

I held out my hand. "Hi. I'm Tally Jones."

Emily looked at my hand as if it were a riddle to be solved before grasping it and giving it a single, bone-wrenching shake.

"You make the ice cream," she said.

I smiled. "Have you tried it? The university is serving cones of honey–vanilla bean, raspberry mascarpone, and chocolate truffle out by the barbecue."

"Diabetic."

"Oh." Alice raved about Emily Clowper's brilliant mind, but she sure couldn't carry a conversation.

She looked at her watch again and sighed.

"Uh, thank you for taking Alice under your wing. She loves working for you."

Emily's mouth softened into something approaching a smile. "The pleasure is mine. This paper she's presenting today on the misogynist subtext of *Robinson Crusoe* is graduate-level work. I'm not a Freudian, but she's made a compelling case for the island as a symbol of dehumanized female sexuality."

"Oh."

"Her mother?"

"What? Oh, no. Aunt. Well, actually first cousin once removed." One of her eyebrows shot up, and I felt as though I'd got caught passing notes in class. "I'm her aunt."

I glanced nervously across the room to where Bree continued to hold court. This woman would make Bree cry.

When I looked back at Emily, her attention had moved to something—or someone—behind me. Now there was no mistaking her smile or the crinkling at the corners of her eyes, the subtle softening of her posture.

"I didn't expect to see you here, Finn," she said.

My heart did a somersault in my chest as I turned to find Finn Harper standing at my shoulder, a camera hanging from a strap around his neck. His mouth curled in a devilish smile, and I couldn't tell whether the heat in his velvet green eyes was for me or for Emily.

Either way, I wanted to curl up in a tiny ball and die.

My relationship with Finn remained uncertain. After a near-twenty-year absence, he had returned to Dalliance about six months ago to take care of his ailing mother. A bizarre set of circumstances threw us together, and I flirted with the notion that we'd pick up our teenage romance right where we'd left off.

But, of course, real life didn't have fairy-tale endings. I still needed to unload a lot of baggage from my marriage and divorce, and I struggled to untangle the dreamy memories of my high school heartthrob from the man he had become. Bottom line, we'd both done a lot of living since I broke his heart in the Tasty-Swirl parking lot.

I still saw him out and about, at the cafés and shops that circled the courthouse square of Dalliance, Texas, and at the various events he covered as a reporter for the *Dalliance News-Letter*. But every single encounter reduced me to a stammering, gelatinous mess.

Dr. Emily Clowper held out her arms, and Finn stepped awkwardly into her embrace. I couldn't bear to look at him, so I studied her, instead, seeing her this time the way a man would see her. Like the eye doctor switching from one lens to the next, my perception of her shifted from awkward and angular to tall and lithe, from cold and abrupt to smart and edgy.

When Finn stepped back, he looked at me, eyes narrowed and appraising. I prayed I didn't look as miserable as I felt.

"Emily and I met when I lived in Minneapolis," Finn offered.

Her smile widened into an almost girlish grin.

"Many years and three moves ago. Back in my wild grad school days."

Finn held up a hand in protest. "Not that long ago. And not *that* wild."

They both laughed, and I forced myself to join in. No matter how long ago they'd been together, their relationship was more recent than ours. And certainly more wild. Emily Clowper had known Finn as an adult, as a self-sufficient man, a person I'd only recently met.

I tried to find something clever to say. "How convenient that fate landed you both in the same Podunk town," I said, then cringed. Even to my ears, my words sounded bitter. "I mean—"

A piercing scream rang through the room, echoing off the high ceiling and leaving an unnatural stillness in its wake.

Alice.

My legs were moving before my brain even finished the thought, but still I was three steps behind Bree as she sprinted across the tile floor of the atrium in her tight dress and hooker heels. I sensed movement behind me, others running toward the cry of distress, which had now settled into a keening wail.

Ahead of me, Bree took the half flight of steps from the atrium into the main body of Sinclair Hall two at a time, then disappeared through the heavy oak doors propped open for the festivities.

I took the corner onto the first floor in a blind panic and nearly fell over Bree, who'd come to a dead stop, staring in horror at the scene in the hall-way.

Alice, our baby girl, stood beneath the harsh fluorescent lights, face the color of chalk, her prim white cotton dress shirt covered in blood.